VERITAS

Visit us at www.boldstrokesbooks.com

Advance Praise for *Veritas*

"Anne Laughlin presents us with a finely nuanced, compelling portrait of Beth Ellis, who has always held life at arm's length. With skill and wry humor, she shows us the realities of a life half lived and what happens when Beth's certainties are blown away by the violence of murder, and the intoxicating thrill of passionate love."—Claire McNab, author of the Carol Ashton and Kylie Kendall mystery series

"*Veritas* is a high-adrenaline read that left me breathless, waiting for the climax. Anne Laughlin plots like a demon and creates memorable characters. But Veritas is more than a satisfying entertainment, as Laughlin paints a dead-perfect picture of corruption and lethal intrigue on a college campus. The novel's emotional force builds as the lives of strong female characters intersect: a beautiful dean with a secret, a determined cop, a mechanic with a gift for no-strings sex. Gripping, fast-paced, smart, and erotically charged—*Veritas* is a winner."—Joan Larkin, award-winning poet and editor

VERITAS

by

Anne Laughlin

2009

VERITAS

ISBN 10: 1-60282-124-0
ISBN 13: 978-1-60282-124-8

This Trade Paperback Original Is Published By
Bold Strokes Books, Inc.
P.O. Box 249
Valley Falls, NY 12185

First Edition: November 2009

Credits
Editors: Cindy Cresap and Stacia Seaman
Production Design: Stacia Seaman
Cover Design By Sheri (graphicartist2020@hotmail.com)

Acknowledgments

For continued medical and gun advice, thanks go to Jim van Bavel. My friend, Jen Earls, an officer with the Chicago Police Department, gave me insight into police procedure and also showed me her ankle holster. Thanks, Crash. As always, I benefited from early readings by Joan Larkin, Maureen Seaton, Linda Braasch, Liz Laughlin, Rita Balzotti, and Michelle Sanford.

Thanks also and hugely to my editor, Cindy Cresap, who provided the kind of professional editorial direction any writer, particularly me, would benefit from. Her input made this a better book.

I spent the month of October 2008 at the Mary Anderson Center for the Arts in Southern Indiana, finishing up the first draft of this book. It was a magical month and a beautiful place, which was promptly and permanently shut down as soon as I checked out. I wonder what I did?

I also got very valuable advice on the opening chapter of this book at the 2008 Lambda Literary Foundation's Emerging Writers Retreat. I workshopped additional chapters at the Advanced Writers Workshop at Story Studio Chicago. Thanks to all of my teachers and fellow students.

I have to thank Radclyffe for giving my manuscript a look and deciding to take both it and me on. Her energy, focus, and leadership are inspiring.

Lastly, and firstly, to Linda, my one true love.

Dedication

In memory of Clarence Braasch, father-in-law extraordinaire

CHAPTER ONE

The president wants to see you."

Dean Beth Ellis stopped at her office door and turned to her assistant, Lillian, who had just delivered the bad news. A meeting with the president of Grafton College was possibly the worst way she could think of to start a day. The promise of the bright April morning evaporated.

"What about?" Beth asked.

Lillian grabbed a fistful of pink message slips from her desk and followed Beth into her inner office.

"He speaketh from on high and deigneth not to tell me," Lillian said, casting her eyes downward.

Beth sighed, hauling herself back up and moving toward the door. She stopped and turned back to Lillian. "How do I look?"

"A little like you're being marched to the guillotine."

"It's not that bad, I guess. I just find him a bit...difficult." She looked down at her dark gray tailored suit, glad that she'd chosen to wear a skirt that day, and tugged on the jacket. She knew she looked fine. She always looked fine. She looked like a forty-year-old dean of a liberal arts college. For a wild and thrilling moment, Beth wished she were about to walk into the president's office in cargo pants, a torn T-shirt, and a slice of her slender midriff showing between shirt and pants.

The president's suite of offices was opposite Beth's on the first floor of Old Main. While Beth felt her own offices were far too lavish for her needs, President Landscome's offices were continually being upgraded to suit his. In the nine months since his appointment as the sixteenth president of Grafton College, Landscome's renovations had given his offices a sort of masculine, clubby feel, a place where you'd expect to see tweedy older gentlemen dotted about the room in leather chairs, snoring behind their copies of the *Financial Times* and wrapped in the womblike comfort of cigar smoke and dark wood.

It did not escape Beth's notice, or she supposed, anyone else's on the faculty, that though the man's name was David N. Landscome, he insisted on being known by his middle name, Nigel. This was in the hope, Beth surmised, that he would be mistaken as someone at least slightly British. His manner of speech was also slightly British, but only in that most irritating of all possible ways, that is, inexpertly done. He sounded like a community theatre actor making his first attempt at *Jeeves and Wooster*. The accent fell away whenever he had to concentrate on his lines.

"Good morning, Cora," Beth said to the president's assistant as she walked into his outer office. "I understand he wants to see me?"

"Go on in. He's waiting." Cora peered at Beth over her reading glasses. Her pinched face and slightly hunched back gave her a rodentlike appearance, which matched her remarkable survival skills.

Beth walked in and found Landscome sitting on a sofa in a corner of the immense room, sipping a cup of tea and reading the morning paper. He was a distinctly pear-shaped man, with thin legs dangling below his great middle. He rose to greet Beth, his plump, ruby red lips forced into a quick smile. His lips appeared to be pasted on his strangely pale, round face. Beth found him thoroughly unattractive.

"Good morning, Dean. I trust you're well?"

"Very well, President Landscome."

"Nigel, please. I think we're at the sort of professional level where some informality is allowed, don't you?"

He gestured toward one of the chairs in front of his desk and took his own chair behind it.

"Of course. And you must call me Beth." She wondered what sort of informality it was that took nine months to get on a first-name basis.

"Beth, I'm leaving this afternoon for a board meeting in London. I wanted to check whether the tenure committee has returned their vote on Dr. Barrow's tenure yet."

A fairly incompetent assistant professor of English had been brought to the college faculty by Landscome, for no apparent reason other than that the man was British. No one seemed to know any details beyond that. His presence was not popular among the faculty, which made no attempt to hide the fact.

"The decision is supposed to be made today. They should send word to me as soon as the vote is taken," Beth said.

"And what's your feel on how that's going to go? It'll be bad business if he's turned down."

Beth's heart sank. The question of whether John Barrow would be awarded tenure was one of the hot topics on campus, and she would inevitably end up right in the middle of the controversy.

"You have to understand the perspective of the faculty, particularly of the tenure committee. Their opinion of Dr. Barrow, and mine as well, is that he's not nearly as qualified as candidates they have turned down in the past. I think we know how they're going to vote today."

Landscome rose slowly from his chair and turned to gaze out the window, his hands clasped behind his back. Beth imagined he was trying to channel Monty at El Alamein, ready to take on the Nazi horde that was the Grafton College faculty. Prior to coming to Grafton, Landscome had been the CEO of a major agricultural corporation. He reportedly ruled his company expecting his wishes to be anticipated and respected by his subordinates, certainly not questioned. This approach might have worked perfectly well in that environment, but Beth wondered how he had been so misinformed about the culture of debate that was the very nature of college life.

Landscome slowly turned to face her.

"Here's what I want you to do. You're to go immediately to the members of the tenure committee and lobby for approval of tenure for Dr. Barrow. Have them postpone their vote if you need to, but make it happen. I'll be most displeased if my veto of their decision is necessary."

Beth just stared at the man, unable to understand why he was trying to ruin the college. He was an occupying force, a foreigner without any respect for the society he'd conquered. The board of trustees hired him believing he could raise enough money as president to rescue the college's imperiled endowment and turn around its fortunes. Beth knew that he was already doing just that, giving him solid backing from the board.

"I don't believe I can do as you request."

Landscome's lips grew redder, and a flush came to his sallow skin. "You will do as I tell you because that is your job. If you want to continue on as dean of the college you'll learn to execute the orders of the president. This is not the first time you've balked in this manner, and I warn you that I have little patience with disloyalty."

Beth remained quiet, determined to not give him the satisfaction of forcing her resignation. She wasn't ready for that yet.

Landscome walked around his desk, escorting Beth to the heavy wooden doors, which he opened as if he were announcing the Prince of Wales. But there on the other side was Cora, typing furiously on her keyboard.

"Don't let me down, Dean. Bring me tenure for Dr. Barrow. We are on a mission to set a new tone here at Grafton and Dr. Barrow is a step in that direction. You'll just have to trust me on that."

Landscome retreated into his office and pulled the big doors shut behind him. Beth turned to go, her heart in her shoes.

"Bloody wanker," Cora said under her breath, demonstrating her own command of British vernacular.

Beth walked out of Old Main to breathe some fresh air and ease the tight feeling in her chest. The building sat on the top of a hill, the apex of Grafton College, with the rest of the campus spread out below, draped around the gentle hill. The small town of Mount Avery lay below the campus and the Midwestern breadbasket stretched for miles beyond that. The fact that the campus was on a hill was a blessing and a curse. It was brutal in the harsh winters with the winds whipping harder the higher she climbed. But Beth was also mindful that the exercise helped her stay slim, which was harder to do as she moved into her forties. Her mother once told her she had the sort of looks that would last well as she aged, but she wasn't certain the same would be said about her body. That ongoing battle would eventually be lost. She wondered if the new battle on campus would also be lost.

Beth spent the rest of the day barricaded in her office feeling angry and ill used. As soon as she heard Lillian say good-bye through her closed office door, Beth left for home. Her house lay just beyond the outer ring of the campus, purchased through a faculty loan program when she arrived at Grafton. It was small and simple and perfectly suited her needs. She was no closer to deciding how she was going to handle the tenure matter, other than knowing she would not do as Landscome ordered and lobby on Barrow's behalf. She was only slightly relieved that the tenure committee had not delivered their decision to her yet. Someone on the committee must be holding up the vote, and Beth idly tried to guess who. It hardly mattered, she knew. Their no vote was inevitable. War between the president and the faculty, it seemed, was inevitable.

The recent April thaw made running outdoors possible again and she looked forward to the exercise. After changing into sweats she jogged around the hill toward the rural road leading out of town. Twenty miles down the road was the state university in Center City, a much larger town that offered many of the things Mount Avery lacked—bookstores, cafés, concerts and theatre, ethnic restaurants, gay and lesbian bars. Over the years Beth had found the university faculty the best source for the only type of relationship she seemed to feel comfortable in—no strings, plenty of sex, and no messy or painful endings. The Grafton College faculty was too insular to pull off that sort of trifecta. She knew from experience that extricating herself from a relationship with a colleague was a complicated matter. Since becoming dean the year before, Beth hadn't found time to visit Center City enough to maintain even these most undemanding of relationships. Her work had rounded that last part of the circle and now encompassed her entire life, a fact that she was aware of but too short on time to resent.

Beth ran hard for forty-five minutes, but as she walked through town on her way back, sweating freely in the cool air, she realized she was still agitated. She passed by Dale and Mel's Auto Repair on the corner of Main and Tenth Avenue and turned in to the open garage bay. A familiar figure stood bent over with her head under the hood of a car. Even swathed in her olive gray coverall, Mel's powerful body was distinct and familiar.

Beth approached quietly, reached over to a battered boom box sitting on top of a tool cart, and turned the volume down on the blaring country music. Mel extracted herself from under the hood and turned around, smiling her slow sexy smile when she saw Beth. Mel was an ace mechanic, far more clever than her brother Dale, and she loved what she did. And when her head wasn't under the hood of a car it could most likely be found under the sheets of someone's bed. Her expertise as a lover was well known in town. It was her stated mission to keep everyone happy, including herself, and that meant no promises, no relationships, no strings. Beth had nothing but admiration for Mel, and, when the mood struck, a fair amount of desire for her as well.

Mel pulled a bandana from her back pocket and wiped her face, then crossed her arms, her filthy hands tucked away. "Professor. Haven't seen you for a while."

Whenever Beth allowed herself to find the relief Mel provided, she allowed herself everything. Her gaze lingered on all six feet of her and her mind started to empty at the thought of that body on top of hers. She stood there mutely, her need blatant.

"Looks like you're about talked out for the day," Mel said. She levered herself off the car and walked over to Beth, leaning in to whisper in her ear. "Why don't I come over so we can spend some quiet time together?"

Beth nodded her head. "Eight o'clock?" she asked.

"See you then." Mel kissed Beth's forehead and then turned

back to the car, bumping up the volume on the boom box before she slipped back into the deep. Beth strolled out of the garage and then broke into a run as she headed back to her house.

❖

By eight o'clock it was dark in Mount Avery. All of the lights were out in Beth's house, except for the night-light in the hallway. It cast an amber glow that barely stretched to the bed, enough so that Beth was able to see Mel, her strong hands gripping her hips, holding her in place. Beth closed her eyes and gave way completely, and she was none too quiet about it. But then she savored the delicious exhaustion and calm the run had not provided her as she lay perfectly still on the bed. Mel eased off Beth and scootched herself up and onto an elbow, trailing her fingers over Beth's shoulders, down her breast, her belly.

"You can talk now, you know," Mel said, reversing her course and heading back up Beth's body.

"I really don't think I can." Beth kept her eyes closed.

Mel lay next to her for a while, and when Beth finally stirred, curling up on her side, she kissed the top of her head and left the bed. Beth opened one eye and watched as Mel put her clothes on. She knew she should say something like "Thanks," or more accurately, "Thanks again." That would be the polite thing to do, but instead she started to drift off. She heard Mel leave the house by the front door, jiggling the handle to make sure it was locked.

CHAPTER TWO

B y the time she reached campus the following morning, Beth felt more willing to face the tenure situation. She realized that what she felt while she was hiding in her office the day before was fear. Not fear of President Landscome or fear of being fired as dean, but fear that a nervous board of trustees and an ass of a president were slowly ruining the college she'd loved for most of her adult life.

When she first arrived at Grafton College Beth had been twenty-seven with a PhD fresh in hand. Moving to Mount Avery felt comparable to moving into a space colony or a biosphere—she was a newcomer in a closed society. She had to make a place for herself in order to survive. The college would provide her safety and community and purpose, and in exchange she would devote her life to the college. The structure remained upright because everyone did their part, but it felt to her that since becoming president, Landscome had been patrolling the campus, pulling out bits and pieces of the foundation. Soon the structure would fall in upon itself and be replaced with some flimflam institution supported by corporate sponsorship, populated by uninspired and unimaginative students and a faculty of frightened part-time teachers. And President Landscome would be proud of the job he'd done.

As Beth walked through the main quad toward Old Main she saw John Barrow, still untenured, heading right toward her. There was no way to avoid him.

"Good morning, Dean." Like Landscome, John Barrow went

for the outdated tweedy, academic look, but unlike Landscome, Barrow managed to carry it off. He was in his mid-thirties, with a full head of wavy dark hair, a neatly trimmed beard, and a wiry build. He was, Beth acknowledged, very handsome, and no doubt used to getting his way. She said her hello and continued walking, hoping Barrow would continue in the opposite direction.

"Dean, if you have a moment there's something I want to call your attention to."

Beth worked to keep her tone pleasant. "If this is about the tenure vote, John, it's not really appropriate for us to discuss it."

"It happens that this is about something entirely unrelated. A past student of yours, as a matter of fact."

"Which student is that?"

"Jennifer Manos, who's in my senior seminar."

"What about Jennifer?"

Barrow came up close to Beth, rocking back and forth on his crepe-soled feet, each forward motion impinging on her personal space. Beth took a step back. "I'm quite concerned, actually. It seems Jennifer has gone missing." He raised an eyebrow at Beth, almost as if he thought Beth had perhaps tucked Jennifer away somewhere.

"What do you mean she's missing?"

"As you know, Jennifer is an avid student, so it caught my attention yesterday when she missed her second seminar session in a row. I took the time to look up her contact information and call her mobile. It went straight into voicemail. I called her house and a flatmate said she hadn't seen Jennifer all week but didn't know where she'd buggered off to."

"John, I doubt she's 'buggered off' anywhere. She's a sensible young woman. I'll contact the dean of students and we'll find out what's up."

"Yes, well, I'm just a bit concerned. She's not seemed quite herself the last few weeks."

"What do you mean?" Beth asked. John had now stopped rocking back and forth and was shifting from one foot to the other.

She wondered if he was hyperactive, though she had always been left more with an impression of sloth than energy. Perhaps he was nervous about the tenure vote.

He spoke more quickly than was normal. "Oh, who knows what goes on in the minds of students? I just sensed she was distracted, if not unhappy. I'd hate to see anything happen to her." Beth doubted he cared about Jennifer's welfare as much as he did about appearing to care.

She excused herself and continued on to her office, where she'd delegate the missing student question to the dean of students as soon as she got in. When she entered Old Main she looked toward Landscome's suite. Landscome was safely away in London, probably for the better part of a week, which gave Beth time to figure out how to play the tenure situation with John Barrow so that she could keep her job as dean, keep the faculty from revolting, and keep Landscome happy. Beth was no stranger to the Machiavellian hornet's nest that was academic politics, so she felt confident, for the first time in a couple of days, that she would figure out this puzzle. As she walked into her office Lillian followed close behind with another wad of message slips.

"Dean Taylor called and she sounds upset. You need to call her right away."

"Okay, I think I know what that's about. Any other emergencies in there?" Beth asked as she settled in behind her desk. Lillian looked at her pityingly.

"Delilah Humphries is on her way over to talk about the tenure vote. She should be here in fifteen minutes."

Beth took a deep breath. "Okay. What else?"

"The board just faxed over a letter saying they are moving up the due date on the annual plan by two weeks. That means you have to get it to them by next Friday."

"Oh, my God." They might as well have said she'd have to write the next *War and Peace* in a day. Suddenly the thought of Mel jumped into Beth's head—uncomplicated Mel and her uncomplicated lovemaking.

"I don't even think that's physically possible, especially with the president out of town. Anything else?"

"That's the worst of it. The rest can wait, though your mother called and said she couldn't get through to you last night at home. She wants you to call today."

"I don't think that's going to happen."

Lillian laughed. "Enjoy the time with her if you possibly can, Dean. Mothers drive you crazy, and suddenly they're gone. Then there's that big void where the irritation used to be."

Irritation was simply one in a palette full of complicated emotions Beth associated with her mother. She wouldn't deny that on the question of her mother she was extraordinarily sensitive. She never volunteered any information about her and when asked she told a version of the truth, that it was just the two of them in the family and that they weren't close. She would not admit to anyone that her mother was a brothel owner in Nevada, not because she was ashamed, but because the news was so flabbergastingly unexpected to everyone who heard it that they could talk of nothing else. Some were no doubt scandalized by the news, while others, struggling to be broadminded, insisted on giving it a literary quality, as if Beth herself were a modern day Moll Flanders. They wanted to hear stories of her mother the madam, how she ran her house, protected her girls, cut deals with the cops and politicians that frequented her house, even though Beth repeatedly reminded them that a legal brothel really wasn't as colorful or dangerous as the illegal sort.

What Beth didn't tell them, what they wouldn't have wanted to hear, were the stories about how her mother neglected her, left her on her own for hours, sometimes looked in on by one of her girls, often not. Or of how her mother ignored her even when they were in the same room, too tired to be bothered. Beth learned soon enough to not ask for what she needed, for that seemed only to make her mother love her less, if in fact she loved Beth at all.

As Lillian walked out of her office, Beth picked up the phone to dial the dean of students, Harriet Taylor. Harriet was in her fourth decade in her position. She knew, intimately, the vast array of stupid things that students did, as well as the great range of their energy and sweetness and eagerness to learn.

When Beth placed the call it was picked up on the first ring and a voice barked, "Taylor."

"It's Beth Ellis, Harriet. I have a message you called."

"Jennifer Manos is missing." Dean Taylor got down to business, as usual.

"God, I was hoping it wasn't true. I just ran into John Barrow and he told me he was concerned that she might be."

"Oh, I bet he's concerned, that son of a bitch." Beth could hear Harriet blow out a breath. "I'll get to him in a minute, but let me tell you what I know. I got a call from a student over at Hadley House where Jennifer lives. Her housemates figured out today that no one has seen Jennifer since Monday morning, when her roommate Mandy saw her still in bed when she left for class. Mandy spent the next two nights over at her boyfriend's room and when she finally got back to Hadley she didn't even think about the fact that Jennifer wasn't around. She figured she'd hooked up with someone."

"Why does she think that's not the case now?" Beth asked.

"When all of the girls in the house compared notes they realized no one had seen her, and that even if she had hooked up with someone she would have come home at some point to change clothes or get books or something. The other thing is that none of the girls think Jennifer is a hook-up kind of girl. As far as they knew there was only one man in her life, and when Mandy took a call from John Barrow telling her that Jennifer hadn't shown up in class this week…"

"Oh, no," Beth said. "Please don't tell me that Barrow is sleeping with Jennifer."

"I wish I could tell you that he is. That would be one way to get him removed from this campus," Harriet said. "But according to her housemates, Jennifer never said they'd gotten together, just that she had a thing for him."

Beth got up from her desk and started to pace. "They have no idea where she might be?"

"None. I've gone ahead and contacted Jennifer's aunt. She's listed as her emergency contact, though I'm not sure yet why her parents aren't."

"Her parents are dead," Beth said, knowing this and several other facts about Jennifer's background. Before she left the English department, Beth had been Jennifer's advisor. "She was ten years old when they were killed in a car wreck and her aunt took her in."

"Well, this keeps getting better, doesn't it? The aunt doesn't have any idea where she is either, and now she's frantic. I think it's time we called the police."

"Absolutely. Keep me up to date and let me know if there's anything I can do." Delilah Humphries entered her outer office and Beth waved her in. "I've got to go, Harriet."

"That's fine, I'll take care of everything, but I've got to tell you, if I find out that one of your faculty has caused harm to one of my students, I'm going to be on the war path." She hung up.

There was no time to react to this crisis with Delilah coming in. Beth retreated behind her desk. There had been a short time, a number of years before, when Beth and Delilah were lovers. She found Delilah's charming insistence that they try a romance tempting enough to ignore her rule about dating colleagues, but once she got up close and personal, charming became eccentric and then eccentric became controlling and off-putting. Beth put an end to things quickly and after an uncomfortable period when Delilah kept trying to get Beth to change her mind, they'd manage to resume a friendship of sorts. Still, Beth was always a little nervous around Delilah.

Delilah swarmed into the office, her presence large and commanding. She was not fat, but she was tall and big boned and seemed twice as large as she really was. She had a great mass of long hair and she wore flowing clothes, simple makeup, flat shoes, and a jangle of rings and bracelets. She whooshed, clanked, and clacked wherever she went, so there was no doubt in anyone's mind when Delilah Humphries was making an entrance. She pulled up immediately in front of Beth's desk, dropped her huge valise with a loud thud, and said, "I'm here to report on the matter of John Barrow."

"Okay."

"As chair of the Tenure and Promotions Committee I have just presided over what I thought would finally be the meeting in which we would vote on Barrow's tenure. However, due to one member's insistence that the vote be delayed until Monday morning, we won't know the answer until then."

Beth didn't know whether to be relieved or concerned. She'd already determined that she would not interfere with the vote, so the delay did not make any difference in terms of her role in the outcome. But if there was some aspect of Jennifer's disappearance that involved John Barrow, she appreciated having additional time to investigate before he became a tenured professor. He would lose tenure for sleeping with a student, certainly his own student, but it was easier to keep it from being granted than taking it away after the fact.

"I take it that the majority still seems to be against tenure?"

"God, yes," Delilah said. "He is one of the least qualified candidates we've ever seen. He hasn't published, he does absolutely nothing on his committee assignments, and even the students think he's lazy." She gave Beth a long look. "Be on the level with me, Beth. What is the reaction of your president going to be if we deliver a no vote on his guy?"

"He is not 'my' president, Dee. He is, unfortunately, the college's president, which gives him the ability to veto your decision. I'm afraid that's what he'll do."

"What the hell is he thinking? Has the man ever been on a college campus before? Does he not have the slightest idea how things work here? He is ruining this place, I swear to God."

Delilah was running her hands through her wild hair, her eyes shut tight. When they opened she whacked the top of the desk with the palms of her hands. "Well, I'll tell you this. If he vetoes our vote on John Barrow, he is going to have a fucking war on his hands and it will be over before he even knows what's hit him. I don't think the board is going to see him as their White Knight if the faculty delivers a unanimous vote of no confidence."

"He's going to remove me as dean if you vote against Barrow."

Delilah's eyes narrowed. "On what grounds?"

"On the grounds that I will have failed to convince you to vote for tenure."

"But that doesn't make sense, even for him." Delilah blew out a long, noisy breath. "This is getting very serious, Beth. We need you as dean to perform whatever damage control is possible while this man is president. If you get tossed back into the ranks with us, he'll replace you with some Barrow-like person."

Beth felt a sickening sensation as she realized something. "No, wait. It does make sense. As soon as I fail to deliver the tenure vote that he wants, which he knows I can't do, he'll veto the vote, get Barrow tenured up, fire me, and then put Barrow in as dean." Beth leaned back in her chair. "It's diabolical."

"It's fucking unacceptable, is what it is." Delilah abruptly turned and stormed out of the office.

Lillian stuck her head in and said, "It's time for you to go to the meeting in town with the mayor."

Beth laid her head down on her desk and moaned.

CHAPTER THREE

The chief of Mount Avery's police department, Sally Sullivan, drove her squad car back toward town to attend the annual luncheon with the mayor, the town council, and whoever the college sent down to represent them. She drove slowly. She would rather direct traffic in a rainstorm than go to the luncheon, but for the most part she accepted that events like this were part of being chief in a small town. She wanted her life to be different than it had been when she'd been with the Chicago Police Department and it absolutely, completely, and totally was as different as she could have imagined.

Sally rolled her window down to let in the fresh April air and let out the stink of the manure clinging to the soles of her boots. She'd just spent the last hour on Harold Johnson's farm, writing him up for letting his bison escape through his rickety fences, for the third time. Two bulls made their way to the parking lot of Glen Parker Elementary School and scared a few dozen first and second graders half to death. Sally grew up in the area and there hadn't been any bison around back then. Now farmers were selling organic buffalo meat at good prices and the bison population was growing every year.

Her cell phone rang and she answered without looking at the number, which she immediately identified as a mistake when she heard the husky voice on the line.

"Detective Sullivan, is that you actually answering your phone?"

The voice belonged to a Chicago cop named Carrie Modenari, a gang team member who was tough as nails on the streets and wildly passionate in bed. Sally had succumbed to Carrie's concerted effort to seduce her when they'd seen each other in the city a few weeks before. That, it turned out, was also a mistake.

"It's Chief Sullivan now, as you know. But you can call me Sally."

"Well, Jesus, I hope so." Carrie laughed. "Unless you wear your new country cop uniform in bed, I'm not going to call you chief."

Sally had really intended their night together to be a solo, but the unrelenting voicemails left by Carrie asking for a call back made it clear that she thought it might be something else.

"So, how come you never returned my call, Sally? I never took you for a love 'em and leave 'em type."

Sally squirmed uncomfortably. She wasn't a one-night-stand kind of person, and this was one of the reasons why. Being physically close seemed to produce complicated feelings, even in women who swore they were just looking for an evening's company. Sally understood that. She never walked away from an encounter without some form of uneasiness. She generally avoided them. But after close to two years in Mount Avery without a girlfriend, Sally just had to take her libido out for the evening. She wouldn't have casual sex with anyone in Mount Avery, though she suspected some of the women she'd met would oblige her. And she hadn't yet met any women in town that she wanted to date.

"Carrie, I'm sorry if you misunderstood anything. I thought it was pretty clear we were just hooking up. I live here in Mount Avery now."

"Which still seems crazy. How can you go from being a big-city murder detective to small-town cop? Aren't you bored to death?"

Sally smiled. She was passing a feed store on the outskirts of town, every truck parked in front of it familiar to her. The high school came into view on her left, the students there frequent enough customers of her police force, but in a different galaxy from the teenagers she and Carrie dealt with in the city.

"I'm not bored. I have my own mini-farm right outside of town. The dogs love it. I love it."

"Mini-farm? What, do you have those little pigs or something? Shetland ponies?"

"Ha ha. It's ten acres with a house and a barn and some corn and soybean fields that people farm for me and it cost about as much as a two-bedroom condo in Chicago."

Carrie's voice sounded brighter. "Maybe I should visit and see what I'm missing."

Oops. Another mistake. Sally pulled into the parking lot of the station and took advantage of her car radio suddenly crackling.

"Carrie, I've got to run. They just called an armed robbery. We'll talk later."

Sally disconnected and cursed herself. Why did she say it was an armed robbery? There hadn't been a single armed robbery in town since she arrived and she knew it sounded made up. And why did she say she'd talk to her later? She had no intention of doing that. Carrie Modenari wasn't going to visit Mount Avery. She wasn't even going to get a return call from Sally. The woman that Sally hoped would be in her future would be nothing like Carrie. She hadn't found her yet in Mount Avery, but she was patient.

The Town Hall for Mount Avery was located at the very north end of Main Street, about a block and a half past the shopping area. The hall was built in the 1970s, and its single-story, cement-block sprawl was now not only ugly, but old as well. It housed the mayor's office, the assessor and tax departments, city clerk, and a few other municipal departments. The biggest room in the building was the conference room where the town council met once a month. Here Mayor Rudy Blaise presided over the six brave citizens who volunteered to serve their town and ponder decisions as diverse as the rezoning of the old Hy-Vee grocery lot to lowering the eligibility age for the annual Pork Queen to fifteen, seeing as there were fewer and fewer high school juniors and seniors actually willing to be a Pork Queen.

Beth trotted up Main, late for the lunch meeting that the town hosted once a year as a gesture of goodwill to the college. Her brain was racing from the multiplying problems that were finding their way to her desk. Problems multiplying on campus were like problems multiplying within Beth herself, white blood cells growing from an infection, making her ill. She knew she should maintain some kind of distance between her personal and professional life, but as they were essentially one and the same, she never could figure out how that was done.

Generally the college and town enjoyed a peaceful relationship, but there were the expected troubles also. Grafton College students, like students everywhere, were hell-bent on getting drunk and acting stupid. Young people of Mount Avery liked to get drunk and act stupid too. Sometimes when this occurred in the same place, all hell broke loose. In a reenactment of an age-old class battle, the students and the working people chose to take sides against one another, usually when they were in a bar and three sheets to the wind. Luckily, none of these dust-ups had led to any real animosity. The college was the town's largest employer outside of the corn sweetener plant, and it needed it in order to survive. The college needed the town to provide it with area services and shopping. The relationship worked fine, but the unspoken difference between the two cultures was always present. It was rare that there was any real social interaction.

As she approached Town Hall, Sally Sullivan emerged from the opposite direction and arrived at the door at the same time as Beth. Sally Sullivan had been hired as chief of police two years before. Beth had seen her around and met her once briefly at a festival, but they were essentially strangers to one another, as much as that was possible in such a small town. Beth had heard a couple things about Sally—that she was an experienced cop, an ex-homicide detective in Chicago, and that she'd taken the job in Mount Avery because she'd grown up in the area and her parents were getting on in years. Beth always thought that sounded a little suspect. Surely there had to be a more complicated reason for moving back to your hometown.

Beth shook herself into the present as Sally opened the door to the building and waited for Beth to walk through. She was dressed in uniform, a navy shirt and pants, black belt and shoes. Knowing that the cut of these uniforms were usually anything but flattering to women, Beth admired how the chief wore hers. Her slim hips allowed her trousers to drape as trousers should, rather than bulge from womanly curves. Beth loved womanly curves, just not in uniforms designed for men, and she blushed when she realized her gaze had lingered a moment too long before she said hello. Sally smiled and waved her hand for Beth to precede her.

"I'm afraid I've forgotten your name, but I know you're from the college," Sally said. "I'm Sally Sullivan, the police chief."

"Yes, I remember. I think we met briefly at the Corn Festival last year. I'm Beth Ellis, the dean of the college." Beth paused in the entry hall. "I'm glad to run into you, Chief. I'm wondering if you've gotten a call yet from our dean of students. It seems we have a student missing."

"I just got off the phone with Dean Taylor. I've put a couple officers to work tracking her down and we'll see what we find out. Who should I be calling on this?" Sally was reaching for a notepad and pen.

"That's Dean Taylor's area. I think she'll just be more upset if I step into this. Thanks for asking, though."

"Is there anything you know about the student that might help us?" Sally glanced at her notepad. "It's Jennifer Manos, correct?"

"That's right. Jennifer is a senior and was a student of mine when I was still teaching in the English department. I was also her advisor, so I got to know her pretty well. She's really, really bright, but kind of a loner. She doesn't make friends easily."

They walked down the hallway to the conference room, their shoes making a huge noise on the linoleum floor, the sound echoing off the concrete block walls. The city offices were closed for the lunch hour, most of the workers having headed home for their sandwiches and soap operas, or over to Lou's Diner down the street.

Sally and Beth entered the conference room to find they were the last to arrive for the luncheon meeting. The mayor and several of the council members had already helped themselves to sandwiches and chips set up on a table along a wall. A tent card with CATERED BY LOU'S DINER had been placed near the soft drinks. Beth happened to love Lou's Diner and ate there frequently with faculty friends. She'd even conducted senior seminars at Lou's, enjoying the intricate and sometimes heated conversations on literature while sitting around the long table in the front of the diner, the table that was occupied by local farmers every morning. She scooped up a sandwich, hesitated over the chips before picking up an apple instead, and took a seat at the conference table. Sally sat next to her a moment later and passed a bag of chips over with a smile. "Here, live a little. You'll just run it off later."

"How do you know I run?" Beth asked.

"Well, I wouldn't be much of a police officer if I didn't notice you running by the station practically every day for the past two years."

"Is that what the police do in this town? I've always wondered. You stare out the window during your shifts and what, compare notes?" Beth realized she sounded a little asinine.

"We observe, Dean. And I've observed you running by the station."

Beth took the bag of chips and arranged her lunch in front of her, glancing once more at Sally. She was like a TV cop, good looking by any Hollywood standard. She appeared to be in her late thirties, tall and angular. Her dark hair was short and beautifully layered, a cut she almost certainly did not get in town at Betty's Hair Salon. Sally seemed perfectly comfortable and sure of herself, which Beth found both intriguing and slightly irritating.

Mayor Blaise sat at the head of the conference table with five of the town council members sitting on either side of him, most of them merchants or professionals in town. The sixth member was a veterinarian who, as usual, was out on an emergency call at a nearby farm. The mayor opened the meeting with a statement he read from an index card, welcoming Beth to their council meeting and noting how much he looked forward to breaking bread with the college representative once a year.

"Now, we like to have these meetings so we can nurture the close relationship we've always enjoyed with the college. Usually we like to see the president attend, no insult intended, Dean. But that's how serious we take this meeting."

Beth had a rather large mouthful of chips to contend with before she managed to reply. The town officials were all looking at her, most of them finished with their meals. "Mr. Mayor, let me just say that it is an honor for me to be here today, and I know the president would feel the same way had circumstances allowed him to attend this meeting. Unfortunately, he was called away on important business out of the country."

"I'm just a little disappointed. I think we all are. It may surprise you to know that since he's been president of the college, no one in this room has had an opportunity to meet him."

"I didn't know that," Beth said. Everyone was still looking at her, except for Sally, who'd gotten up to pour herself a cup of coffee. "Mayor, I sense that you feel a little unhappy about that. Is there anything I can do to improve the situation?"

"I don't know if you can. Part of the reason we get together each year is to talk about how we can have the least division between our two communities. I've noticed that since your president has come on board, there has been a little rise in the friction between the two."

Again with the "your president" thing. It was beginning to feel like being collared by a drowning man in open water. He was threatening to bring her down too. "I've not been made aware of any incidents, Mr. Mayor. Tell me about them."

"Well, as an example, let me have the chief here tell us about some reports she's been getting over the last couple of months."

Sally had just settled back into her seat next to Beth. She appeared a little startled when the mayor called on her.

"You know, Chief, how I was asking you about the way the young people weren't getting along in the taverns lately."

"Well, Mayor, if you're referring to the scuffle outside Werni's last week, I can't say that it was much of a disturbance. We've only been called out about once a month to take care of any disputes over there or at Drexel's bar. And not all of those involved students. I consider that to be a pretty acceptable rate, to speak truthfully."

"It might be an acceptable rate if you're in Chicago," Mayor Blaise said.

"Mayor, if we were in Chicago, these wouldn't even be called incidents." Sally took a drink of her coffee.

Beth could see that the mayor was annoyed. "Mr. Mayor, I feel like we should do something to show you how much we, as a college, value our relationship with the town. Clearly you're concerned, and I would like to address the issue with you. What can we do?"

They spent the next half hour discussing joint projects between town and college, including setting up a scholarship contest for a town student to attend the college.

While Beth said her good-byes to the mayor and council members, she noticed Sally slipping out of the room. She excused herself as quickly as she could and hurried out of the building and onto Main Street where she found Sally talking on the phone and reading something off the notepad in her hand. When Beth reached her, Sally was just putting her phone back on her belt.

"Do you have anything on Jennifer, Chief?" Beth asked.

"No, not yet. We've got people working the phones, and I'll be heading over to interview Jennifer's housemates later."

"What do you think the chances of finding Jennifer are?"

"You shouldn't worry at this point. Your student is probably fine. It's been my experience that when adults go missing, it's more often than not because they don't want to be found." Sally turned her head as a squad car pulled up. "If there's anything to find out, we'll find it out, and I'll keep the college informed."

"Thank you, Chief."

"Try not to worry," Sally said, hesitating before getting in the car.

"Well, I don't think that will happen, but I'll try."

Beth turned toward campus as Sally and the young officer at the wheel took off quickly down Main. She was worried about Jennifer, but the worry hadn't yet moved into a position of prominence. It was being kept at arm's length by worries about the tenure situation, Landscome's reign of terror, the threat to her job, and the changing feel of the campus. She picked up her step and began the uphill climb to Old Main, thinking also about the other thing taking up space in her head—confident, problem-solving Sally Sullivan and how she looked in a uniform. Beth felt a little more out of breath than usual as she continued to climb back to campus.

❖

At the end of the workday Beth picked up her car at home and drove over to the Hy-Vee. Her night stretched in front of her in a comforting way. She planned to buy her favorite foods to eat, watch her favorite movie, and then climb into a hot bath. These things were like pacifiers to her, tried and true methods for zoning out and halting the worry cycle, at least for a few hours. She had never learned to confide in others in the way that came so naturally to most women.

For the most part, Beth's only companions growing up were the young women working for her mother, or the young men who worked security, and though some were very kind to Beth, others were not. None of them stayed very long.

Beth turned her isolation into an opportunity. She fell in love with reading and study and the worlds she could conjure up while she sat with her books. She learned she could leverage this one thing she had on her own, the one thing no one could take from her, into a career, a way of life, a way out of the life she knew in Nevada. She supplemented her mediocre public education with a thorough course of self-study in the classics of literature and philosophy. She aced her college entrance exams, wrote an exquisite application essay, and, of course, had a straight-A average. Her full four-year scholarship to Smith College had her mother sit up and take notice.

"That's an impressive moneymaker," her mother had said, running down the list of scholarship benefits. "I'm glad your hobby paid off. Problem is, it's not an asset you can use over and over, do you know what I mean?"

"Yes, I think so, Mother. I'm idiotically throwing away my youth on academics instead of mindlessly fucking man after man at the Liaison Fantastique. I expect, however, that I'll have a few more options than your girls do at thirty."

"You could take over this ranch someday. I'd never let one of those numbskulls take it over. It would be a damn shame to sell it."

It was true, Beth knew only too well, that her mother trusted no one to administer anything about the workings of the ranch but herself and Beth. Consequently, there was never a time that her mother was not working. She missed all of Beth's graduations except for high school, where everyone in the gymnasium knew what Mae Ellis did for a living. It just seemed sometimes that if there was a way for her mother to make things harder on Beth, she intuitively fell to doing just that.

Beth was just pulling out frozen egg rolls and pizza puffs when she felt the freezer door held open for her. She turned to see Mel, grinning as usual, holding a six-pack of beer under her arm.

"Hello, sweetheart. You have anything to say for yourself tonight?"

Beth laughed and slapped at Mel's arm. "Yes, I do. I want to say thank you for the visit last night. I was entirely selfish, I took advantage of you, and I slept like a baby. So, thanks."

"No problem. You know it's a standing offer." Mel took the cart from Beth and they started walking toward the check-out. "What's up this evening?"

"Are you thinking of asking yourself over? You've never visited two nights in a row, Mel."

"So?" Mel kept pushing the cart, nodding her head at several women along the way. "It doesn't mean anything."

"You're sure? I know we've talked about this, so I don't want to belabor the point, but I don't want you to misunderstand anything."

Mel put her arm around Beth and squeezed her tight. "You're worrying again. It's just friendship with a little sex thrown in. I'm not looking for anything else."

Beth took back the cart and steered it into a check-out lane.

"Okay then. If you want to come over for a movie and junk food, you're welcome. The company would be nice."

"What's the movie?"

"*Top Gun*. It's my favorite." Beth was loading her groceries with a perfectly straight face.

"*Top Gun* is your favorite movie? How is that even possible?"

Beth laughed again. "I know. Yet another thing adding to my mystique."

❖

Sally pulled up to Hadley House, where Jennifer Manos lived with eleven other students. The immediate outer ring of the campus held a number of sturdy old frame houses that were once owned by the solidly middle class in town. As the campus grew and made its way to the edge of these properties, the college bought them up and started to house upper-class students in them. Placement in one of the houses was a privilege of good grades, and the students enjoyed unsupervised living for probably the first time in their lives.

Despite the good academic reputation of the students living in the row of college houses, there was evidence everywhere that the eggheads could drink as much as the jocks. A couple of spent kegs were listing on the porch of the house, and overflowing garbage bins held empty beer cans. Sally knew that she had it easy compared to cops in towns housing the big universities, but still she was sick of corralling kids who were loud, obnoxious, drunker than lords, and constantly sick in her patrol cars and holding tanks. There were times she yearned for the paddy wagons that cleared away Chicago's drunk and disorderly, but those were the only times she thought fondly back to cop life in Chicago. She was still in love with life in a town where the murder rate was zero, and had been for a very long time. The mayor of Chicago sang praise to his crime-reduction efforts when the murder rate fell into the six hundreds.

Officer Ted Benson was in the squad car with Sally. "What do you want me to do while you're inside, Chief?" Ted was in his first year in law enforcement and looked to Sally to be about eighteen years old, though she knew he was more like twenty-two. That still seemed ridiculously young, but he was eager and seemed to learn quickly. She enjoyed training young cops and making them part of her team. They were much easier to work with than some of the older cops she'd inherited from the previous chief, veterans who still had a hard time taking orders from a woman.

"I want you to come in with me and listen and take notes. I'll tell you if I need anything else. We're probably going to search her room, so I'm bringing an evidence bag in with me."

Mandy Orton, Jennifer's roommate, welcomed them into Hadley House. She was a tiny woman and Sally felt huge and old as she moved into the old-fashioned foyer. A stairway with a carved oak balustrade was to the right of the entrance, a living room to the left. After showing the officers into the living room, Mandy asked whether they'd found anything on Jennifer.

"We're hoping that you'll be able to give us a little more information to go on, Mandy. As it is, we have contacted Jennifer's aunt, and she doesn't know where she is, nor does her friend from last year, Tricia. We've contacted almost all of Jennifer's professors, and they don't know where she is. We'd like to go up and see her room and have you tell us what's missing from there," Sally said.

"That's just the thing, Chief Sullivan. I can't see that anything is missing, except her purse." Mandy seemed a little excited that she had police in her house and she leaned forward to take in everything about them. Officer Benson kept his eyes on his tiny notebook, making scribbles even when nothing was being said. Mandy seemed to be trying to catch his eye.

"Mandy, tell me everything you can think of about how Jennifer has been acting recently. Even if it doesn't seem significant at all," Sally said.

"Well, let's see. We've been roommates for the last two years, so I know Jennifer's habits pretty well. She's a real freak about studying and she doesn't party much. That's why I was so surprised when she didn't come home last night. But I thought, you know, that she'd finally hooked up with someone. I mean, it was going to happen sooner or later, right?"

"What's that?" Sally asked.

Mandy tried a coy look. "You know, that she'd hook up with a guy. They say there's someone out there for everyone, and even Jennifer can't stay a virgin forever."

"Do you have any idea who the guy might be?"

"Not really. It's a little confusing. See, Jennifer has a thing for one of her professors, the one with the English accent. His name's John Barrow, which I only know because she says it whenever she can. John this and John that."

"Did Jennifer ever say whether Barrow and she were seeing each other?"

"Well, no, and I'm not sure she would have been able to keep that to herself, do you know what I mean? She'd be too excited, even though he could get into a shitload of trouble for sleeping with one of his students. And it was Barrow who called here looking for Jennifer, and I don't know what to make of that." Mandy was getting wound up, looking back and forth at them and leaning over to stare at Benson's notes.

"Mandy, I need you to concentrate here and tell me everything. Why and when he called, all of it."

"Sure. He called yesterday morning because Jennifer didn't show up for his eight o'clock seminar. He said he was concerned because she'd missed Monday too. You see, the thing is, we didn't realize Jennifer was gone until this morning. I'm not sure I should be saying this in front of a law enforcement officer," Mandy said, casting another look at Ted, "but I spent Monday through Wednesday night with my boyfriend."

"That's okay, Mandy. As far as I know, that's not illegal," Sally said.

"Anyway, I mentioned Jennifer to my housemates at breakfast this morning because it didn't look like she'd come home last night, and we figured out that no one had seen her at all, not since Monday when I left for class."

"You called her cell?"

"Sure. But she didn't answer it. I left one message saying we were worried, and then another telling her the police were looking for her."

"And what was she doing when you left for class?"

"I thought she just decided to cut class and sleep in. That would have been Barrow's class, which should have told me something was wrong. She wouldn't miss a chance to see him. She had the blankets over her head and didn't move while I got ready to go. I guess I thought maybe she was hungover or something."

"Did Jennifer drink a lot?" Sally asked.

"No, she didn't. Jennifer doesn't do much of anything except study and watch a little TV. Her head is always in a book. Or she's mooning about John Barrow, like I said."

They made their way up to the shared room on the second floor. Sally had forgotten how college students lived. Even in this elegant old house, the room two students were expected to share didn't seem big enough for one. It quickly became apparent among Jennifer's highly organized clothing and study materials that nothing was noticeably missing. There were no gaps in the closet or the bookshelves, her clothes drawers were full of neatly folded clothing, her coats and shoes all seemed to be in place in the closet. Her backpack lay next to her bed, filled with textbooks and notebooks.

Sally leaned over to pull open the small drawer in Jennifer's nightstand and stood still. There sitting alone in the drawer was a pregnancy kit, used, its tip showing the + sign that almost certainly meant the tester was pregnant. She took an evidence envelope out of the bag on her shoulder and picked up the pregnancy kit with her gloved hand.

"Looks like Jennifer might have taken care of that virginity issue after all."

"Oh, my God," breathed Mandy. "It's got to be that professor. She would have told me if it was someone else."

Sally and Ted finished up their search of the room and the house and found nothing further. Ted took a copy of the house resident roster and went out front to drive Sally back to the station. Ted would return later to interview the rest of the housemates while Sally tried again to track down John Barrow. He hadn't returned the calls she'd made earlier, and the new information made Sally wonder why.

"I want to thank you for the opportunity with the interviews, Chief," Ted said as they got in the squad.

"You deserve a chance like anyone else. Just don't fuck it up, and I think you know what I mean," Sally said, gesturing back toward the house.

Ted looked appalled. "Oh, Chief, I'd never do anything like that. Jeez."

"Are you going to tell me your mama raised you better than that?"

"Well, she did. She did. And I have a girlfriend already, just so you know." Ted pursed his lips as he drove around the hill toward town.

Coming up on the left was Beth Ellis's house. Sally knew where Beth lived, even if she didn't really know her. She made it her business over the last two years to know just about everything it was legal to know about the citizens of the town, including the college folk. She spent many hours driving around town, taking patrol shifts like the other officers. She knew where people lived, knew what they drove, generally knew who they were seeing, if only because she noticed who was with whom when she was out on the streets or in the town's various stores, restaurants, and bars. Beth's house was modest, but the front yard was nicely landscaped, the paint fresh, the front door a bright shiny red.

After her shift was over, Sally drove back down Tenth Avenue, past Beth's house again. It wasn't on her way home. In fact, it was the opposite direction, but it was one of the routes to the Hy-Vee, albeit a roundabout one. She could use more dog food, she thought. She could also use another look at Beth, curious whether her strong reaction at lunch was repeatable. Maybe it was a singular phenomenon where a hormone surge, blue skies, and a pretty woman converged to produce a false positive attraction—the kind of false positive that had gotten Sally embroiled with the wrong woman on more than one occasion. She didn't think that was the case with Beth. She'd had the same reaction when she first met her at last year's Corn Festival, a brief introduction where only a few words were spoken. It was as if Beth was a magnetic pole and Sally pivoted right toward her. She was captivated by the strong features on her lovely face, expressive and warm and, to Sally, profoundly sexy. She hadn't picked up the slightest hint that Beth felt anything remotely the same in exchange, and soon enough the meeting faded in her memory, revived brilliantly by their meeting today. It seemed unlikely to be a false positive.

As she neared Beth's house a pickup truck approached from the other direction, turning left into Beth's driveway. Mel got out of the truck, a six-pack under her arm. Sally knew what it generally meant when Mel's pickup was parked in a woman's driveway. She hadn't known before that minute that Beth was one of those women.

Chapter Four

The movie was over and the remains of the feast lay on a brightly colored Mexican plate sitting on the coffee table. A few pizza puffs and egg rolls surrounded a bowl of salsa, while bags of chips and cookies were crumpled nearby. Mel's feet were propped up on the coffee table next to Beth's, pointed upright during the movie and now, just as the credits began, starting to move and point at Beth's.

"I thought that stupid movie would never end," Mel said, pulling Beth sideways and moving over her on the sofa. Several empty bottles fell to the floor.

"I refuse to be defensive about *Top Gun*. Kelly McGillis is in it. I think that speaks for itself."

"It's over. That's all I care about." Mel leaned in for a long kiss, so long and intense that Beth eventually put her hands on Mel's shoulders and pushed her up.

"I have to breathe," Beth said.

"Okay." Mel kissed her forehead, her scalp, and then the cowlick on Beth's brow that always made her look just slightly disheveled. There was not a product on earth that hadn't been used in her fight against it.

"That was some kiss," Beth said. "Is there anything going on that I should know about?"

"Don't you start with that. If you don't stop worrying about me making more of this than it is, I'm going to have to stop seeing you altogether." Mel eased back a little and gave Beth room to move up on the sofa.

"No, I don't want that. I just care a lot about you, Mel. I don't want you to get hurt."

"So I shouldn't kiss you like I mean it, is that what you're saying?" Mel smiled.

"It is complicated, isn't it? Sex complicates a friendship."

Mel sighed and reached for her bottle of beer. "Here's the thing, though. Say you and I were not having sex. Would we really be friends? Would you have driven into my repair shop with your VW and thought, 'Jesus, would I like to sit down for a chat with her?' No, I don't think so. Unless you're hiding a deep love for sports and cars, we don't have a whole lot in common. And, I've got to tell you, once you open your mouth about anything to do with the college or books or whatever, I don't know what the hell you're talking about. But once we started sleeping with each other, I'm more relaxed about not having much in common. I'm not bored out of my skull, even if we're not having sex."

"Thanks, I think." Beth had never heard Mel talk for so long. She realized Mel had given all of this quite a bit of thought. "I've always wondered how you've managed to sleep with so many of the women in town and not have any scars as a result. Surely you've angered more than a few, or broken some hearts?"

"Well, I have to say that some are more comfortable about it than others, which I suppose you'd expect," Mel said, flashing another smile. "You're great because a) you're an outstanding kisser; b) you're hot in the sack; c) you're not looking for anything more; and d) I really like you, even though I don't understand you half the time."

"You understand me just fine, Mel. Don't play on that 'I'm just a car mechanic' thing." Beth reached over to touch Mel's leg. "You're smarter and more kind than a lot of the women I've been involved with, and most of them have been college professors." Beth stopped talking as the truth of that statement hit her.

Mel cocked her head to the side, staring at Beth as though she were a painting—an abstract one—and if she viewed her from a different angle she was more likely to figure her out.

"One thing I've never understood about you," she said, "is why you've never had a girlfriend in all the time I've known you. What is that, five years or so?"

"Maybe you've taken all the available women for yourself. Have you thought of that?" Beth teased.

Mel leaned forward and took Beth's hands. "I'm serious. You're a beautiful woman, you're sweet, you're smart, I assume. It doesn't make sense."

Beth rubbed her thumbs along the knuckles of Mel's large, rough hands. "If I did have a girlfriend, you wouldn't be here right now."

"I think you're avoiding the question, darlin'. You have had relationships before, haven't you?"

Beth pulled her hands from Mel's and stood, gathering plates and glasses in her arms. "Mel, being quizzed by you on my relationship history is a little rich, don't you think? What do you know about relationships?"

"I know I want one someday. And don't look alarmed. I don't mean with you."

"Thanks a lot." Beth headed into the kitchen and dumped everything onto the counter. "I've had girlfriends. I just said I did a few minutes ago."

"Have you ever been in love?" Mel was leaning against the kitchen door frame watching Beth rinse dishes and stack them back on the counter.

"Of course I've been in love."

"Once? Twice?"

Beth stepped over to Mel and poked her in the arm. "What are you doing? You've never asked me things like this before. And frankly, that was one of your charms."

"Was?" Mel smiled. She took Beth's hand back into her own. "I'm just curious. If you don't want to tell me what happened, that's fine."

"Good. Subject closed." Beth returned to the living room and gathered up bags of chips and empty bottles.

"Fair enough. How about we take a shower together and just forget it?"

"Maybe," Beth said.

"And I'll say just one final thing. If you want to get a girl, you need to seriously upgrade your taste in movies and food."

"Yes, I'll remember that, Ms. Loose-meat Sandwich Girl." Beth turned toward the kitchen with her arms full. "And who ever said I wanted to 'get a girl,' as you put it?"

If Mel had pushed her further, Beth might have admitted that the thought of something solid had flitted through her mind earlier that day when she sat next to Sally Sullivan at lunch. Not solid in a stodgy way, but firm, present, unlikely to melt or slip away. She shook the image out of her head and passed the phone just as it rang. With her arms full she let it go to voicemail, curious about the 415 area code on the caller ID.

"I'm just going to let this go to voicemail," Beth called out. She didn't know who it could be, and the thought of a shower with Mel was starting to sound good. But when Mel headed back toward the bathroom, Beth found she couldn't resist and she dialed in for her message.

"Dean Ellis? This is Jennifer Manos. It's seven o'clock in San Francisco, so I hope I'm not calling too late. I know the school is probably wondering where I am by this point, so I thought I'd call to let you know I'm okay. I've decided to leave school, but I really can't go into all the reasons why. Maybe I'll be able to come back at some point to finish up. If you need to let me know anything, I've got a new e-mail address—it's JenniferIsGone at yahoo dot com. That should be easy enough to remember. Bye."

"Shit." Beth grabbed the phone and dialed *69. The line rang for a long minute before voicemail picked up and a mechanical voice repeated the number, which Beth wrote down, and asked the caller to leave their message. "Jennifer, it's Beth Ellis. I just missed your call but I'm here at home. Please call me back. We're worried about you, even though you say you're okay. I want to talk to you about school. It sounds so rash to drop out now—you're just a couple months away from graduation. That tells me you're in trouble. Please, please call me back. And here's my cell number so you'll have that too—"

Beth hung up and raked her hands through her hair. She didn't know whether to be relieved or not, though it was undoubtedly a relief to hear Jennifer was not injured or dead. But there was clearly something wrong. Beth headed toward the bathroom and walked through the open door. Standing over by the shower adjusting the water temperature was Mel in all her naked glory. Beth stopped and stared.

"Looks like you started without me," she said.

"Yeah. The water's just about perfect." Mel said, turning to face Beth. She was a beautiful, androgynous vision. Her shoulders were broad, her arms and legs strong and defined, her breasts full and her hips gently curved. Her belly was long and slightly rounded, but still the strength was visible throughout her torso. She stood there as comfortable as if she had her coveralls on.

"I'm sorry, Mel. Truly sorry, believe me. But I think I have to end our evening together. The call I got was from a student we discovered missing today. The police are looking for her, there's a lot of worried people—"

"It's okay. I'll just hang out till you're free." Mel stepped into the shower and pulled the shower curtain closed. Beth could hear her long sigh. "God, that feels really good."

Beth's mouth turned down at the corner as she continued to stare toward Mel, now wondering why this naked woman felt she could make herself at home like this. She crossed the room in a couple of strides and pulled the shower curtain back.

"Mel, you have to leave. I've got a crisis on my hands here."

Mel wiped the water from her face. "Are you kidding me? You're throwing me out after I spent all evening watching Tom Cruise and eating pizza puffs? C'mon, Beth."

Beth grabbed a towel and handed it to Mel. "I didn't know you were expecting something in return," she said.

"Of course I wanted something in return. I don't know if I

expected it." Mel turned the water off and stepped out of the shower. "No, God damn it, I did expect it. Why wouldn't I? That's what you expect when you see me, isn't it? To fuck?"

Beth turned around and headed out of the bathroom. "I don't have time for this, Mel. One minute you're acting like my soul sister, the next you're like some horny guy. I'm calling the police."

"Well, Jesus. Don't call the police. I'm leaving." Mel sounded angry.

"I'm not calling the police about you," Beth yelled back toward the bathroom. "But I'd appreciate it if you weren't here when she arrives."

Beth went back to her kitchen and called the police station. When she told the dispatcher what the call was about, she was patched through to Chief Sullivan's house.

"What can I do for you, Dean?" Sally said. She sounded a little groggy.

"Sounds like I may have woken you, Chief."

"No, it's fine, really. I fell asleep in front of the TV. What's up?"

"I thought you'd want to know right away that Jennifer Manos just called me. Unfortunately, I was busy and didn't pick up the call and it went into voicemail." Beth waited for Sally to respond but there was a longish pause.

"Chief?"

"Sorry. Is she okay?"

"I think so, though she can't really be. She told me she was dropping out of school, but she's just about to graduate. There has to be something really wrong for a student like her to do that. I'm not sure what I should do."

Mel walked into the living room, grabbed her coat, and left. Beth would have to patch things up with her later.

"...better come over," Sally was saying.

"I'm sorry, Chief. I missed that. Someone was just leaving."

"Mel," Sally said.

Beth thought she couldn't be hearing right. "What did you just say?"

"Shit. I didn't mean to say that out loud."

"How did you know Mel was here? Am I under surveillance or something?"

"Of course not. I happened to be driving by earlier this evening and saw Mel pull into your drive."

"Huh. That feels a bit unsettling, like you're stalking me or something."

"I'm not sure you should flatter yourself. I usually have better things to do with my time."

"Well, still," Beth said. She couldn't figure out what was happening with this conversation.

"I think it's just a small-town thing," Sally said. "If we were in Chicago I'd never know who you were seeing."

"I'm not 'seeing' Mel," Beth said. "At least not the way you mean."

"Okay, whatever you say. But I do think I should come over and listen to that voicemail. And there's something I found out today about Jennifer that you should know about."

Fifteen minutes after they talked on the phone, Sally rang the doorbell and Beth opened up to see her for the first time out of uniform. It seemed odd to her now that in the two years Sally had been in town, Beth had only seen her when she was on duty. Now she stood on the front step with faded jeans and Frye boots on, a black leather coat on top. Still a uniform of sorts, Beth thought, and Sally wore this one as well as her cop clothes. As she walked into the living room, Beth had that same sensation of solidness, though it was a feeling that didn't account for the sensation occurring slightly lower in Beth's body. She felt confused by the first, but she knew what physical attraction was. There was no question that she was feeling attracted to Sally.

"I said, why don't you show me where your answering equipment is?" Sally looked at Beth as if she were a bit slow.

"I'm sorry, I'm very distracted," Beth said, leading Sally into the kitchen. "It's been a hellish week and a very long day."

"It's okay. I imagine you're under a lot of stress. Being dean is a big job."

"Well, it's really not the job that gets to me, it's the people. Anyway, here's the phone. It has digital voicemail so I'll have to call in and replay it for you." Beth handed the phone to Sally after she entered her password. Sally listened to the message and hung up.

"And you said Jennifer was calling from a four-one-five number? That's San Francisco."

"That's what the caller ID read. When I called the number back it wasn't her voice on the outgoing message, just a standard recorded greeting. I have no idea what's going on with her." Beth handed her a piece of paper with the phone number and e-mail address as she moved to her small breakfast table and sat. "Have you been able to find out anything about why she left?"

"I think so, but I've got to say that now that she's called in, there really isn't anything more I can do. As I said earlier today, as long as she's moving around of her own free will I'm not in a position to go after her. She's an adult."

"Well, that's where your responsibility and mine are different. Parents expect their children to be reasonably well looked after while they're here, not so distressed that they leave school right before graduation. It's like throwing a hundred fifty thousand dollars down the drain."

"A hundred fifty thousand? Is that how much this school costs?" Sally sat and took her coat off. "That's insane."

"I know. But Jennifer was mostly getting through on scholarships. She's very intelligent."

"Maybe not about everything. It appears that Jennifer is pregnant, and that's likely to be why she left school."

"Oh, shit." Beth began pacing the kitchen. "How could she let that happen? Sorry, it's just that Jennifer has so much promise as a scholar and I know she was looking forward to graduate school. This just doesn't make sense." She stopped and looked at Sally. "I wonder who the father is?"

"According to her housemates, Jennifer only had eyes for this Barrow guy. Her roommate didn't know for sure, but she thinks it's him." Sally stretched her long legs out in front of her and did not appear particularly concerned about Jennifer Manos or John Barrow.

"I don't imagine you much care one way or another about who got who pregnant or whether a gifted student finishes her education, but believe me, this is a big deal. And now with John Barrow possibly involved, the ramifications spread even further. What a fucking mess." Beth sat and put her head in her hands, running her fingers through her hair.

"I don't know if I understand everything that's going on, but I'm happy to help you out in any way I can."

"Why would you want to get involved in a college problem?"

"I don't, really. But I do want to help you. Why don't you tell me the parts I don't know about and we'll see where it goes?"

See where it goes? Beth wondered about Sally's choice of words. Was there a chance Sally was attracted to her? As interesting as that sounded, and as frightening, Beth didn't think there was any room in her head at the moment to cram one more important thing into it.

"If we're going to talk, I think we're going to need some wine."

Beth uncorked a bottle and poured as Sally filled her in on the interviews with the students and with her attempts to find a time to interview John Barrow, who still had not returned Sally's calls or been at home or his office when she tried to find him at those places. Beth described the whole tenure mess, how she found it hard to believe that even John Barrow could be stupid enough to jeopardize an already difficult tenure process by sleeping with a student of his. After she poured a second glass of wine for each of them, she told Sally all about the new president and what a bad fit he was.

"That much I do know about," Sally said. "Even the old-timers at Werni's Tap know that the president of the college is an asshole. What I don't get is why the board of trustees doesn't rein him in a bit."

"I'm not sure anyone has got the guts to tell the board how much the faculty hate Landscome. As long as he continues to bring in new funding commitments the way he's been doing since he arrived, the board will likely let him do almost anything." Sally stared into her wineglass. "I'm surprised that you haven't made the usual smart remark about the horrors of academic politics."

Sally smiled ruefully. "It's not that different or worse than police department politics, at least in big cities like Chicago. But professors, unlike cops, aren't wired for violence. You have that much going for you."

"You wouldn't say that if you'd seen the Committee on Committees in action last week."

"You have a Committee on Committees?" Sally looked truly horrified.

"Oh, yes. And the chair of the Committee on Committees is very powerful. In a small school like this, the quality of life of each faculty member is largely determined by what committees they end up serving on. The lobbying for positions puts Washington politicking to shame."

"And where there's power, there is corruption. I've lived in Chicago, so I know."

"I am a little worried about integrity starting to take a backseat on campus. I hate to sound like an anticorporate academic, but the fact is that I'm an anticorporate academic. I see the corporate sensibilities of our new president starting to create rifts in the faculty, and the problems are going to get worse before they get better."

They were quiet for a moment. Beth realized she felt better sharing the details of her troubles with Sally, that they felt smaller, maybe a little absurd, whereas the usual feeling for her when campus problems were particularly problematic was to feel threatened.

"Why would Jennifer go to San Francisco? I've never heard her say anything about that city." Beth moved to pour her more wine, but Sally placed her hand over her glass.

"If Jennifer is pregnant, she's looking for a place to have the baby or terminate the pregnancy, and she can do both there, of course. Maybe a friend of hers lives there?"

"Can you look into the number she gave me, see who the

phone is registered to or where she called from or something?" Beth asked.

"Sure, I can do that."

Beth stared at Sally's hands, one resting on the table, the other twirling her empty wineglass. They were surprisingly delicate hands, the fingers long and tapered, the skin smooth and soft looking. The nails were well cared for. Beth tried to imagine Sally preparing for bed in the evening, smoothing hand cream on, filing her nails. She had a hard time picturing it. But why? Why shouldn't Sally do the same things other women do? Because she was really tall, commanding, in a position of power? Beth knew such assumptions could be so wrong. How many people assumed that all she read was Austen and Elliot, or whatever appeared on the Booker Prize long list, when in fact her favorite novels were mysteries and thrillers?

Lost in her thoughts, Beth was startled when Sally pushed her chair back and stood.

"I better get going. My dogs will want to go out."

"Oh. You have dogs."

Sally smiled. "That surprises you?"

"I guess not. It's just that I realized it's the first thing you've told me about yourself."

Sally put her jacket on as she regarded Beth. "You haven't asked me anything."

Beth opened her mouth to protest, but Sally had already turned and headed toward the front door. Beth followed behind. "I'm sorry. I must seem self-centered to you."

"No, you don't. You have a lot going on, and I don't."

"You must have someone keeping you busy, Chief. Are you saying you don't have a girlfriend?" She hoped the answer was no.

Sally paused at the door. "You just assumed I'm a lesbian?"

"Let's just say it wasn't a big leap."

"Since you're asking, no, I don't have a girlfriend." She opened the door and stepped out, turning back to Beth. "And I don't have a Mel, either. Good night, Beth."

Chapter Five

The following morning, Beth sat with the dean of students, dean of admissions, and department heads for their regularly scheduled Friday meeting to coordinate the ongoing projects and policies of the college. After each of these meetings she would summarize the gist for Landscome, thus obviating any need for him to attend. It was a report she gladly wrote. Before the start of the meeting Beth took a few minutes to tell Dean Taylor about the voicemail message from Jennifer Manos and the news of her apparent safety.

"You didn't feel a phone call to me was in order? I would have appreciated being spared another night's worry." There was no mistaking Harriet's displeasure. Beth just kept herself from cringing.

"You're absolutely right to be annoyed with me, Harriet. I can't imagine why I didn't call you."

Perhaps because too much was happening, too fast? Because she simply forgot? Because Sally came to her house and sat for a chat and everything else flew out of her head? Beth didn't bother offering up any excuse. Harriet would reject it out of hand. Beth endured another few moments of glaring before taking her seat to start the meeting, refusing to appear chastised. It was a bit much, she thought, to be condemned by Harriet Taylor for thoughtlessness. She couldn't remember the last time Harriet had actually inquired about anything pleasantly, said a kind word, or eagerly shared good news. She tried to think what it was she always said she admired about Harriet. Maybe it was simply that she never made a mistake. Ever. And her manner was so supremely self-assured, Beth couldn't imagine Harriet would even feel bad in the unlikely event she did err in some way. Was that what she admired, even tried to emulate? A person so tightly in control no outside force could upset her?

The weekly meeting was held in the large conference room in Old Main, an ornate but stately room, decorated by fluted sconces, beamed ceiling, wood-paneled walls, and an immense mahogany conference table that comfortably seated twenty in wide wooden armchairs. The board of trustees met semiannually in the room and Beth imagined they all loved the Ivy League feel of it. She knew that President Landscome was not alone in being enamored of the elitist feel of academe. She had been in thrall to it most of her adult life.

As Beth was pouring a cup of coffee at the side board, she listened in on a conversation between the dean of admissions, Ed Baker, and the director of the library, Andi Vancaro. Ed was nearly a giant—close to seven feet tall and corpulent as well. He picked up a large croissant from the tray next to the coffee and it looked like an animal cracker in his hand. Andi Vancaro, who Beth thought of as the first Goth librarian in the Midwest, was petite and ghostly pale. Ed tried to keep his voice low as he talked to her, but what sounded muted to him rang clear as a bell to everyone nearby.

"What I heard was that several of the members of the committee wanted to vote him in, and Delilah delayed the vote in order to win them over," Ed said. He took a bite of the croissant and it was nearly gone.

"How will she do that?" Andi asked. She had no trouble whispering—she was a librarian, after all—which forced Ed to bend nearly in half to bring his ear close enough to hear her.

"I'm not sure she can," Ed said. "From what I hear, Landscome's got his folks just as much for Barrow as Delilah has hers against him. She may be able to win on a simple majority vote, but she wants a full one hundred percent to try to avoid his veto."

Andi's dark red lips moved and Ed leaned down again. "Sorry, I didn't catch that."

"I think she said that it's fucked up," Beth offered. Andi nodded.

"Well, she's right about that, Dean. I know the president is offering his people something in return for their vote. I heard Andrews in Sociology is getting the London/Florence program next year. If word gets out on how this president is awarding tenure, my recruitment efforts will be seriously damaged."

"But the president doesn't award tenure. The faculty does," said Beth.

"I'm never on the right committees," said Andi, looking fierce.

Some of the others approached, wanting in on everyone's favorite topic of conversation.

"All right, let's start the meeting so we can get out of here. You know I can't talk about this with you guys."

Beth presided over the meeting, cranky that she could neither participate in the tenure vote nor gossip about it. She had been forced to cut back on faculty gossip because deans were supposed to be above that, but Beth doubted she was. It wasn't like her to purse her lips when a bit of gossip broke out at a party. She wanted to dive in and dig in the dirt with the rest of them. There wasn't that much about being dean that Beth thought was fun, which disappointed her. She was proud of being dean, but she wondered sometimes if she was happy. She missed teaching.

She looked forward to her evening plans and the chance to put everything out of her mind for a bit. She was driving into Center City to have dinner with an old friend, an activist and bookstore owner who was not an academic, not an ex-lover, not a love interest. Just a friend, an acquaintance really, which was exactly what Beth needed. She thought back to Sally's parting words the night before, that she didn't have a girlfriend and she didn't have "a Mel" either. She didn't know exactly what that was supposed to imply. Sally didn't sound judgmental, as in "no, I don't have a girlfriend or a sex buddy either." It was more along the lines of "no, I don't have a girlfriend, or a cat either." It was just a fact, but she wanted Beth to know she was unencumbered. She didn't know if Beth really was. That must be it.

Good lord, thought Beth. What if Sally really was attracted to her and was interested in dating, or having a relationship? That was what solid people did. It wasn't what Beth did. She trotted out her sexual self on a fairly regular basis, but her heart she kept on a very tight rein. Once it had gotten loose. Just once. Her heart made a run for it and got picked up right away by a fellow grad student who swatted it in the air for a while for a bit of fun, and then *wham!* Her heart was batted down to the ground and stepped on. She was so devastated she couldn't even talk to a therapist about it. She couldn't seem to get over the heartache, but when she thought about getting help, the very idea of opening her mouth and actually articulating how terrible the abandonment felt was absolutely paralyzing.

Now she felt a little tug in that same area and it terrified her.

❖

Sally was just turning off her computer and getting ready to leave for the day when her cell phone rang. She glanced at the display and smiled.

"Hi, Mom. I was just about to leave the station."

"I'm glad I caught you, then. I need you to go by Werni's and pick up your dad." Sally's mother, Nancy, wasn't big on small talk.

"What's he doing there?" Neither of Sally's parents were big drinkers, but Mike Sullivan always had a beer at the end of the day.

"I forgot to pick up his beer at the store today and we are completely out. He came in from work, opened the fridge, and looked at me like I'd just slashed his tires. Stormed out without saying a word, so I imagine he went straight to Werni's."

"Why don't you just let him sit there for a while? We can wait dinner on him. I'll go get the dogs and come on over to the house."

"Humor me," Nancy said. "You wouldn't want one of your officers picking him up for a DUI, would you?"

"God, you worry about him too much." Sally turned off her

desk lamp and headed out of her office, leaving the station by the back door, her phone at her ear.

"I worry about you too, but that's a whole 'nother conversation. Now go on and get your dogs and your father. We're having a roast chicken tonight."

Sally couldn't think of a single Friday night since she moved back to Mount Avery that she didn't have one of several conversations with her mother as she got ready to leave work and join her parents for their weekly dinner together. Her mother either wanted Sally to pick up something at the Hy-Vee that she needed for the meal, or she wanted her to pick up her father at one of the town taverns, or she just wanted to make sure Sally was coming.

Sally got into her Jeep Cherokee and headed out of town toward her house. When she moved back to Mount Avery she'd bought a property about two miles from the center of town, ten acres of mostly wooded land, some tillable, with a small frame house and an old barn. It had once been the focal point of a much larger holding, with the thousand acres behind it long ago swallowed up by one of the area's corporate farms. The property represented everything Sally's life in Chicago had not been—simple, quiet, in harmony with something other than street violence and bad memories of more despair and ugliness than she thought it would be possible to see.

As she pulled into the long drive leading to the house, she could see the faces of her two dogs pressed against the living room window. They weren't barking or jumping up and down. They were checking out who was arriving. Their faces disappeared as they ran to the kitchen to meet her at the door. They were both Labs, one chocolate, one black, both on the small side. Sally had picked the smallest from two litters just a week after she'd closed on the property. She named one Betty and the other Lou, and almost immediately began to wonder how she'd ever lived without dogs. She opened the door to let them out, pausing for a few licks and head rubs before following them into the yard.

The dogs did their business and then started exploring the yard as if they'd never seen it before. Sally watched them with her hands in her pockets, her mind wandering to the conversation with Beth the night before, a topic she had returned to repeatedly throughout the day. She felt confused by it. Despite the fact that there was nothing overtly flirtatious about their time together in Beth's kitchen, Sally sensed that Beth was growing more comfortable and more interested as the evening passed. Why then did Sally end the altogether pleasant time together with the remark about Mel? She didn't even know for a fact that Beth was sleeping with Mel, though she'd be shocked if she wasn't. Mentioning it was out of line, though. There had to be something in Beth's question about girlfriends. Women didn't ask that unless they were looking for a specific answer.

While the dogs gobbled down some dinner, Sally changed into jeans and a sweater, and then the three of them left to pick up her dad. The dogs followed her into Werni's, a tavern that often had a dog wrapped around the bottom of every other bar stool. Betty and Lou were not regulars like some of the dogs there, but they were known. Their entrance was barely noticed by the Labs and spaniels already hunkered down for a night of drinking with their people. Sally stood at the door for a moment to look for her father, but it didn't take more than that to spot him. Werni's was a small place, a simple rectangle of a saloon with a long wooden bar on the left, a pool table at the right rear, and a few tables in the right front. A small back room past the end of the bar had a service window. From here Werni served up his blue plate specials to the workers at the corn sweetener plant who came in for their dinner breaks, and on Fridays he sat there and cashed checks for the same workers. Quite a bit of the cash he handed to them through the window made its way back into his till by the end of the night. It was a clean place that mostly had town drinkers, but there was a group of college students with several empty pitchers of beer on their table. There were also a couple of the town boys playing pool. The college students didn't even seem aware of the pool players' presence, but Sally figured they would be before the end of the night. She sighed.

Her father was sitting at the bar down near the end, his mug of beer empty. Sally could hear him laughing as he talked to the bartender, Marilyn, who'd been tending bar at Werni's since Sally was a teenager. She was tiny and vibrant and as healthy as you can imagine any seventy-year-old to be, which amazed Sally when she thought of where she spent her days. There was enough secondhand smoke in the bar to do a person in. She loved flirting with all the regulars at the bar, even the semi-regulars like Mike Sullivan. He picked up her lighter and touched her cigarette with it, snapping the Zippo closed when she pulled away from the flame. Sally rolled her eyes and took the stool next to him.

"Mr. Gallant."

"What's that?" he said.

"Never mind. Mom says I need to drive you home so that I don't have to arrest you for operating a vehicle while under the influence. Have you exceeded your limit, sir?"

He grinned. "Officer, I admit it's true. My limit is usually one beer. Tonight I've had two. Do your duty, if you must."

"Sorry. I'm off duty. Let's have one more and head home. You can apologize to Mom for being a pig today."

"What are you talking about?" He looked at Marilyn and back at Sally. "I haven't done anything."

"You stormed out of the house like a brat because Mom forgot to pick up your six-pack. What are you, twelve?"

Marilyn laughed and started to walk away. "Honey, they're all twelve. You're just smart enough to not keep company with men, so you tend to forget."

"Oh, Christ. Don't go bringing that up," her father said. He turned his head to the Cubs game on the television over their heads. Another season of woe was just getting under way.

"Dad, are you still afraid to hear people actually say that I'm gay? Here's a news flash for you—everyone knows. The officers who work for me know, and guess what? They still have my back."

"You're their boss. They know they have to have your back." He got up from his stool and leaned down to pat Betty. "You know I don't like to talk about this. I haven't said anything about the way you live, so you should just let me have my ways too."

Sally drank her beer and let her father change the subject to the Cubs, an old standby that either of them could talk about at length. She didn't really care about the Cubs.

❖

Sally and her parents were on their second *Law & Order* rerun. Nancy and Mike loved it when Sally pointed out where the show was inaccurate in matters of police procedure. Sometimes Sally illustrated a point with a made-up story, just because they got such a kick out of it. Sally's cell phone rang just as the second show was getting under way.

"Chief, it's dispatch. We have a dead body reported."

Sally stood at the excited tone in Dave's voice. She walked into the kitchen with the phone at her ear, her parents following right behind her.

"Give me the address, Dave. Give me everything the caller said."

"I don't know what all. Let's see. The address is four-twelve West Third and the guy just said the body's dead and that it looks like he'd been shot."

"Third Street or Third Avenue?"

"Third Avenue."

Sally recognized the address. It was the home of Professor John Barrow. She'd driven by his house several times over the past two days.

"Have you called paramedics?"

"No, Chief, I called you first. I never had a murder here."

Sally was walking out the door to her car.

"You have to do your job now, Dave. Get me an ambulance and at least four squads at that address. I'm on my way."

"We'll watch the dogs," Nancy called as Sally waved and reversed quickly out of the drive, on her way to her first murder scene in Mount Avery.

CHAPTER SIX

The nights in Mount Avery were so dark, the streets so wide and uncluttered that Sally felt she was driving to an emergency scene in a place that couldn't possibly have an emergency. In Chicago, the night was never really dark. The pale blue streetlights cast their glare on every block and the streets themselves were so full of legally and illegally parked vehicles, never mind sidewalks full of hydrants, trash cans, streetlight poles, traffic light poles, newspaper boxes, mailboxes, and people, that emergency vehicles were forced to pull up to a scene in any way they could. That's after they fought the traffic and other obstacles to get there in the first place. As Sally neared the address on Third Avenue, there were two patrol cars and an ambulance in front of and behind her, lights and sirens going. They all pulled neatly to the curb in front of the house where a man and a dog stood in the yard, the man waving his arm, the dog straining at his leash. The dispatcher had relayed to all units that the victim was reported to be dead, but still Sally and the others ran at speed to the body lying in the doorway of the dark house. She sent two officers around back. The paramedics knelt and did a quick assessment.

The body was of a younger man, dressed in corduroy trousers and button-down shirt, blood blossoming a stain in the middle of the chest. He lay flat on his back, eyes pointed straight up, arms at his sides, as if he were playing a dead man in a play. Most of his body lay within the living room of the house, with his feet jutting out the doorway, propping the screen door open. The house itself was dark and the paramedics used flashlights.

"He's dead, Chief," said Tonya Mitchell, the senior paramedic in the fire department. "Looks like a bullet to the chest."

Sally took stock of the people standing around her. There were her two patrol officers on the second shift, Jake Edmunds and Bob Geddings. Bob was a veteran who was training Jake, but neither of them had ever worked a murder scene. They were staring at the body as if they couldn't believe it. Tonya had been around for a good while, but her experience of dead bodies had come in Iraq, where she'd just completed a second tour of duty. The man and his dog were standing quietly out of the way. Instead of being excitable about his find, the man seemed reverent, as if quiet and respect were what were called for. Sally thought they were, but no one ever seemed to get that. Sally had been at countless murder scenes, and she was accustomed to irreverence from the professionals on the job. Now she was the only officer around with any murder experience.

"Okay, here's what we do," Sally said. "We'll use red tape to mark off the body and the area surrounding. Do not walk past the red tape for any reason. If you destroy evidence, I will fire you. Jake, you take care of that and also set up our perimeter. Bob, you need to call Dr. Rice out here on the double, and then put a call in to State to get a forensics team in as soon as possible. And, Tonya, you just hang back, all right? We'll need you to take the body in to the hospital morgue in Center City, but it's going to be a while yet." Sally pointed at a group of officers standing in the back of the crowd around her. "I'm going to take you three and clear the inside of the house."

Sally led the way to the back of the house and entered, the team spreading through the house, each room entered and swept with guns at the ready. There was no one in the small two-bedroom house. She made note of the fact that not a single light was on and the blinds were all drawn. There was nothing on the kitchen counters or in the bathroom that would indicate Barrow, or an intruder for that matter, had been interrupted in the middle of anything, other than the open bottle of wine and the half-filled glass. No mess that would have been made if a burglar was ransacking the house and been interrupted by Barrow's return. She didn't see a laptop anywhere, but the things normally taken in a home invasion—desktop computers and other electronics—appeared to be present. A more thorough search would have to wait for the forensics team.

Out back again, Sally put an officer in charge of maintaining the log that would record the name of everyone entering and exiting the house. Then she stepped over to the middle-aged man and his dog, who were now sitting on the lawn. Sally crouched down to talk.

"Sir, I'm Sally Sullivan, the chief of the Mount Avery Police Department. Can you give me your name, please?"

"Sure, sure. I'm Andrew Thompson. I live next door." Thompson reached over to pat his dog, a young beagle.

"Would you take me through what you saw, everything that happened tonight?"

"I came out to walk the dog at the same time as usual. His last walk is around eleven and we always head this way so we can go into the park. Morgan here started whining almost right away and pulling at his leash. He was really yanking me toward John's yard here so I followed him a bit, gave him some leeway. I noticed that the front door was open and then I saw the body lying right where it is now. I ran up to see what I could do, but I could tell right away he wasn't alive. I felt his wrist for a pulse and checked his breathing. He definitely seemed dead. I didn't touch anything, just called nine-one-one on my cell. That's it, really."

"Who is John? Is that the owner of the house lying here?"

"Yeah, his name is John Barrow and I think he rents the place. I know him because we both work at the college. I probably wouldn't know him otherwise. He lives alone and really keeps to himself."

"Did you notice whether there were any lights on in the house? Both earlier this evening and when you saw the body?"

"I don't think I noticed one way or the other when I got home from work. It wasn't dark then. Just now, I'd have to say the house was dark. I do remember that the room was dark behind him."

"And you didn't turn any lights off yourself?"

The man looked horrified. "No. Why in the world would I do that?"

Sally felt Bob coming up behind her and turned around.

"State is sending over a scene of crime team. Should be about an hour before they all get here," Bob said. "And, Chief, we've got a pretty good crowd gathering around here. What do you want me to tell them?"

In addition to the flashing lights of the emergency vehicles, the street was lit up by the front porch lights of every house on the block. Neighbors in bathrobes were as close as the sidewalk in front of the house, while Jake was winding crime scene tape around a tree at the side of the yard. "Bob, get over and tell those folks to move the hell back, and don't be nice about it. I want them way back. No, I want them home, but since they won't do that, you and Jake need to push them way, way back. Get that perimeter set up. And get a couple more officers down here. We're going to need to talk to every one of these folks."

Sally stood. "Mr. Thompson, we're going to have to get a full statement from you later, so I want you to sit tight at home now. Just tell me whether you saw anyone around this evening, or anytime today, who went to Mr. Barrow's home, parked in front, anything at all."

"Nothing." Thompson looked sorrowful at this.

"And you didn't see anyone leaving the house?"

"I'm sorry, no."

"It's nothing to be sorry for. It just is," Sally said. "If you'd write your name and contact information down here for me, I can let you go inside your house."

As Thompson wrote in Sally's notebook, she once again surveyed the scene. There was a line of cars now on Third Avenue as the whole town became aware of something big happening. Mel's truck pulled up. Sally could plainly see a young woman in the truck with her, sitting close to Mel on the bench seat. On the other side of the street, Beth was walking toward the taped-off area. Sally met her at the tape, motioning her inside it. Maybe Beth hadn't seen Mel. Or better yet, maybe she had.

"What are you doing here?"

Beth looked perplexed. "The same as everyone else. I wanted to find out what happened."

"I would have been calling you anyway, because you're dean. John Barrow's been shot, dead."

"What?" Beth looked shocked.

"That's literally all I know, but I'm going to need to talk to you later. For right now would you get me the next of kin information so we can notify the proper person?"

Beth stood with her mouth slightly open, her eyes set straight in front of her. She blinked once, said, "I'll go get that," and then turned and walked back the way she came. Sally frowned as she watched her blend back into the crowd. She wanted to follow her, take her by the hand, reassure her. She wanted Beth to squeeze her hand back. She knew that hearing of the murder of someone you knew was a shock for almost anyone, but Beth seemed completely dazed.

"Chief, the ME's here," Tanya said, tapping Sally on the shoulder. Dr. Tom Rice was an internist in town and the medical examiner for the county. He had the lanky build of a long-distance runner, and Sally often saw him out running the same routes that Beth did. She had not worked with him other than at a teen suicide the year before. Now he was kneeling next to the body, pulling instruments from his bag. Sally knelt beside him.

"The man who found the body tried to read a wrist pulse, but otherwise nothing's been touched, Doc. This is just as he was found."

"Is this one of the college people?" Rice asked. He was opening Barrow's shirt and examining the wound. "I think I recognize him."

"His name is John Barrow, a professor of English. Any idea how long ago this happened?"

"He's not cold yet, but definitely cooling. Let me get his temperature."

The ME made a small incision and inserted a thermometer directly into the liver.

"His body temp is less than a degree under normal, so he probably died within the hour. That's just preliminary, of course."

"I understand." Sally said. "While you're rooting around the body, will you see if he has a wallet and any cash in his pockets?"

Rice reached into a back pocket and pulled out a well-worn wallet. There was over a hundred in cash and his credit cards in the wallet, plus a driver's license from the U.K. The rest of his pockets were empty.

It was several hours before Sally was able to leave the scene and head to the station. A few reporters and one media truck had arrived, and they agreed to Sally's request that they not release any name or identifying information until she had informed the next of kin. She knew it wouldn't take long for them to get his name on their own, so she shared the information with them as long as they played by her rules. Beth had called with a number in suburban London for Barrow's mother, and Sally would place the call soon. She needed to organize not only her team and the investigation, but her thoughts as well. She posted one of her men out front to keep kids and the curious away from the crime scene. Preliminary canvassing of the neighborhood by her officers had not produced any reported sighting of anyone approaching or leaving Barrow's house, nor of anyone even hearing the gunshot. A preliminary search inside Barrow's house came up equally empty of clues, though she still needed a full analysis of his files, his computer, and the contents of his office at the school. She also had in hand Barrow's briefcase, which contained several files related to his tenure situation. Based on her conversation with Beth the evening before, she felt the tenure fight was as good a place as any to start her investigation. And given the probability that Barrow was the father of a student's child, that angle needed to be explored as well. Sally made a note to confirm Jennifer Manos's presence in San Francisco at the first opportunity.

The state scene of crime team had been thorough, but Sally was not hopeful they would find any useful fiber, hair, cigarette butt, or footprint evidence. It appeared to her that the victim had opened the door, probably to someone he knew, and was then shot in the chest at point-blank range. The presence of the wallet and cash made robbery an unlikely motive. The spent bullet casing was found lodged under a decorative rock to the right side of the front door, which would also support the theory that the shooter was facing the front door. But why was Barrow in his house in the dark? Even if he'd just arrived home, wasn't turning on at least one light the first thing he'd do upon entering? Barrow wasn't wearing pajamas and the beds were all made. Perhaps he'd fallen asleep on the sofa during daylight and woken up with the arrival of his killer at the door. Perhaps. And why had no one heard the shot?

It was only a few hours before dawn now, and Sally was wrung out. The adrenaline that had fired her up when she took the call at her parents' house was now out of her system, and she knew she'd need to get some sleep if she hoped to be at all effective the next day. The call to the scene had reminded her of so many similar calls in Chicago, but the differences between a big-city investigation and this one were starting to sink in. Sally had taken a call from a state police lieutenant who wanted to know if she had the manpower she needed to get the job done, which she said she did. She didn't need the state boys and their Smokey Bear hats trying to run her investigation. But she'd lied when she said she had the staff she needed. She really didn't have adequate staff to properly serve the town when it was quiet, let alone when a murderer was on the loose. She would have to delegate what she could and get to work on the rest. First, though, she'd catch a couple hours of sleep on the cot in the back room of the station.

Sally let the overnight dispatcher know where she was and tried to settle down in the cot. By some miracle of bad design it was both lumpy and thin and her body felt exhausted and restless. She knew that the feeling didn't come solely from the murder investigation. It took her back to the endless string of homicides she worked in Chicago, often around the clock in the frenzy of activity common for the early hours of an investigation. The physical exhaustion hadn't driven her from the city she loved. It was the soul-numbing sameness of it. The awful sameness of it. Over and over she'd arrived at crime scenes where the victim was not an innocent but rather a participant in an explosion of violence brought about by an event of infinitesimal importance. Usually an argument over respect, a commodity so valued in the ravaged, gang-ruled neighborhoods that taking a life over the granting or withholding of it was considered honorable, at least by those doing the shooting. The real victims, the ones Sally cared about, were the families trapped in their homes, terrified for their children. When those children, those families, were shot in the cross fire of these disputes, she could barely compartmentalize her feelings sufficiently to do her job properly.

The spillover into her off-hours finally became unbearable. A visit home to her parents and an opportunity with the Mount Avery PD inspired her move, a life change so enormous that this murder in town felt like a shock to her too, as if she'd forgotten what people were capable of.

Still, she recognized that the case was very different than the usual sort in Chicago, and would, in fact, require some real investigation—as opposed to the usual rousting of rival gang members and bargaining for confessions. She also recognized how much she had changed. Instead of a dreary rotation of three emotions—anger, frustration, and sorrow—she felt plenty of others. Contentment, amusement, engagement, enthusiasm, love, felt at appropriate times, not draped over her life like an impenetrable, low-lying cloud cover. If she had any frustration in Mount Avery it was that she hadn't yet found someone to share this new life with. She wondered if Beth Ellis could be what she'd been waiting for.

CHAPTER SEVEN

When Beth arrived at her office to begin dealing with the consequences of the murder, she did not pretend to be grieving over the death of John Barrow. She didn't know him well, and what she did know she didn't like. She was not given to pretending sentiment that didn't exist, but she understood that there would be plenty of people upset about a murder on campus, not the least being the parents of the students. The first thing she did was put a call in to Sally Sullivan to get an update on the investigation. She was patched through to her cell phone.

"Good morning, Chief. I hope you got some sleep last night," Beth said.

"I managed a few hours. How about you?"

"The same. I'm afraid it's hard to fall asleep after a faculty member gets murdered. Maybe you're more used to it."

"It's not something we're going to get used to in Mount Avery. I can guarantee you that," Sally said.

"Chief—"

"Sally. You should call me Sally."

"Well, you should call me Beth."

"I'd like to. That's how I think of you anyway."

Beth thought this sounded mildly flirtatious and something fluttered inside her a bit.

"Are you driving right now?" Beth asked.

"Yeah. I'm on my way back from Center City."

"Where are we in the investigation? I have to call the president when we hang up and I'd like to have as much information as possible to give him."

"That won't be much. We have no witnesses, no physical evidence at the scene that we can determine at this time, the autopsy was performed this morning, we're still reviewing evidence from the victim's home and office, and we're developing the lines of our investigation."

"I'll pass that along to the president."

"I need to see you to go over a few things. Is eleven in your office convenient?" Sally asked.

Beth didn't think Sally's voice sounded flirtatious now, but that fluttering continued. With all hell breaking loose around her she found this distraction to be not only untimely, but also alarming. It felt suspiciously like the last and only time she'd fallen in love. The last time she'd placed her trust in someone else, her lover ran off with one of Beth's best friends—fairly mundane in the grand scheme of things, but devastating to Beth. It seemed irrefutable that when someone claimed that they loved her they asserted some right, never granted by her, to not only say that they loved her but also to inflict terrible hurt through their actions, as if the two things went together.

"I'll come to the station. You've got enough going on to worry about my convenience. Have you contacted John's mother in England?" Beth asked.

"Yep, and put a call in to the media afterward with the bare-bones facts. I think you can expect a number of calls this morning from reporters."

"Yes, they're already coming in. Thanks, Chief. I'll see you at eleven." Beth hung up, unsettled.

Beth called in to her voicemail and took down five messages from various local and wire service reporters. Then she tried to summon the will to put a call in to Landscome. She wondered how long it would take him to accuse her of murdering John Barrow to avoid having him get tenure. She dialed his cell number, which she knew would be with him, because he'd made it a point of telling everyone that he could be "reached anywhere in the U.K. on my mobile."

"Nigel Landscome here."

"It's Dean Ellis, sir. I'm afraid I have some bad news."

"Oh, dear. I don't like the sound of that."

"John Barrow was murdered at his home last night."

"What? I must have misheard that."

"I'm afraid not. It happened about eleven last night, we think. The police are investigating, of course, but there doesn't seem to be the slightest clue as to who might have done it." Beth filled in Landscome with the rest of the information given to her by Sally, and by the end she could hear him begin to sputter.

"And just so you know they are covering all possibilities," Beth said, "I have told the chief of police about the tenure controversy. I think the fact that you were the only one in favor of John's being granted tenure puts you the most in the clear at this time."

"I don't feel that this is the best time for you to be glib, Dean Ellis. Hopefully, you'll have been dealing with the media and a grieving campus in a more professional manner."

"Of course. The media has been given a statement by the chief, and I thought you and I would discuss how you'd like to handle our further dealings with them."

"Hold them off until I can get back into town. Just say we are making plans for a memorial service, assisting in the investigation, etc. I want you to maintain as much of the status quo as possible until I get back. I'm not filled with confidence in your abilities at the moment, Dean. Not only did you fail in my absence to deliver the tenure vote I asked for, but the tenure candidate has been murdered."

Beth looked at her watch. It had taken five minutes for him to blame her for the murder, about what she expected.

"As you wish. I take it that means you don't want me to make any arrangements for increased campus security?"

"No, you should take care of that immediately, and put out an announcement to the entire campus that it's being done. Christ, this is a bloody nightmare. Has the board been notified?"

"They haven't. Should I wait on that as well?"

"I'll take care of the board from here. You just do everything else that needs to be done, Dean. I'll be on the next flight home."

Beth started to make a cursory to-do list, which was unlike any to-do list she'd ever written. She was numbering down the side of the paper when Delilah Humphries swept into her office, dressed entirely in fleece, her preferred Saturday look, though not a particularly good one. The fleece cape gave the ensemble the Delilah touch.

"I suppose you all think I murdered the man." She sat in the seat in front of Beth's desk and thrust her chin forward. "Which is ridiculous. I wouldn't waste that amount of time on him."

"Oh, I don't know, Dee. It doesn't take all that much time to kill someone, does it?"

"I wouldn't know. I have to say that this does eliminate a few vexing problems."

"Actually, Dee, you don't have to say that. It's in poor taste, don't you think? I'd at least wait a little while before remarking on the positives."

"How long do you think that should be, exactly? I'm wondering if I should postpone my party tomorrow."

Every quarter, Delilah hosted a faculty party at her house, Sunday afternoon affairs that were among the best attended of the countless faculty parties given throughout the year. With a couple hundred very smart people set down on an isolated outpost, the social life with colleagues was of perhaps unnatural importance. While most employees in workplaces of all sorts enjoy some interaction with colleagues outside of office hours, in the world of the small campus, the social activity of a faculty member is almost exclusively with colleagues. The potential for drama and in-fighting is endless, the gossip mill constantly overworked, the mutation of cliques and alliances ongoing and unpredictable. Delilah's parties were showcases for all of these things to play out, and it was a rare quarter that went by when there wasn't some scene that was talked about for weeks.

"I'm not really prepared to make a call about your party," Beth said. "I have a few dozen other things to sort out here." She pointed at her list, hoping Delilah would leave. When she didn't, she added, "And I have to leave in a minute for the police station."

"Really? You have to go spend time with that good-looking chief of police? Poor you."

"Please, don't start. We've just had a murder on campus. Aren't you concerned about that?"

Delilah stood and picked up her bag. "I think I'll go ahead and have the party. Everyone's going to want a place to talk to others about this. It might as well be my house. You should tell your police chief to come by. Maybe she can arrest Professor Mustard in the drawing room with the candlestick."

The fact was that Delilah did have a drawing room. Hers was a large Victorian frame house that had three levels and a full basement. It was several times too large for her, but she'd managed to fill it with more stuff than most people could accumulate in five lifetimes. Most of the first floor rooms were kept fairly uncluttered, simply so she could host her parties. But those who ventured beyond these rooms were flabbergasted at the sight of towering piles of magazines, boxes and boxes of books, dishes, collectibles of every kind—the usual pack-rat collections that are the subject of TV pieces on how to organize the world's most disorganized people. The thing the producers of these stories don't seem to get is that the appalling mountain of stuff in the house of a pack rat has little to do with lack of organizational ability and everything to do with the inability to let go of things. Suggesting to Delilah that she simply get out the bin and start throwing things away would be like telling an alcoholic that all she had to do was limit herself to one lovely cocktail per evening and all would be well. Beth had tried once to talk to Delilah about possibly throwing out some of her stuff, and the mere suggestion sent Delilah on a binge of buying, clearing out the new item racks at three different Dollar Stores.

Before heading over to the police station, Beth spent some time coordinating extra security with both the police department and the private firm that contracted with the college. She wrote a press release for the media and a campus-wide release, which she worked on with Dean Taylor and the security chief. She made preliminary plans for a campus memorial and put a condolence call in to John Barrow's mother. She worked down her list and wished fervently that it would be enough to put her world back in order. Then she left for the station.

Chapter Eight

With an early morning autopsy already behind her, Sally drove to Katie Murphy's house on Saturday morning. The tenure fight was the most obvious line of inquiry to follow and Katie the most obvious beneficiary of Barrow's death.

Sally pulled up in front of the college-owned duplex rented by Katie, set among a row of similar units housing assistant professors and other adjuncts. Katie was locking her door as Sally approached and identified herself.

"This must be about John Barrow's death," Katie said. She was composed and casual, her young face serious but not frowning with concern or anxiety, clad in tailored slacks and a light turtleneck, a canvas bag slung over her shoulder. "I just heard the news a little while ago."

"I'd like to speak with you for a moment about it."

"Sure. Let's go back in." Katie unlocked the front door, which opened directly on the front room of the small house. It was furnished a notch above student level—one end of the room held an oak veneer dining table covered with papers, files, and laptop, the other end a small TV and a love seat with canvas slipcover. They sat side by side on it.

"Dr. Murphy—"

"Please, it's Katie."

"Katie, I understand that you are an adjunct professor in the English department, where John Barrow was an assistant professor."

"That's correct." Katie was sitting forward, slightly turned toward Sally.

"I also understand that he was recently placed in that position at the president's request, thereby taking a tenure-track position that you were hopeful of securing yourself."

"And you're thinking that would provide a motive for me to murder John Barrow?"

"I'm a long way from forming any opinions," Sally said. "I'm just gathering and confirming information at this point."

Katie's composure had not faltered in the least, and Sally thought she seemed interested in the conversation, as if they were at a dinner party discussing campus politics and not her possible motive for murder.

"The dean's office would certainly confirm that I was one of several candidates interviewing for the tenure-track position when Barrow got the job. You should also consider the fact that if Barrow had not been granted tenure, that position would most likely be available again. The tradition is that a teacher moves on from the campus that denies him or her tenure."

"What did you think Barrow's chances of getting tenure were?"

Katie smiled. "The information I had was that the committee was far more against tenure than for it."

"And your source?" Sally already knew who Katie's source was likely to be, having seen Katie leave Delilah's house early in the morning on more than one occasion. She was always surprised what she discovered as she drove around town on patrol, most of it irrelevant, but much of it interesting.

Katie looked uncomfortable for the first time. "My source? Chief, a college campus itself is a source. You can cross the quad between classes and be three rumors richer than when you started out."

"So you're saying that you don't have access to a reliable source of information on what goes on in the tenure committee?"

"I don't see the relevance. I'm uncomfortable giving out names of people who might have told me things. It doesn't feel right."

Sally shifted her position on the sofa, as if signaling a shift in topic. She noticed Katie visibly relax again.

"I'm just wondering if your source isn't Delilah Humphries. I know she's chair of the tenure committee and I believe the two of you are close."

"Close?"

"As in I've seen you leaving her house in the early morning close."

Now Katie got up from the sofa and walked to the other side of the room. "Have you been watching me for some reason, Chief?"

The trouble with this kind of information, Sally thought, was that people thought she was some kind of loser for having it. She must be stalking because she was either a right wing law-enforcement nut patrolling the streets 24/7, a lovesick lesbian parked in front of her adored's house, or simply a loner with nothing better to do with her time. The last description fit a little too closely for comfort.

"I just happened to be driving by on patrol. I assumed you were sleeping with Delilah. I apologize if I assumed incorrectly."

Katie gazed out her front window for a moment before turning back to Sally. "No, you're correct. We didn't want anyone to know during the tenure battle since it would appear to be a conflict of interest if Delilah was pushing for a no vote on the committee. She told me that it appeared the committee was going to vote against Barrow but that Landscome was threatening to veto that."

"Thank you. Just one other question for now. Will you tell me where you were last night?"

Katie smiled. "You did just make this easier for me, as it turns out. I was with Delilah at her house all evening, and I slept there last night."

"And neither of you left the house for any reason?"

"No."

"And Delilah Humphries will say the same?"

"Well, I hope so. I fell asleep around ten, so unless she saw me sleepwalking she'll say that I was there." Katie picked up her keys and her bag. "If that's all, Chief, I have to run my car to the shop for servicing and then meet a student on campus."

Sally handed over one of her cards and left, not even a rumor richer than when she set out. As she drove back to the station along Main Street she noticed that there was more foot traffic out than she was used to seeing, the weather still being fine and the pedestrians clearly enjoying the beginning of their weekend. Delilah Humphries was coming out of the pharmacy, a small plastic bag in her hand. Sally pulled over and lowered the passenger window, calling out her name. Delilah turned her head and moved over to the car.

"Did you want to speak to me, Ms. Chief of Police?" Delilah lowered her face to the open window. "I didn't know you even knew who I was."

"Well, I know you are the chair of the Tenure and Promotions Committee and I wondered if you could speak to me for a few minutes about John Barrow."

Delilah looked a bit put out, as if that wouldn't be the number one thing on the mind of the chief the morning after a murder in town. As if she'd be the number one thing on Sally's mind. "I suppose I have a few minutes. Where would you like to talk?"

"I have some things I have to do now. Why don't I come by your house later this afternoon? Will you be at home?" Sally asked.

"Yes. I suppose you know where that is," Delilah said.

"I'll find it," Sally said, pulling away without another word.

As soon as she got back to the station she called the state lab, trying to mobilize their weekend staff to view her case with at least some urgency. CSI team members were working their way through bags of the detritus found around John Barrow's body, but all they were coming up with was dirt that was the same as the dirt around the front door, fibers that were the same as the fibers in the clothes the victim wore, and no extraneous match, pin, earring, pocket lint, or other form of matter that might qualify in any sense as a clue. They did not expect that the remainder of the untested material would be any more revealing.

She called the ballistics lab next to find out if there was any useful information found on the bullet or the casing. Sally had delivered the bullet and casing to the lab in Center City immediately after the medical examiner extracted the bullet from John Barrow's heart. The autopsy was without surprise. No other wounds were found on the body, and the only other finding worth note was the appearance of the wound itself. The compact stippling around it confirmed that the shot was fired from two or three feet away.

Sally missed the sort of connections she had in the city, missed knowing who to call to help speed up the processing of information. With so little crime actually happening in Mount Avery, certainly little of the sort that needed to involve the state labs, she hadn't had occasion to get to know the experts and technicians that turned evidence into useful information. She picked up the phone to call and make her best case with whoever they assigned in the ballistics lab. She was transferred to a lab supervisor named David Zimmerman.

"Chief Sullivan? I was just going to call you. We put a rush on the material we received from you this morning and I think I have some information for you."

"We need every bit of it that we can get here."

"I guess you can say you got lucky on this one. Normally, a bullet and casing don't tell us enough to identify the make of gun that shot them. I can tell you to look for a gun that shoots three-eighties, for instance, but not which of the many, many guns shoot that bullet."

"Yeah, I know that. What's different about this?"

"There are certain ejector type markings on this casing that can only be made by a Walther PPK."

"You're kidding."

"No, ma'am. I've only seen this once before, and that was in Chicago."

Sally sat up further. "That gives us a lot more focus, and we can use that. I'm a little surprised at the gun, though."

"Yeah, the James Bond gun. Haven't seen one of those ever used around here, but they're not that uncommon nationwide," Dave said.

"I had one myself as a backup gun a long time ago. They're nice and small, easy to conceal. How certain are you?"

"Pretty damn. Of course, you get me a gun and I can tie it all up for you with this bullet. Until then it's just something for you to watch out for."

"Well, that's more than I had before. Can you fax that report over to me?"

Sally hung up and called Bob Geddings into her office.

"Bob, have you heard anything more on the cell phone?"

Geddings looked down at a fist full of notes in his hand and sat to start shuffling through them. "I did get confirmation that the phone was bought by a Jennifer Manos in San Francisco on Wednesday, two days before the shooting. But that doesn't help us place her at the time of the murder."

"Nope, it doesn't." She thought about her refusal to let any of the state police help in her investigation and wondered if it was her pride or her desire to not be bogged down by their bureaucracy that really was behind that. Certainly she could use a few experienced hands. "Bob, you work on getting some background info on John Barrow. He was at the London School of Economics shortly before coming to Grafton last fall—start tracking back from there. And send your trainee in to me, Jake. I'm going to get him started on something else."

Sally assigned Jake to tracking down any sales of Walther PPKs in the surrounding multistate area. Then she checked the time and realized that Beth would be on her way over. She went to the break room to brew more coffee.

Beth was shown into Sally's office by Henry, the desk sergeant, and she saw immediately that Sally was running on fumes. Her eyes were red and there were dark circles under them, her hair was a little wild and her smile absent when she looked up to welcome Beth. She motioned her to the empty chair in front of her desk. There was only room for one. Her office was exactly as Beth had expected—small, beige, without personal touch, fairly well organized without appearing obsessively neat, and efficient.

"How are you holding up?" Beth asked her. "You look exhausted."

"Do I? I probably look like shit, but I feel okay. Just trying to get to as much of this stuff as I can while we're in the first hours of the investigation."

"Yes, they always say that on TV, that the first forty-eight hours are the most important time for catching whoever committed a crime." Beth took her jacket off and put it behind her back. She was exhausted as well and leaned back, stretching her legs in front of her.

"They got that one detail right, then."

"Hmm." They looked at each other.

"Thanks for getting me that information so quickly last night. I did talk to the victim's mother, and I have to say, my impression was more that she was thankful for my kindness in calling her than really upset by the news."

"The British are terribly polite, as we know," Beth said. "But that was my impression too. I just talked to her an hour ago. Maybe she didn't like him either."

"It seems there was a lot of that going on. I want to review with you the story you told me Thursday night about the fight over John Barrow's tenure."

"Thursday night was a far more enjoyable time. I practically feel nostalgic about it. It seems incredible now that the tenure fight I described then, as ugly as it was, could lead to this."

"We're looking into it, of course. I'm not certain that it's the reason Barrow was murdered. He seemed to be a very unpopular man."

"If I remember correctly," Beth said, "you were a homicide detective in Chicago."

"That's right."

Beth waited for Sally to give her a little more background but there was only silence.

"That should help you considerably in your investigation."

Sally smiled briefly. "Let's hope so. As it stands now we don't have much physical evidence to go on." She opened a file and read from some handwritten notes. Beth tried to surreptitiously read Sally's notes upside down, but Sally closed the file. She was all business now.

"Let me see if I understand the two basic positions on this question. The faculty in general, and the Tenure and Promotions Committee in particular, were against tenure because they thought Barrow unqualified, and they were outraged because they felt this is a faculty and committee decision that the president had no business threatening to veto. How did they know the president threatened to veto their vote?"

"Because I told Delilah Humphries, something akin to publishing the news on the campus network. I hoped that by letting them know about the veto, the tenure committee would deliver a unanimous vote and the faculty would be prepared to back them up, if necessary."

"Wouldn't this put you in a bad position with the president?" Sally looked at her with some concern.

"It will, if he finds out, but at this point I don't see how it puts me in any worse trouble with him. He knows I'm opposed to Barrow. Or was. I don't know, it's all such a mess. I wish that the college could go back to the way it was."

"What way was that?"

"Definitely pre-Landscome. Since he's been here there's been a constant battle to defend how we do things. Defending academic integrity and excellence, for instance, is not about ego, as Landscome alleges. It's about maintaining the system that provides the best education for the students."

"Excuse me for saying so, but that does sound a little, I don't know, conservative? Stodgy? As if new ways of doing things is bad."

"I guess I can only describe it this way. Imagine a large family with opinionated but loving children and trusting but protective parents. The family operates well because they understand their shared mission—to support and love each other as they pursue individual excellence. All of a sudden one of the parents—the most important one for setting and maintaining that tone—well, something terrible happens and that parent is replaced by a stepparent. The evil, greedy, short-sighted stepparent that every kid fears and loathes. Now the common mission of the family members changes quite rapidly to one of survival, maintenance, anger, and resentment. It's no longer a place where its members thrive. It's a sorrowful place."

Sally was silent for a another moment. "Has anyone ever said to you that it's just a job? That your work isn't your life? Friends used to say that to me all the time in Chicago."

Beth felt her nose wrinkle. "You sound like my mother."

"I take it that's not a good thing?"

"I'm talking specifically about the irony of her urging me to separate my work life from my private life, something that she never once even attempted to do. She's a big 'do as I say, not as I do' person."

Sally had opened the file again and had her finger on the notes as she listened to Beth talk. "We should probably get back to the interview."

"Of course."

"The other thing I don't quite understand is why President Landscome cared so much about Barrow. You said at one point that he brought Barrow in from another college. Do you know anything more about that?"

"President Landscome arrived on campus late last summer, and it must have been his first week on the job when he told me a new English professor would be joining the faculty."

"Is that the usual way faculty members are hired?" Sally asked.

"Not at all. Quite the opposite, in fact. It so happened that we did have a tenure-track position open because I left the faculty when I became dean. The feeling was that Katie Murphy would be moved out of adjunct status and into the tenure-track position, but the department conducted the usual search anyway. That's protocol. Before that decision had been made, the new president made a very heavy-handed plea that Barrow be given the position."

"I don't really understand all the ins and outs of this. Can't he just hire who he wants?"

"That's just not the way it traditionally works regarding the hiring of academics. But certainly the president has a lot of power and can lobby for his man. In this case he convinced enough people in the English department to hire Barrow. There are rumors that he gave them something in exchange for the votes."

"And what was your position on the question of hiring John Barrow?"

"I made it very clear that I thought Katie Murphy should be given the position. She was well liked by faculty and students, highly qualified, and already in place here. She deserved the spot. I don't think taking that stand got me off on the right foot with the president, but I just didn't see that John Barrow was much of an addition to the college."

"Did you receive any background information on Barrow?"

Beth placed an envelope on Sally's desk.

"I've brought his file in for you, but there's not much there. His CV is quite short. I did confirm his last adjunct position at the London School of Economics. The letters of recommendation have still not been provided to me, though President Landscome keeps assuring me he has them. Not much else there, I'm afraid."

"Would it be accurate to say that Katie Murphy potentially benefited from John Barrow's death?"

"Yes, she would be well positioned to get that spot in the English department and in line for tenure. But I can tell you that there is no way that she killed John Barrow."

"You say that based on what?" Sally asked.

"Just knowing her. There's just no possibility of it."

Sally made a note on the pad in front of her. "I'm going to need the names of all of the faculty and others who had a say in both the hiring of John Barrow and the vote on his tenure."

Beth hesitated. "All right, I'll make those available to you." She rose and put her jacket back on. "What about Jennifer Manos? Have you looked into her situation at all?"

"Why? Do you think she was capable of murdering Barrow?"

"My guess is that she had a motive," Beth said. "I imagine

Jennifer told Barrow that she's pregnant and he dropped her like a box of rocks."

"I imagine that's so, and that's why she left. Whether she murdered him is now also a question of opportunity. She supposedly was in San Francisco the evening of the murder, when she called you, and if that's the case, she's clear. But I did track down the phone number she gave you on her voicemail. The phone was one of the pre-paid minute jobs, and we can't trace back her location. We're working on tracing where she bought it, and we've left messages for her, of course."

Sally got up and led Beth out of the office. "Anything I tell you is not to be released to the press, and all updates about the investigation need to come from my office only. I want to keep you informed, but I can't have what I tell you getting out to the press and from there to the killer."

"I understand. I will gladly refer the press to you." They headed to the door of the station together. "None of this seems like motivation for murder, though, does it? Would anyone care so much about Barrow getting tenure that they'd murder him? And would Jennifer kill the father of her child, eliminating any chance of them getting together?" Beth asked.

Sally stopped at the door of the station. People were out and about, running errands and enjoying the first truly springlike day of the season. The sun was out and jackets were open. "A murder in the city is usually a pretty clear-cut case of gang-related killing or domestic violence of some sort. Looks like I'm going to have to dust off some real detecting skills for this."

Beth smiled. "I think we're in good hands. Thanks for letting me know what's going on." Beth opened the door to head out. "Good luck with the president. He'll be wanting an explanation from you as to why you haven't caught anyone yet."

"Don't worry, we will. And, Beth, your president doesn't scare me."

"He's not my president!"

❖

As Beth walked across campus she saw students milling about in groups, talking excitedly among themselves. News of John Barrow's murder had reached them by now, along with word that the murderer was still at large. She headed toward the Annex, the coffee shop/café/hangout located in the Student Union and visited on a daily basis by nearly every student and faculty member. The food was good and cheap, the seating plentiful, and the coffee always fresh. In the middle of the Annex was a large fireplace surrounded by lounge furniture. These were the seats that were always taken first, and it was where Beth was scheduled to address students for the first time since the murder the night before. Beth was joined by Dean Taylor, who set up a portable microphone and amplifier with the efficiency of a band roadie. Harriet flipped on the microphone and began to speak as a growing crowd of students listened.

"Students, Dean Ellis and I have joined you here today to make a preliminary attempt to answer your questions about the terrible incident last night. As you all read on the campus network, Professor John Barrow was killed last night in his home by an unknown assailant. Dr. Barrow's family in England have been notified and will be arriving tomorrow to retrieve the body. Obviously, the police are hard at work trying to apprehend whoever killed Dr. Barrow, but as far as I know there have been no arrests."

Harriet looked to Beth for confirmation, which she gave with a nod of her head.

"Our primary concern at the moment is the safety of the student body. We want to assure you that security has been increased to a level that will make it impossible for any unauthorized person to access your dorms. It's at a level that you will undoubtedly find annoying, but we must ask for your patience during this time. I'll now turn this over to Dean Ellis, who would like to say a few words."

Beth took the microphone. Some of the faces in the crowd had the stupefied look of any eighteen-year-old just out of bed at noon on a Saturday, while others appeared both somber and attentive.

"Someone has shattered something we have taken for granted here at Grafton. Our active, exciting, insular, and safe world has been invaded just long enough to turn that world upside down. We don't know who killed Dr. Barrow, or why, but we do know that we lost one of our members, one of us, and that is painful and frightening.

"As Dean Taylor indicated, we have increased security and will keep it in place until the threat to anyone here on campus is gone. We are cooperating fully with Chief Sullivan's investigation, and ask that you do as well should she or any of her officers need information from you."

A shaggy-haired boy raised his hand and she pointed at him.

"Dean, I don't think we're particularly freaked out, in terms of our own safety, I mean. Somebody didn't like Barrow, but it's not like this was a random campus shooting where a student starts taking down other students."

Other students were nodding. She suspected they were starting to imagine what it would be like to have uniformed officers at the doors to their dorms, patrolling the campus day and night, putting a distinct crimp in their style. She wouldn't have liked it either.

"I agree that this is different than those campus tragedies. This seems to be a situation with an intended victim. Your name is Craig, right?" Beth asked the student. He looked a little surprised that she knew who he was. "We have to acknowledge that even though it doesn't seem likely any of you would be targeted by the same killer, it's not impossible. And our job is to keep you as safe as we can. I truly believe that it won't last long and that you don't have to feel you're living in a police state. Unless you're breaking the law, the officers won't bother you."

Another student piped up, a senior English major whom Beth knew well. Amanda was a born leader and organizer.

"Dean Ellis, a number of us are really sad about Dr. Barrow's death, and we're sickened by the gun violence in this country. We'd like to pay our respects to Dr. Barrow and demonstrate against gun violence by having a candlelight vigil on campus tonight."

Beth smothered a groan. She admitted she had lost her enthusiasm for things like vigils and protests, but the idea seemed particularly wearying at the moment. Still, the students seemed eager, so there was nothing to do but support it.

"That's a great idea, Amanda. Why don't we speak after you get your plans set and I'll make sure security is there to work with you. I'm going to turn this back to Dean Taylor, who will tell you about the upcoming memorial service and the presence on campus of therapists and counselors, should anyone want to speak about their reaction to this."

That was greeted with a few snorts and groans, but Beth could see that the students were genuinely stunned by what happened. Murder at Grafton had seemed as likely to them as a campus concert by Radiohead or some other major band. You had to go to school at an entirely different sort of place for those things to happen—both the good and the bad.

Beth made her way through the crowd and headed out into the sunny spring day, the sort of day that made her want to dance and play and laugh and have sex, except that she was dean of Grafton College and there was a murderer running loose, and why would she even be thinking about such things? In fact, with her world in crisis, Beth felt herself less willing to focus on crisis management than on when she would see Sally again, a lapse so foreign to her she blushed at the recognition of it. The worst part of this wandering attention, of having her eye off the ball and squarely on the girl, was that it felt disorienting. Her entire world was the college and now that the college was truly in a crisis, her mind kept wandering back to a woman she barely knew. Sally's request for the personnel files of the faculty was something she would normally have fought, but she conceded instantly because it was something she could give to Sally. The physical pull was there, it was real, but she'd experienced attraction with any number of women. Wanting to give something, just for the sake of giving? That was different.

Katie Murphy emerged from Bart Hall and trotted down the steps, her heavy bag bouncing off her hip. Beth hadn't seen Katie for a few weeks—unusual on a campus so small—and she was struck again by how young Katie looked, though she was now in her mid-thirties. Her hair was braided in a single rope down her back, her clear skin and eyes were untouched by makeup, her clothes well cut, comfortable, and familiar. Katie appeared to believe in buying quality, not quantity, and seeing her wear the same outfits quite frequently was not a hardship. Beth had no trouble understanding why Katie was popular with the students. She was simply pleasant to be around, serious about her field but lighthearted about life.

Katie had set herself on a collision course with Beth and would have run right into her had Beth not said her name and stepped out of her path.

"God, I'm sorry, Beth. My mind is somewhere else, I'm afraid."

Now that they were close together, Beth saw that Katie seemed a little agitated. Clearly the tenure battle for the position in the English department had taken its toll, Katie's first meaningful chance at tenure being derailed by John Barrow. His death would be a complicated event for her.

"Are you okay, Katie? Everyone's upset, of course, but I know this affects you in particular."

Katie's eyes snapped onto Beth's. "You don't think I had anything to do with Barrow's death, do you? It's one thing to be questioned by the police about it, but if people I know are thinking—"

"No. God, no. There were plenty of people who disliked Barrow as much as you and I did. Has Chief Sullivan already spoken to you?"

"This morning. I don't have anything to hide from her, but it's unsettling." Katie looked at her shoes. Beth thought she was trying to decide how inappropriate it might be to ask about the tenure position now that the top candidate was dead.

"Beth, I want to ask you about something."

"Okay." Beth thought it actually was a little inappropriate to ask this soon.

"I think you know a woman I met this morning. I had to take my car in for service and I had quite a conversation with the mechanic there."

"Wow. That's not what I expected you to ask about."

"It's a little soon to ask about tenure, don't you think? And I don't even know what to say about the murder. It seems unreal. I hope they catch the person quickly."

"Why do you say I know Mel?" As if every lesbian in town (and there were a lot of them) didn't know Mel.

"I never said her name was Mel, so there's one clue. But mainly it's because she told me. When I said I was with the college she mentioned you."

Beth felt alarmed. She also felt a blush come to her face. "What did she say when she mentioned me?"

"Only that she knew you." Katie seemed to study Beth's face for a moment. "I wanted to ask you about Mel because she was flirting with me, and I found that I was flirting back. But if you have something going with her, I won't pursue this at all."

Beth grinned. "Katie, you obviously have not heard of Mel before today, though how that is possible I'm not sure."

"What do you mean?"

"Mel has a good heart, but she also has an outsized libido. Her mission, and I quote her, is to spread the loving wherever it's needed, and in this town it's needed by a fair share of the women, single or not."

Katie looked crestfallen. "You mean she sleeps around."

"Oh, yes."

"She's a cad?"

"A lovable one." Beth could see that Katie was confused. "It doesn't mean she wasn't sincere when she was flirting with you. Mel has tremendous focus. But you need to be forewarned if you think you may have more than a passing interest in her. You'll just get your heart broken."

Katie looked behind her, as if she could see into Mel's shop and figure out how she could have been misled. Then she turned back. "I don't know what I feel. Frankly, I thought she was sexy as hell, but I don't want to be the housewife to her milkman. Milkwoman."

"Milkmaid?" Beth offered.

They both cracked up, the thought of Mel in apron and bonnet akin to über drag.

"Anyway, thanks for the heads up, Beth."

"As to the tenure situation, let's just get through the memorial and all of the chaos right now, and then we'll sit down and talk about it. We'll bring Delilah into it and figure out how to move forward from here. Frankly, at this point I'd like to see us dispense with the full search and interview process, but that's not totally my decision."

Katie gave Beth a wan smile and moved off, her step not as light as it had been a few minutes before. Beth felt like going to Mel's and telling her to keep her pants on for once, but she knew it wasn't her place. She was Katie's dean, not her Mother Superior. And she'd be an appalling hypocrite to boot.

❖

Beth walked quickly toward home, ready for a glass of wine and a few hours alone. She would go back on campus at eight o'clock to show her face at the vigil. She loved that the students felt a strong reaction to Barrow's death and that they wanted to make a statement about gun laws. She believed it was a student's duty to feel things keenly and react to them strongly no matter what the issue at hand, to ignore shades of gray and political expediency, to go straight to claims of corporate greed, right-wing conspiracy, and the alienation of our culture as a whole. Society needed the young to voice these things because it seemed so many lost the nerve or the energy to do so once they got out of school. She seriously doubted that any law banning the possession of handguns would have saved John Barrow's life; someone wanted him dead and would have found a way to make it happen. Still, the vigil was harmless and might make some feel better.

With her mind wrapping itself around these thoughts, Beth stepped off the curb onto the street ringing the campus, turning after the fact to look to her left. She saw the squad car in time to jump back out of its way, just as it hit its brakes hard. Adrenaline flooded her body. As she shook and tingled, Sally Sullivan, naturally, got out of the car. Beth sat on the curb and awaited her lecture about looking both ways before crossing.

"I don't think it would improve town-gown relations to have the chief of police run over the dean of the college," Sally said as she walked around the front of her squad and stood in front of Beth. The sun was directly behind her, making her seem like a dark column surrounded by light, mystical in some way, with her arms akimbo, fists resting on her gun belt. The image reminded Beth of something, some fetish or iconic figure. Her mind raced through a catalogue of images and literary references, finding comfort in the familiar academic discourse in her brain, the brush with death she'd just experienced finally pushing her beyond what she could comfortably process in any twenty-four-hour period.

Sally squatted before her and looked intently into Beth's face. "Beth?"

With the sun no longer shadowing her, Sally's face popped into view. "Sorry I almost ran into your car," Beth said.

"I wouldn't worry about the car in that encounter. I am a little worried about you."

"Why?" Beth scootched down the curb a little as Sally sat next to her. She noticed Sally's perfectly pleated pants and shiny shoes and wondered if she sat in front of the TV at night buffing those clunky shoes, or stood ironing those straight creases. There was something reassuringly competent about the way Sally was all spit and polish.

Sally continued to stare at Beth, as if watching for signs of concussion even though a collision had been avoided. "You don't seem well. Is there anything I can do?"

"Catch the killer, for a start. The students are scared, but they don't want to show it. The faculty's scared too."

"Are you scared?" Sally asked.

"I think I'm numb. A lot has been going on lately and some part of me is threatening to shut down. I think I just need some time alone."

Sally sat on the curb and put her arm around Beth's shoulder, and Beth couldn't have been more surprised if Sally had stood up and danced a jig. She turned toward her and saw the concerned look on her face, felt her squeezing her shoulder gently. She felt cared for, she felt attracted, and she felt arousal—all things she'd felt around Sally before, but all when she had the ability to keep everything on a theoretical plane. Now the physical barrier was breached, and not only did her interest and arousal shoot up, but so did her fear. She turned toward Sally, drawing her shoulders in, making herself small and tense within the circle of her arm. Sally withdrew it.

"I promise you I will catch who did this," Sally said. "My gut tells me that this is a purpose killing, that the killer doesn't have any further targets in mind. But I also promise you that we'll keep everyone safe on campus until we do catch him."

"Thanks."

"And as far as your alone time goes? I just drove by your house and saw a car in the driveway."

"Yeah?" Beth frowned slightly. Who was parked there? And why did Sally always know who was in her driveway?

"Yeah." Sally stood, smoothing down her pants before offering Beth a hand up. "Looked like a Cadillac Escalade with Nevada plates."

The adrenaline coursed back through Beth's body, now a signal of an entirely new fear. She turned from Sally and started sprinting toward her house, praying that her mother had not come for a visit.

❖

It was midafternoon when Sally pulled into the drive of Delilah's big house. Despite the bright day, lamps shone throughout the first floor and as Sally approached the front door she could smell the delicious aroma of baked bread. She realized she hadn't eaten since that morning when she had a Pop-Tart.

The front door stood open and Sally peered through the screen after ringing the doorbell. The large living room was really a double parlor with the walls between the rooms removed. There were a couple of comfortable-looking seating areas, but it was designed to be open space, conducive to entertaining. Sally supposed it was used for the faculty parties she'd heard about, but of course never been invited to.

Delilah emerged and moved quickly toward the front door. Her sweatsuit was now covered by an apron, her hair piled high on her large head. She was at least as tall as Sally, but outweighed her by a fair amount, and Sally guessed that weight wasn't all flab, either. Delilah looked like someone who could easily sling Sally over her shoulder if the situation called for it.

"Good afternoon, Chief," Delilah said, opening the screen door for Sally and looking her over as she entered. "I just put the first batch of cookies in. If you're here longer than fifteen minutes I'll be able to serve you some."

"That sounds great. I'm afraid I missed lunch."

"Well, come on." Delilah led Sally down a hall into a large kitchen. Bowls, dripping spatulas, mixing machine, food processor, open bags of flour, oats, sugar, baking powder, and all sorts of dried fruit, nuts, and chocolate were spread about the generous countertop space as well as the breakfast table. Delilah cleared some space at the table and sat Sally down, then filled two mugs of coffee from a thermos before joining her.

"All this mess you see here is preparation for the faculty bash tomorrow. I hold a regular party here, but we'll keep it to a properly somber tone tomorrow."

Sally didn't say anything as Delilah settled herself at the table, her two hands wrapped around her coffee mug. The rings on each of her fingers were smudged with flour. The unpainted nails started clicking loudly on the ceramic mug.

"Chief, I'm actually glad you're here. I have something to tell you, and I would have come in on my own initiative, but your request for this interview beat me to it." Delilah looked straight at Sally, her eyes defiant.

"I'm listening." She remained far back in her chair as Delilah leaned toward her across the table.

"It's just that I imagine all possible motives for killing John Barrow are being explored. He wasn't much liked, so I bet you have a number of motives to pick from."

"Did you have a motive?" Sally asked.

"No, I didn't. But I am the chair of the tenure committee and I'm sure you've heard about the controversy over whether to grant tenure to him or not."

"I'm familiar with the situation."

"One of the reasons some of us didn't want Barrow to get tenure is because it would make it unlikely Katie Murphy would be put on a tenure track in the English department. She's clearly more qualified than Barrow."

"That's been mentioned."

"I've been sleeping with Katie."

Delilah kept the defiant look on her face. Sally imagined she was disappointed to not have Sally react with surprise to her news.

"So, because you have a personal relationship with Katie, you have an even greater reason to want to deny tenure to John Barrow."

"I imagine that's how it looks, so I wanted to be up front about it. Katie and I have been keeping the relationship quiet until after the tenure vote, which now will never come." Delilah stared into her coffee mug as a few moments of silence ticked by. Then she looked back at Sally. "Aren't you going to ask me anything?"

Sally had investigated enough murders and other crimes to know that a variety of techniques were used by people to throw suspicion off of themselves, or, for the attention seekers, onto themselves. If you are guilty of something, you might bring up the thing that makes you look most suspicious simply to make yourself look like someone who isn't guilty. She knew this could be true of Delilah. Sally thought it more likely, however, that Delilah didn't much like the fact that she wasn't playing a significant role in the college drama. Her commanding position as the chair of the tenure committee was now less relevant, her fabled faculty party was co-opted as a memorial party, and her girlfriend did not need her influence any longer.

"So if I understand what you're saying, Professor, the fact that John Barrow was likely to become tenured upset you because it would hurt Katie's chances of obtaining tenure."

"Yes, that and the fact that it's a step toward lowering the overall quality of our faculty. That reflects on all of us."

"And this made you angry?"

"It did. It most definitely did. I guess the question really is whether it's the kind of thing that would anger one enough to kill? What do you think, Chief?"

"I think that people in academia take things far more seriously than outsiders ever imagined. I'm starting to see that. And I've seen lesser motives for murder. But I think the question at this moment is whether it angered you enough to kill."

Delilah looked pleased with the discourse. Sally didn't doubt that Delilah expected to find Sally to be bumpkinish, unworthy of intellectual feint and parry.

"You're right, of course. I can tell you, Chief, that it angered me a good deal. But murdering John Barrow accords him more importance than I think he deserves. He wouldn't be worth the risk, the bother."

"That makes it sound like some people would be worth the risk and the bother."

"I'm afraid my habit of being glib makes me appear to be unfeeling. I'm not. I'm sorry that anyone here at the college has been murdered, even John Barrow. And I admit that I'm crazy about Katie."

"Would you please tell me where you were last night between nine p.m. and midnight?"

The kitchen timer rang and Delilah got up to take a tray of chocolate chip cookies out of the oven, moving the cookies onto a wire rack and starting to scoop more dough onto the cookie sheet. She seemed lost in the task.

"Delilah, you haven't answered my question. What were you doing last night?"

"Oh, was that question for real?" Delilah opened the oven door and slid the new tray in. "Well, one thing I did last evening was go over to the Hy-Vee for some of these ingredients, and while I was there I saw your friend Dean Ellis and Mel getting supplies for a cozy night in."

Even though Sally already knew this, the mention of it made her feel a little queasy. The last time she'd had this kind of visceral reaction to a woman, she'd ended up in a long relationship, one that was beautiful while it lasted but very ugly as it ended.

"I guess there must be a point in you telling me this?"

"You like her, don't you?" Delilah looked over at Sally, who sat. "Just call it a sixth sense, but I can tell you two would be perfect together. Mel is a problem, though. She beds as many women in town as she can, keeps them all wanting more, and you never know how deep she's got her claws in. I think Beth's been under her spell for a long time."

"I'll ask you now for a third time—where were you last night? And I want an answer."

"Oh, lighten up, Chief. I'm just having some fun with you. Last night I was with Katie from about eight o'clock on, and she left here first thing in the morning. I suppose you could confirm that with her, but I'd appreciate it if you'd keep it to yourself. I know she wants to keep our relationship a secret until this whole thing settles a bit."

Sally got up to leave. "Thank you for your time. If you think of anything further, please call me at the station."

Delilah walked Sally to the door. "Chief, I hope you'll come to my party tomorrow. Wouldn't it be a good opportunity to observe, get to know the players a bit more?"

"Sure, I'll stop by. I won't stay long, though."

Delilah smiled. "Wonderful. And, Chief? I wouldn't worry about Beth and Mel too much."

"What makes you think I'm worried at all?"

"You see, I used to date Beth. Not for terribly long, but it was intense. She has a way of going for something all-out, and then walking away without a second thought. Chances are she'll get sick of Mel at some point."

Sally shook her head as she trotted down the front steps. "I'll keep that in mind."

She got into her squad car and pulled into the street, irritated by Delilah's teasing, flabbergasted at the thought of Delilah and Beth together. She was less willing to acknowledge how irritating she found the idea of Mel with Beth.

CHAPTER NINE

Beth ran as fast as her moccasins would allow, heading straight into the eye of the storm rather than away from it. It was counterintuitive, she knew, like steering into a spin when you've lost control of your car. There always seemed to be chaos wherever her mother was and right now things at Grafton College were quite chaotic enough on their own. Her mother had a way of inserting herself into the middle of every situation she came upon, charming everyone along her path and leaving Beth feeling lumpy and dull. She didn't think she could cope with it this time.

Mae had only been to Mount Avery once before to visit Beth, dropping in unannounced ten years earlier after attending an "industry convention" in Chicago. Beth recalled looking over the panels and workshops in the program her mother kept as a souvenir, trying to imagine attending any of them. "Management Ethics: How to Get the Most From the Best Girls," which sounded a little suspect in the ethics department. A panel called "When Do You Run That Charge Card?" discussed, according to its description, whether it was better to have the front desk come in with the card charger when the employee and her client were in flagrante delicto, and thus more likely to be adding on some services, or during some negotiation when the client arrived at the ranch. The program was nearly as thick as the one for the Modern Language Association convention Beth attended annually, and there any resemblance ended. Mae spent most of the twenty-four hours of her visit asleep, recovering, she said, from the endless "networking" they were forced to do.

As she turned the corner onto First Avenue, Beth saw the Escalade in her driveway, her mother standing at the rear of the giant vehicle, dwarfed by it, yanking on a large hard-sided suitcase that would hold enough clothing for a long stay. Mae Ellis was a small woman, just 5'3" and not much over 100 pounds. She was stylishly dressed in the sort of travel suit ladies of a certain age might wear their first day at sea on a luxury cruise: comfortable but perfectly coordinated, every detail and accessory carefully thought out. Her elegant appearance was at odds with the string of profanity being directed at the suitcase she was wrestling to the ground.

Beth practically screeched to a halt next to the car, reaching a hand forward to lift the suitcase back in the car.

"No point in taking the bag out of the car, Mae. You're not staying here." She'd always called her Mae, since she was a tiny girl. Mae didn't feel the word "mother" should be used in the brothel. She was concerned it would make the clients uncomfortable. Beth was mostly kept out of sight for the same reason, though once she was old enough to look after herself she was free to go wherever she liked. Mae's determination of a child being old enough to take care of herself came much earlier than most parents'. At eight Beth could pretty much come and go as she pleased, though the lack of places to go limited her freedom. Her mother certainly didn't.

Mae stepped back and stared at Beth, her mouth open and her hand at her chest. "Where the hell did you come from? It's like you popped out of the sky."

"I'd say it's more like you popped out of the sky," Beth said. She shoved the suitcase into the rear of the car and slammed the hatch shut. "What are you doing here?"

"Visiting you, obviously. Or trying to. I'm on my way east and wanted to see you."

"Well, you can't stay here."

"Beth, I can't leave. Not just yet. I've driven twelve hours today and I'm tired."

Mae opened the hatch again and yanked at the suitcase until it teetered at the edge of the cargo area and then fell to the ground.

"I don't understand why you're here. Couldn't you have told

me you were planning this? We just talked on the phone the other day."

"I could have, but I wanted to surprise you."

"Score one for you, then. It's just that you've arrived at the worst possible time." Beth reached down to pick up the suitcase and Mae moved to block her by standing on it.

"Relax, Beth. If there's trouble, I can help you. I'm very good with trouble." Beth laughed out loud at that, thinking truer words were rarely spoken.

Out of the corner of her eye Beth could see her neighbor Stephanie come out of her house and head down the drive to retrieve her garbage can from the street. As soon as she saw Beth she made a beeline over to join them by the Escalade.

"It's Mrs. Ellis, isn't it?" Stephanie asked, reaching over to shake Mae's hand. "How nice of you to be here for the dean during this very difficult time."

Mae's eyebrow went up and she turned back to Beth. "What is going on?"

Stephanie leaned in, unwilling to let Beth tell the news once it became clear that Mae hadn't heard it. "One of the faculty was murdered last night. The whole campus is in an uproar."

Beth gave Stephanie a stern look before moving her mother off the suitcase with one hand and then picking it up with the other. "I think I'll just get Mother inside, Stephanie, if you wouldn't mind excusing us."

"Of course. It's all very upsetting, I know. But don't you worry about the dean, Mrs. Ellis. She's got all sorts of people looking out for her, including the police chief."

Beth gave her neighbor a murderous glare before turning to her mother.

"Come on. We'll get the rest of your things in a bit." Beth hauled the suitcase toward her front door with Mae at her heels, aiming her key fob over her shoulder to lock her car doors. Beth could hear Stephanie shuffling in her slippers back into her own house, eager, no doubt, to get on the phone and tell whoever would listen that Beth's mother had come for a visit and Beth didn't seem any too pleased about it. Since Beth became dean, Stephanie found every aspect of Beth's life to have some social or political importance. She was the widow of a college administrator and naturally suspicious of the academic. If only Stephanie knew the whole story. That Mae was visiting from Liaisons Fantastique Pleasure Ranch located sixty miles outside of Las Vegas, where prostitution was perfectly legal but still as stigmatized as when ladies of a much earlier time served the "needs" of the miners in the area. Beth didn't doubt that Stephanie would have plenty of listeners for news like that.

Once inside the house Beth carried the suitcase down the short hallway leading to the bedrooms. The guest room was across the hall from Beth's room. The third bedroom at the end of the hall was used as a study. Beth flung the heavy suitcase on the guest room bed.

"You're welcome to stay tonight. God knows I don't want you driving into a ditch. I don't know how you even drive that ridiculous car. You look like a peanut behind the wheel."

"I want to stay a few nights. I'm not expected in New York until next week."

"It's too much. I can't do that."

"Why is it too much? I'm just going to sit around. You don't even have to talk to me."

"Right." Beth knew her mother didn't understand, wasn't capable of understanding. She barely understood herself why merely being near her felt so triggery. She felt anxious, a little short of breath. She wanted to relax around Mae and just enjoy the maddening, outrageous person she was. She wasn't going to change. She certainly would never become a candidate for Mother of the Year. But wanting to relax and be herself around her mother and actually being able to do it were very different things. Beth also wanted world peace and an end to hunger. None of these things seemed like they'd ever actually happen.

Beth made to leave the room, but Mae again blocked her way, standing at the door, legs apart and fists on her hips.

"Jesus H. Christ, you are a brat. Do you know that?"

"I'm sorry, Mother, am I not acting the way you want me to? Sorry to irritate you."

"I don't know how it is that you don't irritate yourself."

"Oh, I do. Believe me."

Mae relaxed a hip and a smile raised one corner of her mouth. She reached out to Beth and took her gently by the forearm, pulling her down with her to sit on the bed. "What was that woman talking about, a murder on campus?"

Mae settled in to listen to a good story. She'd want all the details, and she'd get them. Beth would give way to the inevitable. She'd succumb, as everyone did, to Mae's persuasiveness, no matter how uncomfortable or anxious she felt. Growing up, Beth could count on only a few minutes a day with her mother, usually the time after school when the yellow bus dropped Beth off a half mile from the ranch. When Beth walked into the kitchen in the small private residence they shared, her mother would be sitting at the table, yawning from the nap she'd just woken from, her hands wrapped around a cup of coffee. She'd pour some for Beth, having practically weaned her from breast milk to caffeine, and then have Beth tell her stories from her day. Not snippets of this or that, but stories with a beginning, middle, and end. Usually the stories featured villains, the nasty kids who teased her about what her mother did for a living. It made for a Dickensian childhood, but Mae was fascinated by the stories and usually she found a way to turn them around in order to ridicule or pity Beth's tormentors. The attention from Mae made the teasing at school easier to take, and the temptation to embellish the stories or simply make them up was almost impossible to resist.

As long as Beth didn't whine, Mae would be sympathetic and would advise her on how to handle bullies, cliques, and the occasional friend. If Beth whined about the difficulties at school, her mother would walk out of the room. She had no time for victims. Now Beth found herself telling Mae her latest horror story from school, the entire background on John Barrow and President Landscome, and the little that was known at this point about the murder and its investigation.

"See, this is the thing, Bethy. You have always thought that your world of faculties and PhDs and elevated thinking would be like living in a cloister. The one murder we had at the ranch wasn't even as nasty as this is. Do you remember that?"

"It would be a little hard to forget."

"Isn't that the truth? But really, when you think about it, it was just an old-fashioned gunfight over a woman. It was just like *High Noon* there in the lounge."

"*High Noon* without the moral imperative, you mean. I just remember coming in to get a soda from Ernie and all of a sudden the bar stools went flying and there was a little popping sound and this big fat guy fell over like a redwood. Then Ernie had me by the collar and out of that room."

"Ernie was a wonderful man, wasn't he? May he rest in peace."

"What happened to him again? You told me, but I can't remember." Half the time when Mae called, Beth continued to work and heard only bits and pieces of her mother's news reports.

"It was prostate cancer. I swear, that's an epidemic and it's affecting my business. You know, once the disease progresses men have a hell of a time with an erection. Gets so they don't even try, and that's not good for us."

"'Erection' is a pretty clinical term for you, Mother."

"It's business. And business hasn't been great lately."

Beth sighed. She was sure her mother would devise an effective marketing strategy to counteract this loss of business. Free Viagra at the door, penis pumps discreetly stashed in the bathrooms. Mae was nothing if not inventive.

"Maybe I can help you while I'm here," Mae proposed. She popped open her suitcase, the inside filled with carefully labeled packing cubes, removing the one on top and holding it in her lap. "That is, if you'll let me stay for a day or two."

"I'm not sure pimping and whoring are exactly the skills that are needed just now, but I'll check with Chief Sullivan if you'd like."

"Don't be so crass, Beth. I was actually proposing taking care of you a bit while all this is going on. I'm sure you have your hands full. I could cook, for instance. Do the shopping. Whatever you need, sweetheart." She looked at Beth with a sincerity so intense that Beth completely mistrusted it.

"Let's just see how things go today. And don't unpack everything. One cube—that's it."

"Agreed. I've missed you, Beth. It will be good to spend time together. You won't regret it."

"I'm sure that's not true. Please promise me you won't go out unless you're with me. I'm dean of the college now, remember. Your eagerness to talk about the ranch's success isn't something I want spread around campus."

"It doesn't seem like that would make much of an impression around here," Mae said. "Murder trumps prostitution any day."

Chapter Ten

Sally steered her car toward the station, her thoughts divided between what she still needed to do before the end of the day and the interview she'd just concluded with Delilah. The only thing she'd learned was that Delilah and Beth had been an item a while back, a fact not relevant to the investigation perhaps, but Sally felt its impact. Beth seemed to be attracted to women with big personalities, and while Mel couldn't be more different than Delilah, they did have something in common—they both sucked a little more air out of a room than the average person did.

Her mood was on a steady downward course. She had a murder investigation that was stalled and she didn't seem to be able to get it unstuck. The only thing she felt capable of doing was going through the motions of the investigation, but she knew that methodically doing so formed the bulk of police work. Inspiration would have to wait.

Sally walked into the station through the back door, making her way unseen to her small office. On Saturdays there was a skeletal administrative staff, but the front was overseen by old Henry Barda, retired from the force several years ago and happy to play desk sergeant/dispatcher on the usually quiet weekends. Most of the rest of the daytime roster were out recanvassing Barrow's neighborhood or on patrol. Sally picked up her phone and called the front desk.

"Henry, it's the chief."

"Yeah, Chief."

"Send Ted Benson in to see you me, will you? And maybe brew up a fresh pot of coffee. I can smell that burnt pot from my office."

Sally put the phone down without saying good-bye. She knew she'd sounded short on the phone, which she didn't like to be with her staff. Sometimes unfriendly was the best she could do. Compared to some of the superior officers she'd worked for, she figured she had a light touch most of the time. She pulled her file on the Barrow murder off the top of the growing pile of paperwork on her desk, wondering again whether she should call in some help from the state police.

"Hey there, Chief. Henry said you wanted to see me." Ted Benson stood just outside her office door.

"I need a report from you."

Ted took a step into the office and assumed an at-ease position.

"Ted, I thought we'd talked about this at-ease thing you keep doing. Now come in and sit down."

"Ma'am, I'm more comfortable giving my report while standing." Ted relaxed his posture somewhat, but kept his eyes straight ahead and his hands behind his back.

"Officer Benson, sit down in the fucking chair. That's an order."

"Yes, ma'am." Ted moved quickly to sit in the chair in front of Sally's desk.

"You're doing the ma'am thing also."

"Sorry, Chief."

"Okay, let's hear what you got off the computer from Barrow's house."

"I've been through ninety percent of it, Chief, and there doesn't seem to be anything interesting, though he does have some porn on there."

"What kind of porn?"

Ted looked confused. "What kind? I guess the kind you'd expect. People doing it."

"Adult people? Vanilla sex or BDSM? Professional or amateur? There are clues in a man's taste in porn."

"Well, I guess it was regular, then. Men and women just doing it. I couldn't look long, Chief, with women walking by in the station."

"Ted, I am a woman, remember? I have seen porn where people are doing things that your mind, in particular, would never be able to think up. And so will you before your career's over."

"There wasn't anything like that. And the rest of the files in the computer all seemed to be about his school work."

Sally leaned back and sighed. "Okay. Finish going through that and then check with Bob on his look into John Barrow's background."

"Uh, Chief. I was supposed to be off today. I was thinking I might be able to leave soon."

Sally stared at Ted, who had the good sense to look sheepish.

"Do you have somewhere else you want to be, Officer?"

"Well, it's just that—"

"Because I don't know if you recall that we have a murderer running around Mount Avery. Did you forget that?"

"No, ma'am. It's just that it's my girlfriend's birthday and she's kind of expecting me. And there's the fact that the murderer is likely to be long gone."

Sally stared even harder at Ted, the silence growing longer and strangely louder, until Ted squirmed in his little chair.

"Officer Benson, you're absolutely right. We don't know whether the murderer is long gone or not. In fact, we don't know shit. And we'll continue to not know shit as long as we have half-assed officers like you working on this investigation."

Sally stood. "Officer, stand at attention."

Ted stood and snapped to attention, his eyes fixed straight ahead. Sally positioned herself so she could look back at him. "If you want to be some kind of lifelong, half-assed cop who doesn't care about anything beyond his pension, keeping his girlfriend happy, and complaining about his work conditions, then go ahead. There's plenty like that on every force. Probably the vast majority, in fact. You'll have a nice, boring, but very long career ahead of you. Is that what you want, Officer Benson?"

"No, Chief."

"I happen to think you might have a little more on the ball than that. Did you know that I thought that?"

"I was hoping you'd give me opportunities to show you."

"And I have. And you're responding to a giant opportunity to show me what you've got by asking if you can go to a birthday party."

"No, Chief. It's just that…"

"I don't care. The only thing I care about is catching this guy. You can leave now if you choose, but think carefully before you do."

"I'll stay, Chief."

Sally looked at him for a bit longer before sitting back in her chair. "At ease, Officer. Continue your report."

"After working most of the morning on the computer, I joined the other officers on Third Avenue who were re-interviewing the victim's neighbors. I'll bring in the statements, but the short story is that no one heard anything or saw anything. Not at the time we think Barrow was shot or at anytime yesterday."

"That's just damn odd," Sally said. "It's not that I don't believe them. I think they'd leap at the chance to be involved in the investigation. But a gunshot outdoors should have been heard by someone in a quiet neighborhood. What do you think, Ted?"

"Silencer?"

"Precisely. A silencer used on a James Bond gun to shoot an unpopular English professor in the middle of rural America. What does that suggest to you?"

Ted looked stumped at this one. "I'm afraid I can't guess, Chief."

"It suggests a professional hit. I'm not saying that's what it was, but it doesn't have the feel of a crime of passion. There's no sign of struggle, no one heard any noise, no one reports ever seeing Barrow even with another person."

"Except for that college girl, Jennifer," Ted remembered.

"Yep. We need to get her tracked down."

Sally thought about this some more before getting up and

moving around her desk. "Let's see if Henry made a new pot. I need some coffee."

"There's one other thing to report," Ted said as Sally led them down the hall to the break room. She smiled for the first time in hours when she saw the fresh pot.

"What else do you have, Ted?" Sally poured and handed Ted a mug.

"Jake was working on tracking down any purchases of Walther PPKs in the area. When he got called out to an accident scene he asked me to tell you he hadn't come up with anything."

"Did you take a look at what he did?"

"Yes, Chief. He did finish e-mailing and calling every gun shop in the eastern part of the state. No record so far of anyone buying a Walther anytime in the last few years. We're still waiting for some responses."

"We know it's unlikely we'll find the killer from a list of registered gun owners. He will have picked the gun up some other way." Sally drank some coffee and thought for a bit. "Okay. Put that stuff on my desk, and the interview statements too. Then you can go be with your girlfriend."

Ted looked surprised, and then resolute. "No, ma'am. I'll stay on."

"No, you'll go now, and I appreciate the work you've done today. But if something comes up tonight, I'll haul you back in here. That understood?"

"Yes, ma'am."

"Chief."

"I mean Chief. Thanks."

Ted left the room before Sally could change her mind again. She poured herself more coffee before she returned to her office. Ted's files were already on her desk, and as she sat to review them Henry rang to announce that a Jennifer Manos was at the front desk to see her. Sally was reminded why she liked to work so much; usually there wasn't time to think about anything else when she was on the job.

When she reached the front of the station, Jennifer was

standing near Henry's desk. Her age and the backpack slung over her shoulder gave her away as a college student, but she showed none of the vibrant health Sally would expect to see. Her skin was pasty, her face was broken out, her hair greasy and pulled back into a tight ponytail, stretching the skin around her temples. Her clothes were too tight and the hand holding the strap of her pack looked doughy, as if a dimple would appear if you pressed a finger in the flesh. Sally was just able to recognize Jennifer from the photo that had been given to her when she went missing.

"So, you're back in town, Jennifer."

"I'm here because my roommates said you wanted to talk to me." She didn't smile, offer her hand, or look Sally in the eye. Her gaze was directed at about badge level.

"It's good to see you safe and sound. There were people at the college who were very worried about you."

She shrugged. "Not everyone at the college was worried."

Sally saw Henry shaking his head, still convinced after years on the Mount Avery force that Grafton College students were spoiled rotten. She regarded Jennifer. "Well, thanks for coming in. Why don't we go to my office and talk?"

After they'd settled in and Jennifer had refused an offer of coffee or tea, Sally asked, "What do you know about what's been going on here since you took your unscheduled vacation to San Francisco?"

Jennifer responded in a clipped, impatient voice. "It was hardly a vacation, not that it's any business of yours. Nonetheless, in answer to your question, I am aware that Professor Barrow was murdered last night."

"Wasn't Professor Barrow the reason you left town?"

"No. I don't know why you'd think that. I went to California to be with my cousin."

"With school in the middle of the semester? And graduation coming up? That doesn't sound like the honors student people described to me when I spent a good amount of man-hours trying to track you down."

Jennifer was unperturbed. "I'm not sure why I'm here, Chief

Sullivan. Why would Professor Barrow be the reason for me going to San Francisco?"

"I talked to some of your housemates and they seemed to think you may have had a crush on him, and—"

"A crush?" Jennifer's voice climbed a few octaves at this. "A crush is something one has from afar, Chief. A crush is something a schoolgirl has. A crush is not what a woman feels for her lover." Jennifer crossed her arms around the backpack sitting on her lap and held it close to her chest.

"Jennifer, was John Barrow your lover?" Sally tried to speak gently.

"I don't have to speak to you about that. It's not any of your business."

"That's where you're wrong, I'm afraid. I'd love for your romantic life to not be my business, believe me. But John Barrow was murdered and it's my job to find out who killed him, and everything is my business until I do."

Sally flipped open her file and pulled out a morgue shot of Barrow. He looked pale, but not gruesome. The hole in his chest was not huge. It almost appeared as if he were napping.

"Here's your lover, Jennifer. Don't you want to help me find who did this to him?"

Jennifer could not avert her eyes in time. Her hand flew to her mouth as she tried to hold back a sob. "Oh, God." She was clearly trying to contain her reaction, but racking sobs overtook her and she rocked back and forth in her chair, her pack tumbling to the floor as both her hands now cradled her face. Sally sighed as she got up to look for some tissues. She thought it unlikely Jennifer had killed Barrow, but her passion for him was clear. And passion equaled motive to kill, more often than Sally ever thought was possible.

When the sobs subsided and the snuffling and eye rubbing began, Sally resumed her questioning.

"Jennifer, whatever the story is between you and Barrow, I have to hear it. We're not concerned with anything except who did this to him. Now, were you and John Barrow lovers?"

Jennifer held her head high. "Yes."

"For how long?"

"Since fall term."

"While you were missing from campus I was asked by the college to try to find you. Dean Ellis, in particular, was concerned. I searched your room."

"You what?" This came out as a shriek. "Am I living in a gulag? You can't search my room."

"I can, and I did. I found a pregnancy test kit that was positive. Are you pregnant?"

Jennifer hesitated. Her spotty, pasty face was now swollen from tears, her red eyes almost closed shut. "No, I'm not."

Sally watched her closely. "Let me rephrase that. Were you pregnant?"

The hesitation was a little longer this time. She picked her pack up and held it again to her chest. "These are very personal questions and I will not answer them. Sorry." She didn't look particularly sorry.

Sally leaned back in her chair and picked up the phone. "Henry, will you get Becky Reynolds back in the station, please?"

"What are you doing?" Jennifer squeezed her bag more tightly to her.

"I'm getting another female officer in here. It looks like I may end up having to arrest you and I'll want Officer Reynolds to process you."

Jennifer bolted up from her chair, her pack swinging wildly from her arm, knocking Sally's coffee cup off the desk and into the garbage. "Arrest me! You can't arrest me. I haven't done anything."

"Sit down," Sally snapped. Jennifer sat, her eyes now huge in her face. Sally didn't know if it was anger or fear behind them. She didn't really care. "By not answering my questions you are not cooperating with my investigation. You have a motive for killing John Barrow, whether it's that he dumped you because you were pregnant with his child or he dumped you simply because he was bored."

"No! He didn't dump me because he wanted to. He was forced

to. He had to make sure he got tenure in order to secure our future. He definitely didn't dump me. It was just a break."

Sally continued as if not hearing her. "In addition to motive, you had opportunity. We only have your word that you were in San Francisco last night."

Now Jennifer's mouth dropped open. "Am I in *Mayberry R.F.D.* here? If you're looking for an alibi, I have several suggestions on how you can confirm my whereabouts. Like number one, I was on a flight this morning from San Francisco."

"This morning is not last night, and there are lots of flights between San Francisco and Chicago. You could have been here, flown to San Francisco, and then been back here again."

"Why would I do that? And can't you check whether I was on any of those flights, if they even exist?"

"I have checked that out, Jennifer, and the flight times do work. You are only listed as being on the one flight this morning, however."

Jennifer smiled, but it wasn't a cheerful smile. It was a smile of triumph. "There you go. I just told you I wasn't on any other flight."

"But you could have used an alias and false identification."

A small, sturdy woman in uniform appeared at her door. "Henry said you wanted me, Chief?"

"Yeah, Becky. Grab yourself some coffee and sit tight. I'll be with you in a few."

"Sure thing." Becky had the slightest smile at the corner of her mouth as she looked at Jennifer. Her opinion of college students ran along the same lines as Henry's. Jennifer watched her walk away and turned back to Sally. She now seemed to be edging more toward fear and away from anger.

"Chief Sullivan, you cannot arrest me. It would be wrong. I haven't done anything. You just can't arrest me."

"So you keep saying, but of course the fact is that I can, and I will. As I've said, motive, opportunity. That's enough right now. We'll find the weapon."

Sally gazed at Jennifer as if she were a little bored, as if she

were watching a Cubs game at the end of the season, no hope that
the game would mean a damn thing, but there was nothing else to
watch. It was going to take something big—a triple or a home run
or something—for Sally to change her attitude. The disinterest was
meant to worry Jennifer, and it appeared to work.

"Chief, if you want to check on my alibi I can give you my
cousin's name and she can give you the names of the other people
we were with Friday night."

Sally pushed a pen and paper over to Jennifer, who scribbled
a name and number on the pad. "Now tell me why you went out
there."

"Why? What difference does that make to you?"

"I'm still investigating Barrow's murder and you were the
closest person to him, it seems. I want to know why you ran away
just days before he was killed."

Jennifer glared at Sally. "I had an abortion, okay? Are you
satisfied now?"

"And Barrow was the father?"

"Of course he was. He's the only man I've ever slept with."

"It probably made you pretty mad that he didn't want to have
anything to do with the baby. I mean, who wouldn't be furious to be
seduced like that and then cast aside."

"I wasn't cast aside! How many times do you need to hear this?
We were taking a break. John just thought it was a terrible time to
have a baby, what with the tenure situation and the problem with me
being a student and him a professor. No one would understand."

Sally didn't think Jennifer was hiding anything more, but she
let her sit there in silence for a little while, just to see if anything else
erupted from her. If she was delusional enough to think Barrow was
just taking a break from their relationship, then she wouldn't have
killed him.

"I'm going to check things out with your cousin and if
everything is as you say it is, then we have nothing more to worry
about. Okay?"

"It will check out. I haven't told you any lies." Jennifer got up and slung her bag back on her shoulder. "But I've told you more than I'd want anyone to know."

"Don't worry. I don't think this has to go any further than between us. One other thing, though. Since you were so intimate with Professor Barrow, did you pick up on any enemies he may have had, any personal problems that may have been troubling him?"

"The only thing he ever talked about was tenure. And he really hated all the people who wanted to take it from him. He thought they were all anti-British."

"Anti-British?"

"Whatever. I just mean that they all seemed to hate him because he wasn't from here and he was a favorite of Landscome's. Dean Ellis hated him, and so did Professor Humphries."

"Do you know if they had words?"

"I don't know. Not that he told me. He just said that once he got tenure he would be able to do what he wanted and things would be fine for us. I just had to graduate."

"Why did you say you were quitting school when you called Dean Ellis?"

Jennifer looked confused, as if keeping track of the melodrama that was her life was impossible without a script. "I don't know. That was, like, four days ago."

"Did you change your mind because of anything Barrow said to you? Or any change in his circumstance?"

"Listen, I've told you all of what I know. Maybe I felt like quitting when I called Dean Ellis, but it seems stupid now."

"All right. I think that's it for now. Just stay in town for a bit, all right? And if you think of anything else that might be helpful, give me a call."

Sally walked Jennifer out. Becky and Henry were drinking coffee by the front desk. "What did you need me for, Chief?" Becky asked.

"I thought I was going to be able to arrest someone for the Barrow murder, but it turns out she has an alibi." Sally turned around and started walking back to her office.

"Where you going from here, Chief?" Henry asked.

"Back to square one."

Sally returned to her office to check the alibi Jennifer gave her, doing it for form's sake. She had no doubt it would be confirmed.

CHAPTER ELEVEN

Beth finished washing the dinner dishes, her mother at her side wiping them down with a soggy dish towel and then rooting around Beth's cabinets, looking for a place to put them. Their conversation had been safely stalled on kitchen logistics for the past fifteen minutes, and what Beth guessed to be the normalcy of it struck her as not only unfamiliar but also strangely pleasing.

Moments such as this were rare growing up on the prostitution ranch, a term Beth used deliberately to conjure up an image of herds of whores, tended through their prime and then moved off the ranch to meet their fate. Beth never knew what happened to the women who quietly left the ranch, usually when they were closing in on thirty. Many of the women who worked at the ranch were putting themselves through college and graduate school, so their departures were celebrated. Others bided their time until the day they were called into Mae's office and given a generous amount of notice that their work at the ranch was coming to an end. Beth rarely got to know any of them well, except for the few who became her babysitters. These were the young women who were not proving to be customer pleasers at the ranch but whom Mae did not have the heart to fire. They watched Beth while Mae tended to ranch business, and inevitably they left after several months. After having her heart broken several times, Beth learned to not grow close to her minders.

Mae continued her analysis of Beth's kitchen. "Most people in this day and age have dishwashers. You're really the only one I know who has a kitchen like this." She was on her tippytoes, sliding a bowl onto a cabinet shelf.

"Like what?"

"Your appliances are ancient, your cabinets are horrible, and your countertops are not only Formica, but really old Formica."

"The appliances work fine. There's no reason to replace them. And there's no place for a dishwasher, even if I were to buy one." Beth stood and looked at her kitchen, finding it perfectly satisfactory.

"You have no vision. What you should do is knock this wall out, tear everything down to the studs, and put in a new kitchen that opens up to your family room there. You'll love it." Mae swept her arm from side to side, painting a picture of a modern kitchen/great room filled with the latest appliances and finishes.

"You're doing it again, Mother."

"Doing what again?"

"Trying to control me. You're already redecorating. You arrive here unannounced, which is a way of controlling me, because you know you'll get your way. Am I supposed to throw my own mother out of my house?"

"Good Lord. Are you this way with your friends? Do you even have friends?"

Beth left the kitchen and headed to her room, with Mae close behind. As Beth pulled clothes out of her closet and started to change, Mae said, "Why don't we open a bottle of wine and play Scrabble or something?"

"Normally, I'd love the opportunity to kick your ass in Scrabble, but I have to go somewhere."

"Where? Can I go?"

Beth ignored the question. "I have to go on campus for a bit. The students are having a candlelight vigil to honor Professor Barrow and to protest gun violence."

"Oh, gag."

Beth went back down the hall and into the bathroom, with Mae still close behind. She closed the door on her mother, who kept right on talking. "I can't believe students would protest one of their own constitutional rights. That's so shortsighted."

"What right would that be, mother? The right to be violent?"

"The right to bear arms, Ms. PhD. It's fundamental."

"Sounds like you are too. You've been in Nevada too long."

Beth came out of the bathroom and put a coat on from her front closet.

"Here, let me grab a coat and go with you. I want to see this candlelight vigil." Mae reached into the closet for her fringed and beaded leather jacket.

"No. I can't worry about you up there. I'm dean of the college, for God's sake. Even your best behavior I'll worry about what people are thinking of you."

"Actually, that's not true. You'll be worrying about what people think about you, Beth. And that's always been your problem."

Beth turned to open her front door. "My problems right now are numerous. Please don't add to them. I'll be back in an hour."

Beth left her house and her mother and walked across the street to start climbing the hill to campus. She prayed that her mother would take pity on her and actually do as she asked. If she appeared on campus, the likelihood was high that someone would learn about Liaisons Fantastique. Mae was, if nothing else, an unwaveringly honest person when it came to what people knew about her. With the campus in crisis, Beth didn't want her leadership diluted by the news that the dean was raised in a brothel. Even if everyone else on campus was understanding, she was sure Landscome would look for a way to use it against her.

It was fully dark and Beth could see the glow of candles from the lawn in front of the church that stood at the top of the hill, next to Old Main. From here the bells of the Methodist church had rung for over a century until a decade ago, when the church and the college were separated. While the union between them had become unhappy, the breakup was amicable. Townspeople, faculty, staff, and students still worshipped in the church on Sundays, but there was no affiliation with the college. The bells had been silenced as part of the separation agreement. The imposing church, with its towering spire, loomed over the large group of students standing on the lawn, holding candles sputtering in the breeze that was always present at the top of the hill. They faced a young man who spoke passionately about the need for new laws eliminating all handguns in the United States. There were a few students goofing around, but for the most part it was a serious group. The speaker was replaced by a young woman who started to exhort the crowd to sing a protest song, one Beth did not recognize. What happened to "Blowing in the Wind"? Wouldn't that be perfect for a protest of gun violence? A few minutes before, Beth had felt like a fourteen-year-old as she argued with her mother. Now she just felt old.

As she made her way to the other side of the gathering, Beth stopped several times to speak with students. Campus security officers were positioned around the periphery, and a couple of the town's police officers were also present. She scanned the crowd looking for Sally, spotting her as she approached the side of the crowd that Beth had just abandoned, her hands jammed into her jacket pockets. Sally stopped and also searched the crowd, nodding to her officers and then resting her gaze on Beth. An unmistakable hormone surge blasted through Beth's body and she gave a little shudder. A delicious shudder. No matter what chaos reigned in her mind, her body was clear. She wanted Sally Sullivan and there was something more powerful about the attraction than she'd ever felt before. This was not an intellectual or aesthetic attraction. This was a full-bore attraction that was brought about by physical proximity but found its power in so much more than that. Now that she acknowledged it, she felt backed into a corner. If she didn't act on it, would it torment her every time she saw Sally? If she did act on it, how long did she have before her heart was broken?

Beth began to make her way back across the crowd when she saw her mother striding right up to Sally. Mae tugged on Sally's sleeve and said something to her. Sally took Mae by the elbow and guided her in Beth's direction. Beth froze like a rabbit, unable to move and half hoping that by holding completely still she would become invisible. She couldn't quite cope with the idea of a chat with her mother and Sally. Perhaps they would walk right past her, talking about how much in love Sally was with her and how it would be perfect for them to get married in Mae's wedding chapel in

Nevada, recently converted from its colorful past as a brothel. The fantasy felt lovely for the moment Beth was allowed to indulge in it before she heard her name called. She turned to see Amanda, the student organizer extraordinaire, who was saying something to her.

"I'm sorry, Amanda. I didn't catch that."

Amanda leaned in closer, her earnest face creased with concern. "Are you okay, Dean? You don't look well."

"Don't I? It's been a very trying day."

Beth could hear her mother's voice saying, "There she is," as she and Sally drew nearer.

"Amanda, would it be appropriate for me to say a few words? It seems there's a little break between songs." Beth started walking toward the front of the crowd before Amanda could answer.

"We would love that, Dean. The administration's support is really important." Amanda was trying to keep up with Beth, who was practically running. When she reached the front of the crowd, she moved the microphone stand away from the young woman who was tuning her guitar for another song. In the relatively silent crowd, Beth could hear her mother say, "What the hell is she doing?"

Beth launched into a five-minute salute to those who fight against gun violence, a one-minute eulogy of John Barrow, and another three minutes on the importance of community during troubled times. She then stepped away from the microphone and plunged into the crowd on the side opposite of Mae and Sally, hurrying back home before either could catch up with her.

As she let herself back into her little house, Beth felt almost overcome with dissatisfaction—with her life and, most of all, with herself. She was tired of being the person whose fantasy was that her mother owned a Las Vegas wedding chapel, because that was a big step up from the truth. She was tired of stretching her arms around every brick of Grafton College, trying to keep any part of it from changing. She was tired of being afraid of falling in love. What about Sally was frightening? She couldn't think of a thing. And yet she realized she was looking for some sort of guarantee that she wouldn't be hurt again if she gave her heart to someone. She thought it was guaranteed that she'd always love Grafton the way she had passionately loved it for years, and yet now she felt increasingly distanced from it, alienated by a leader who didn't seem to share a single opinion with her about what made the college great. People simply differed from each other, and those differences brought about unpredictable events. There were no guarantees. Beth wondered how it was that she could understand something intellectually but have no control over it emotionally. That her mind was not strong enough to control everything in her life was frustrating beyond belief. She went into her sadly dated kitchen and made a drink, downing it as she stood at the sink. Then she made another and carried it into her bedroom, locking the door behind her. She could decide to stay locked away and protected from the hurt the unpredictable could bring, or she could throw in with the living. She wasn't yet sure which it would be.

CHAPTER TWELVE

Sally was at her desk early Sunday morning, reviewing her files, putting together a murder book, determined to find some thread to follow. The only motive for Barrow's death that she could see was the determination of someone that he not receive tenure. Though Sally had heard of crazier motives for murder, it still struck her as improbable. But it was all she had.

She was jotting down points to cover that day when Henry called her from the front desk. She glanced at her watch and saw that it was past seven already. The weekend day shift would be settling in.

"Chief, what are you doing back there? I was just calling to leave a message."

"What've you got, Henry?"

"I just got off the phone with the college president, a Nigel Landscome. Says he's back in town and wants a call from you. Kind of sounds like he's expecting you to report to him."

"Can't say that surprises me. Give me his number."

After going over a few day-shift matters with Henry, Sally hung up. She went into the kitchen to make a new pot of coffee, not anxious to give Landscome the impression that she was willing to drop everything to return his call. But after the coffee brewed and she'd fixed a cup, she couldn't stand to wait any longer. She took her coffee back to her office and picked up the phone.

"Nigel Landscome here."

Sally introduced herself and asked him when he had arrived back in Mount Avery.

"Flew in from Heathrow and arrived late last night. Earliest flight I could get on and it was terribly uncomfortable, I don't mind telling you. No business class upgrades left me in a middle seat in coach."

Sally ignored his whining. "President Landscome, I need to speak with you as soon as possible. Obviously you know that John Barrow has been murdered."

"Of course. That's why I flew back on that awful flight."

"You should know that Dean Ellis has been very cooperative and I am confident we have security issues on campus well covered."

"I'll have to take your word on that for the moment. I haven't had a chance to suss anything quite yet."

Sally gritted her teeth. She knew that "suss" meant to figure something out; she'd read a fair share of British mysteries. And none of it mattered, neither his ridiculous adoption of British slang nor her irritation with it. At the moment, though, she hated him for it. Hated his absurdity and his thoughtlessness. She held her tongue and let the silence lengthen.

"I don't have all day, Chief. Report on your progress. It's been over a day now since the murder occurred. I have an hysterical campus here and we need results."

"First of all, the campus is anything but hysterical. As I said, Dean Ellis has done a great job reassuring the students, and there are security officers positioned around the clock. Secondly, the purpose of my call is not to report to you but rather to ask you some questions. I'll be at your house in ten minutes."

"Now, wait just a minute. I didn't agree to any such meeting. I'm dead on my feet and was just going in for a lie-down."

"I really don't care whether you were going in for a wank. Ten minutes."

Sally hung up the phone and blew out a breath. She wanted to arrest him just for the hell of it. She thought about the possibility of Landscome being the murderer, but his London trip and the fact that he'd recruited Barrow and put him up for tenure made that seem only wishful thinking on her part. She grabbed Ted Benson on her way out the door. Ted was just coming on shift, his first cup of coffee slopping over the sides of his paper cup as he trotted behind Sally to the car.

"Did your girl have a nice birthday, Ted?"

"She did, Chief. I should have told you last night that the reason I was anxious to get over to her place was I decided to ask her to marry me." Ted held on to his cup with both hands as Sally squealed out of the station house parking lot.

"No kidding? Well, congratulations." Sally shot Ted a look. "She did say yes, didn't she?"

"Yes, she did. I can't believe it. I mean, I can believe she said yes, 'cause I know she loves me. I just can't believe I'm getting married."

"Yeah, well, we'll celebrate later. We've got to knock something loose on this case, today. I'm going to find out why this stick-up-his-ass president wanted John Barrow to get tenure. It sounds like he was going out on a limb to make sure it happened. Why?"

"'Cause he liked him?" Ted offered.

"Maybe. But liked him in what way? It doesn't seem likely they were lovers, since Barrow made a habit of sleeping with female students."

Sally pulled into the wide brick drive of Landscome's house, located a block off campus on a stately street with large homes on huge lots. The doctors and lawyers of the town lived in this area, along with business owners, auto and implement dealers, the town's two real estate brokers, and those families coming from "old Mount Avery" money. The president's home was the largest of them all, its lawn well tended by work-study students, the wooden shutters and window trim freshly painted, the front door a glossy black, just like you'd see in London. The house was way too large for one man, but as far as Sally knew the widowed president lived alone.

The front door was yanked open as soon as Sally rang the bell. Landscome stood holding the door, the wisps of his remaining hair standing upright, his blue cotton oxford shirt wrinkled and wet under the armpits. He looked like he'd just gotten off a long flight, not arrived the night before, but he still managed to seem imperious as he scanned Sally and Ted from head to toe.

"The mayor will be hearing about your rudeness, Chief. I'm sure he won't be happy," Landscome said, blocking the door.

"You be sure to let me know how that goes, Mr. Landscome. We're here to ask you some questions about the murder of one of your faculty members and we're going to stay here until we get some answers. If you'd rather do it while we're out here on your front steps, or even better, down at the station, that's just fine with me."

Landscome headed down the center hall of the house, veering left into a dark study, Sally and Ted close behind. He sat behind a large wooden desk placed in front of the bay window. The curtains were drawn and the room was messy and smelled sour. Sally thought it felt like the elegant surroundings of a rich, bottoming-out crackhead.

"Let's get this over with, Chief. First off, I want to know what your investigation has turned up so far. Have you found anything that would qualify as a clue?"

"A clue? Do you mean like a cigarette with lipstick on it? Or a smoking gun? I'm afraid things aren't quite as neatly laid out for us as that."

Landscome ran his hands over the top of his head and then began to massage his temples. "I'm glad you find this all amusing, Chief. Let me ask you more directly. Have you found anything at the scene or on the body that may indicate why the murder occurred?"

"And I'll ask you again, more directly, just what sort of thing you have in mind?"

"Oh for God's sake," Landscome spat. "I am trying to find out from you if we know why this happened. Is that such an odd question?"

"Just oddly put, I'd say. But to answer the question, I'll say that we are still exploring all possible leads. We have nothing conclusive at this time."

Landscome slumped back in his chair. "Fine. I will get your report after I've had a chance to talk to the mayor. Now, what do you want to ask me? I can't imagine what it could be."

"I've talked to several people about the fight over whether to grant tenure to Professor Barrow. I've also learned that you were very much in the camp wanting it, that in fact you brought him in to the college and put him into the tenure-track position over the objections of some members of his department. Do I have that about right?"

"That's more or less correct. However, he did pass his department's tenure review and was standing legitimately before the full tenure committee."

"And this made some people pretty upset, didn't it?" Sally asked.

"If there's one thing I've learned since coming to Grafton College, it's that it doesn't take much to upset faculty members. They take turns writing scathing memos and disrupting meetings over the most inane dribble you can imagine."

"But this issue has been particularly sensitive, hasn't it?"

"I don't think I have the longevity here to answer that question, Chief Sullivan. They seemed upset to me, but that had no effect on my decision making. I am the president of the college, and in my opinion John Barrow would have made an excellent permanent member of our faculty. That's why I brought him to Grafton." He picked up a mug of something from the desk and grimaced as he took a drink. "It's bloody awful he's dead."

"Where did you meet John Barrow? What was so special about him that you were willing to bring him here from England, with no guarantee of tenure, and against the wishes of the faculty you were just getting to know?"

Landscome snorted at that. "I'm the president, as I said, and I don't let the whining of a spoiled faculty influence how I run the college. John Barrow represents everything that is noble about the academic life—devotion to scholarship, dedication to teaching and to students, publishing in his field. He has the highest recommendations from his former colleagues at the London School of Economics, which is how I heard of him."

"I'd like to see those recommendations. There was nothing like that in his personnel file."

"Certainly. But you'll have to wait until tomorrow when Cora can get them for you. I haven't any idea where she may have filed that information."

"Why don't we give her a call right now and ask her to meet us at your office?"

Landscome looked exasperated. "Why does any of that matter? What possible connection can his past recommendations have with his murder? Are you sure you're not in over your head, Chief?"

Sally sat in one of the leather chairs in front of Landscome's desk. "Here's what I see, Mr. Landscome. I see an unpopular president increase his unpopularity with the faculty by trying to force them to grant tenure to a teacher who I've heard described as lazy and of mediocre quality. There is real tension between the faculty and the administration because of this. No one knows why you care so much about this Barrow fellow."

"I don't care that much about Barrow. That wasn't the point. The point was that I need to show the faculty who the decision maker is and that I won't be cowed by their hysteria. And I still don't see what my actions could have to do with Barrow's murder."

Sally picked up the desk phone and handed it to Landscome. "Call your secretary and arrange for her to meet Officer Benson at your office. Tell her to get us copies of the letters of recommendation. I'm seeking information at this time, not forming opinions. If you fail to cooperate, that's another bit of information for me."

Landscome took the phone and hit a speed-dial number. He asked Cora to meet him at his office in an hour, without providing an explanation as to why. He hung up without saying good-bye.

"I just can't imagine why people don't like you, Landscome, as charming as you are," Sally said. "Now, one last thing before I leave. Where were you on Friday night around eleven p.m. central time?"

"You know very well that I was in London. I just arrived back late last night."

"There have been stranger things than people flying back and forth from places trying to fake an alibi. I actually don't know where you were on Friday night."

"I was staying at Brown's Hotel in London, if you must know. I checked out shortly after Dean Ellis called me with the news."

Sally handed a card to him.

"We'll be following up on all this. In the meantime, give me a call if you think of anything else."

Landscome stood as Sally and Ted walked toward the door. "I expect to be kept fully informed, Chief."

Sally ignored him, leaving by the front door without a word of farewell, Ted behind her. When they were in their squad buckling up, Ted said, "He's kind of a jerk."

"Yeah, I went in expecting as much. I didn't expect to find him so agitated."

"What do you mean? He just seemed to want to pick a fight."

"He seemed very anxious to find out what we knew, what we might have found," Sally said.

"Like there should have been something there that was incriminating to someone, right?"

Sally pulled into traffic and headed back to the station. "I think there's only one person President Landscome ever worries about, and that's himself. So I wonder what he was expecting that we'd find?"

"Shouldn't we go back and ask him, Chief? Interrogate him or something?" Ted was getting that eager look in his eyes, like he was about to see some action.

"Actually, Ted, I was thinking of waterboarding. That usually gets an answer out of a suspect pretty quickly. What do you think?"

Ted studied Sally's face. "I think you're messing with me, that's what. But really, Chief, if you think he's hiding something, why wouldn't we go ask him?"

"It's a fair question. I just don't want to put him on the defensive. It seems he might be worried that we'll find something specific, so I'd like to exploit his nerves a bit more and try to get him to spill what he knows. First I'm going to take another look at everything we found at the scene and at Barrow's office. Maybe there was something I missed the first time through."

❖

An hour later Sally threw a file into a bankers box and closed the lid. She felt like screaming, and might have done so if Henry weren't down the hall. She had just reviewed all of the files taken from John Barrow's office at school as well as from the file cabinet and desk drawers in his home office. There was nothing that jumped out at Sally any more than upon their initial review.

The collection included financial records, which did not reveal any evidence that Barrow was threatened by debt or enriched through blackmail. Barrow had the modest income and significant school loans of most younger academics. He maintained a file labeled *Ongoing Research*, which seemed pretty thin to Sally. There were two large boxes filled with the working drafts of his dissertation and a paper he had published in an academic journal. Its title was "Shakespeare's Sister—The Real Bard? How Feminist Fantasies Have Twisted the Established Research." Sally would have to ask Beth about that. Was this controversial? Enough to kill over? She was beginning to suspect that all things academic were potent grounds for violence.

The desktop computer removed from Barrow's home office was now set up on Sally's desk. She'd explored every corner of both the onboard hard drive and the external backup drive, just as Ted had. His browser history and bookmarks showed a liking for Internet porn, but Sally was so used to seeing that in the course of investigations that she almost considered it normal. Barrow's tastes in porn were heterosexual and fairly vanilla, with an emphasis on enormous breasts. It was pretty tame, as far as these things went.

The computer in Barrow's office at school was networked and shared with an office mate. Ted had examined it the morning following the murder and found that there was nothing there that Barrow would not be comfortable having someone else see. Sally was still left with a single possible motive for Barrow's death—that someone really didn't want him to get tenure. That or a random act of violence that had the killer ringing a stranger's doorbell and shooting when the door opened. She wasn't sure which seemed more improbable.

Ted had been dispatched to meet Landscome's assistant. Sally called his cell to see if he'd found the letters of recommendation.

"The secretary's going through some files now, Chief. She's already said she doesn't think she has anything like that here and that any letter of recommendation should be in the dean's file."

"They're not there. I reviewed the original file myself. The dean said she didn't consider the file to be complete and has asked Landscome for the letters several times."

"So what do you want me to do? Should I go get Landscome and bring him here?" Ted asked.

"No, let's let him think we're not focusing on him. There's something up with him bringing Barrow here. I'll ask the dean to contact the school in London and get the letters from them, if in fact they exist. You just stay there until the secretary finishes and then meet me at Katie Murphy's house."

She gave Ted Katie's address and hung up, then called Katie. A groggy voice answered on the third ring.

"Is this Katie Murphy?" Sally asked.

"Yes."

"This is Sally Sullivan, Mount Avery Police."

No response. Sally could hear some sounds of movement and then someone in the background asking who was calling this early on a Sunday morning. Sally thought it sounded like Mel.

"I'm sorry, Chief Sullivan. I was sound asleep. What can I do for you?"

"I'd like to talk to you this morning, at your convenience. I have some additional questions for you."

There was another silence before Katie said, "It never occurred to me that I would be considered a suspect."

Sally heard a very clear "What the fuck?" in the background, followed by a shush. Now she was sure it was Mel.

"I'm not treating you as a suspect. I'm just following up on the tenure controversy we discussed before."

"I see. I'm not sure what help I'll be, but I'm happy to answer your questions. Should I come to you?"

"No, I'll come by your place."

"That would be fine, Chief."

Sally wondered if Mel's truck would be parked in front when she arrived, or whether she'd parked it where it couldn't be seen by Delilah.

Next she called Beth at home. Mae answered the phone.

"Good morning, Mrs. Ellis. It's Sally Sullivan. We met last night on campus?"

"Of course, Chief. I wouldn't forget you. But if you're calling for Beth, I'm afraid she's not here. She went out for a run some time ago."

"Okay, will you have—"

"Is there anything I can help you with? I'm worried about Beth, with so much going on."

"No, if you'd just have her—"

"I mean, talk about a rough business. Who'd ever think a college could be so full of nasty people? It makes my business look like a convent. Well, maybe not a convent, but you know what I mean. People I deal with are straight up. What you see is what you get and all that."

"I'm afraid I don't know what business you're in. Beth hasn't mentioned it."

"Really?" Mae said, her mock surprise evident. "I'm surprised it wasn't the first thing out of her mouth. Oh, wait a minute. She's just coming in now. Hold on, Chief."

Sally heard the phone being put down and then some muffled conversation. "Chief? Sorry to keep you waiting," Beth said. She sounded slightly out of breath.

Sally smiled with the sound of Beth's voice. The image of her came instantly to mind, clad in her running clothes as she'd seen her so many times, running past the police station on her way out of town.

"I thought you were going to call me Sally."

"Right. Is this a social call?"

"I wish it was, but it's not. I'm trying to track down the letters of recommendation for John Barrow, the ones you said you tried to get from Landscome."

"Have you asked him?"

"Yep. And so far he can't produce them. I don't want to waste much more time trying to find out if they exist or not."

"I take it you think they might not."

"That's the feeling I have, but I need it confirmed. Would you call that school in London—I forget what it's called—and request copies?"

"The London School of Economics. And yes, I'll call, but it's Sunday afternoon there. I'll have to wait until first thing tomorrow morning."

"Or the middle of the night. That would work also," Sally said.

"That doesn't work so well for me, but I'll see what I can do."

"Thanks."

"You're welcome. When I called the LSE at the time Barrow was hired, they did confirm that he had been teaching there as a part-time instructor in English. I didn't ask for his letters because Landscome kept telling me he had copies for our file. It seems stupid of me now."

"Don't second-guess yourself. You haven't done anything wrong."

A silence hung on the line. Sally was reluctant to hang up, wanting the contact with Beth, but not much good at small talk. Then she remembered the party. "Are you going to Delilah Humphries's party later?" she asked.

"Yes. It's essentially mandatory attendance for me."

"She invited me and I thought I'd drop in at least. Maybe someone will just come up to me and confess to the murder."

"Where there's hope, there's life, Chief."

"Sally."

Beth paused. "Yes. Sally."

They hung up and Sally checked her hands to see if they were trembling. She felt something akin to an adrenaline rush, the fight-or-flight response to danger that most cops were familiar with. But this had been a low-watt conversation about letters of recommendation. Danger? Maybe. But when wasn't it a risk trying to love someone? From the extent of her physical reaction to Beth, Sally guessed the reward would far outweigh the risk.

Sally shoved the thoughts of Beth to the back of her mind and left the station to interview Katie. The phone on her belt rang just as Sally was pulling out of the parking lot.

"Good morning, Chief. It's Rudy Blaise."

"Good morning, Mr. Mayor."

"Word is that you're out and about early today."

"I think I can guess who passed that word along to you."

The mayor laughed. "That and a few other choice words, some of which I can't say I understood. But the point was clear enough. The president thinks you're in over your head, Chief. Says you're grasping at straws."

"And what do you think, sir?"

"I think he's an ass and a half, is what I think, but I don't suppose it would hurt to ask if you need any help."

Sally paused for just a moment. "No, sir, I have the staff I need. We are following up on a few things and I hope to have something to report soon. Do you feel any obligation to do as President Landscome asks?"

"None whatsoever. But if you want anything from me, just let me know. I don't know who the state or county could send our way who'd be more qualified than a former Chicago homicide detective."

Mayor Blaise loved to bring up the fact that his chief of police was a murder dick in Chicago. If Sally told him that they actually were called "dicks" within the department, he'd be over the moon. It was all Mickey Spillane to him.

"Thanks for the vote of confidence. I'll let you know how things progress," Sally said.

Sally flipped her phone closed as she turned onto Katie's street. Heading toward her was Mel's truck, which braked to a stop in the middle of the road. Sally pulled her squad car up alongside and lowered her window.

"Is there a reason you're obstructing traffic?" Sally asked.

Mel had her elbow out the window of her F-150 pickup. The truck was black and gleaming, the interior black leather, the stereo system obviously enhanced. Mel reached over to shut it off and turned back to Sally with a smile on her face.

"There's no one else on the street, Chief. And I'd probably still be asleep myself if you hadn't called Katie this morning."

"I thought that was you swearing in the background. Is she okay with you spreading the word about your latest conquest?"

Now Mel frowned. Sally thought she was guileless, which was probably one of her charms. You always knew what was going on with Mel. She either wore it plainly on her face or told you straight out. Sally knew this much from the time she'd spent in proximity to Mel at Werni's Tap. Everyone there loved her, teased her, and perhaps, most importantly, respected her limits. When Mel stopped smiling, you could be sure that she wasn't happy at all. That unhappiness directed at someone could be an impressive display, and only the most naïve pushed her one step beyond.

"I believe that the word *conquest* sounds a little disrespectful, Chief. I'm sure you don't mean that."

"No disrespect to Katie Murphy was intended."

"That's good. She's a very classy lady. I'm lucky she wanted to spend time with me."

"Uh-huh." Sally wondered whether Mel was as grateful as she seemed. No wonder the women loved her. Mel seemed to worship each and every one of them.

"She's about to tell you about our getting together herself. We don't want any secrets when you're prowling around town investigating a murder. And I know that Katie's in the middle of the story, though I don't pretend to understand all that tenure crap."

Sally smiled. "Yeah. If you do figure it out, clue me in, okay? Those academics are the champions of obfuscation."

"You sound like one of them with that big word."

"That's because it's a word that describes what people do to make something really unclear, and any police detective will be very much familiar with obfuscation."

"I think here they just call it bullshit."

Sally put her car back in drive. "I'll go see Katie now."

"Don't you beat up on her, now. She's a nice lady."

Mel touched the bill of her Mopar baseball cap and drove away, a smile back on her face. Sally felt a little queasy. Mel seemed so at ease, all the time. She had a lightness about her that Sally would never have. Even if she adopted Mel's ways and tried to pick up as many women as possible, she'd strike out right and left. She was gloom to Mel's cheer, reserve to Mel's openness. No wonder Beth liked Mel. Maybe even loved her.

Sally pulled the squad up to the curb in front of Katie's house. The screen door swung open and Katie stepped out to greet Sally. She wore loose blue jeans and a tight T-shirt, her young face relaxed but her eyes worried.

"Come in, Chief. I have a pot of coffee on."

"I'd love a cup," Sally said. Katie led her into the small kitchen. The stove and refrigerator were compact size, the cabinets were painted metal, and the floor was covered with industrial-grade linoleum.

"I know this place seems a little grim," Katie said. "I had better digs when I was a grad student."

"It's not so bad. Convenient."

"And cheap. I'm lucky to have it."

Katie poured the coffee, passed the cream, and led Sally back to the front room. She sat next to Sally on the sofa.

"What can I tell you?"

"Was that Mel I heard here when I called this morning?"

"You know it was, Chief. I just saw the two of you talking down the street."

"Mel is not a kiss-and-tell kind of person, which I suppose is how she stays alive in this town."

"What does this have to do with anything?" Katie asked.

"I'm not sure yet. But look at this from my point of view. When

I talked with you yesterday morning, the alibi you gave for the time of the murder was that you were in Delilah's bed. Delilah's alibi is that you were in her bed. Now I come to discover that you're sleeping with Mel. That makes the alibis a little suspect, like you and Delilah both agreed to provide them for each other."

"Because Delilah and I conspired to murder John Barrow? That's absurd."

There was a knock on the door and Ted came in.

"Ted, this is Katie Murphy from the college. Sit down and take notes and I'll fill you in later." Ted pulled a chair over from the dining table and took out his notebook.

Katie looked worried. "Chief, I'll be the first to admit that I wasn't a big fan of John Barrow, but that simply put me with the majority on this campus. Delilah was quite vocal about disliking him, but it wouldn't occur to her to murder him. She's many things, but she's not a murderer."

"You're right that there are a lot of people who disliked Barrow. But you're the only one who would benefit directly from his death. It isn't guaranteed, I understand, but it's very likely that you will take his position in the English department. I can certainly see wanting to move out of here."

"You think I would murder someone so I could move into a better apartment? That's the craziest thing I've heard. I wasn't even sure I wanted to stay at Grafton, so I sure as hell wouldn't murder someone to ensure that I can. And if Delilah and I were supplying alibis for each other, what was her motive?"

"That's easy. She's in love with you."

Katie leaned back on the sofa, her arms wrapped around her middle. "Should I get a lawyer?"

"That's up to you, but it's only going to impede the investigation. If you're innocent, you'll want the investigation concluded as soon as possible."

"I guess. It's hard to know what's right."

"I just have a couple more things to cover. Bear with me here. The first is for you to tell me what you would expect to happen as far as tenure now that Barrow is dead."

"I really don't know that I expected anything. Dean Ellis told me yesterday that she'd like to avoid the whole formal interview process and just put me into the English department as an assistant professor. I have no idea if that will fly or not."

Sally paused for a moment while Ted scribbled furiously.

"The second thing is for you to tell me where you stand with Mel and Delilah. I'm not being nosy. I just need to know what is going on with all the players."

"I don't really care if you know. Delilah and I have only been seeing each other for a short while. I'm not even sure how it started, and I've been pretty sure all along that it wasn't going to last. She's so intense. But Mel feels so different to me. She says she wants to see me again, and I definitely want to see her. I'm going to break up with Delilah."

"She'll be very unhappy."

"Probably, but I can't be responsible for that, can I?"

Sally stood. "Ted, take these cups into the kitchen, will you, and meet me outside?"

"Sure, Chief." He leaned over in front of Katie to pick up a cup and said, "Excuse me, ma'am." When he'd gathered the cups he stepped into the kitchen. Sally heard water running.

"Don't wash them, Ted. Just put them on the counter."

Ted came back out and headed for the door. "Sorry, Chief. Ma'am."

Katie turned to Sally. "What's with the 'ma'am' thing? I'm thirty-four years old."

"Old habit, I think. Listen, Katie, I need you to stay here in town while we're continuing our investigation, okay?"

"Am I really a suspect?"

"Right now everyone is, but you are the only one that has a motive that's clear cut and I can't eliminate anyone from consideration at this time."

Katie went to the door and held the screen open for Sally. "I hope you find the murderer quickly."

Sally just nodded good-bye and walked through the door. Ted

was standing by her squad car, his own pulled up right behind it. A neighbor out walking her dog looked at them curiously.

"What's next, Chief?"

"Head over to the station and get the keys to Barrow's house out of the locker, then meet me at Barrow's place."

"Are we looking for anything special?"

"At this point, we're looking for anything. There's got to be something we missed."

"It wasn't us that searched the place anyway. Didn't the state boys just go through and then bag everything up?" Ted asked.

"Yeah. And I've been through that stuff twice. Let's just take a look to satisfy my curiosity, okay?"

"Sure, Chief. I'll see you over there."

As Ted pulled away, Sally called Henry at the station.

"Henry, Ted's on his way to pick up Barrow's house keys, so will you grab those for him?"

"No problem. Anything else?"

"I want you to put your detective's hat on for me and run down an alibi. We're looking to confirm that Nigel Landscome was registered in Brown's Hotel in London, England, last Friday, including any evidence of when he checked out of the hotel."

"In London?"

"You can do it, Henry. They speak English. They have phones."

"Okay, Chief. I'll get back to you."

Sally hung up and drove toward John Barrow's house. The yellow crime scene tape was still in place on Barrow's property. The red tape around the area where the body was found had been removed by the state CSI team when they left the scene. Ted pulled up as Sally stood on the patch where Barrow had fallen, looking out to the street to see what she could see. There was one house directly across from Barrow's, but two interviews with the owners had produced only one answer to their question—they hadn't heard or seen a thing. They were sound asleep at 11:00 p.m. on Friday, just as they were every night. Just as was most everyone on the street.

Asleep or cocooned in their living rooms with their eyes and ears focused on their TVs.

Sally took the keys from Ted and they went into the house. The look and feel of the place was familiar to Sally from the many murder scenes she'd worked in Chicago. Surfaces were covered with fingerprint dust, every bit of paper and ephemera bagged and removed, along with any sense that a person had lived in the place. Ted held his arms carefully at his sides, as if he'd just entered an overstuffed antiques shop.

"You can't hurt anything," Sally said. "Just put on your gloves and let's go through every drawer and closet again. It shouldn't take long."

Ted headed to the kitchen. Sally went to the answering machine attached to the living room phone. She had stopped by on Saturday to check it for messages, and there'd been none. Now she saw the red light blinking.

"Mr. Barrow? This is Karl over at It's Geek to Me in Center City. Say, we've got your laptop ready. You had a virus, that's why it was frozen, but we decontaminated her and she's running fine. I updated your security software, no charge. Anyway, we're open today, Saturday, till five but closed on Sunday. It's here waiting for you."

Sally picked up her cell and called directory assistance for the store's number and jotted it down while she was being connected. The call went right into voicemail and Sally left a message telling anyone at the store to call her regarding John Barrow's laptop. Then she yelled for Ted.

"I don't know if this will turn out to be anything, but I'm counting on you to run this down. Barrow did have a laptop, but it's been in a repair shop in Center City. I don't have the address—here's the name and phone number. Get down there and get me that laptop."

"Are they open today?"

"Nope. You need to find the owner and get him to the shop. Don't let me see you again until you have that computer in your hands."

Ted looked both eager and uncertain. "I'll try my best, Chief."

"Ted, you need to walk out of here knowing you can do this. You're a police officer. You're gathering evidence. This is what we do."

"Yes, ma'am. I just hope I can find him."

"My guess is this shop is in a strip mall, or somewhere with other shops nearby. Ask those folks for his name. Use the Internet. You'll find him."

"I'll call you when I have something," Ted said.

"You do that. And don't let me down."

Sally spent the next couple of hours going through every nook and cranny of the house, not finding a thing. She hoped Ted was going to bring back a laptop full of clues.

Late Sunday afternoon, Beth put her macaroni-and-cheese casserole into a thermal tote and walked to Delilah's house. The quarterly faculty parties began promptly at 4:00 on Sunday, as they had for the past ten years. Each year, Delilah sent out an announcement right after New Year's Day so that faculty members could mark their calendars with the correct dates. Not every professor attended, regularly or otherwise. The hard sciences, for instance, were poorly represented, but that still made for a large gathering. As Beth neared Delilah's house she could see others approaching from every direction, each carrying something to contribute. She knew that Sally planned on stopping by the party and her body did that flippity-flop thing in her stomach again when she thought about it.

The afternoon was sunny and warm, a hint of cool air coming in on a breeze. Delilah stood at her front door, holding the screen open and ushering people in. Beth could see the look on her face, the one that seemed more impatient than welcoming, as if all of these college professors were tardy. She would have the same demeanor at the end of the party, which always came promptly at 7:00, holding the screen door open again and guiding the slightly wobbly back out the door. In between, everyone seemed to have a good time.

As Beth climbed the steps to the front door, Delilah waved her hand, hurrying her up. Then she clasped a hand on Beth's forearm, holding her in place as Roy Thibedeau from History and his wife scooted through the door.

"Margaret, you know where to put the salmon mousse," Delilah said to them, a forced smile on her face. She turned back to Beth after the Thibedeaus had gone in. "Honest to God, hasn't she gotten it through her bonnet that no one eats her damn mousse? It looks like the one house standing after a tornado when people are done eating, and still she brings it to every party."

"Dee, you're gripping my arm like a vise. What's going on?"

Delilah closed the screen door and pulled Beth to the far side of the front porch. She waved as Sandy Anderson from Sociology entered the house, holding hands with a young woman.

"Who's she with?" asked Delilah.

"Grad student from State. They've been together for a while now."

"Well, no one told me." Delilah stared after them.

"Delilah, it's been two years since you and Sandy broke up. And you ended it, remember? No one told you because you have a huge reaction to little things. It's tiresome."

Delilah was about to argue the point, but then stopped and took a long breath. "I don't have time now to tell you, again, just how wrong you are. Or to point out that you are the biggest sponge on campus. You take everything in and never change shape—it's like you have no reaction to anything. I'd rather err on the side of standing up for myself, thanks very much."

Delilah crossed her arms and looked a bit triumphant. "Let's see if this gets a rise out of you. I just heard from a reliable source that Landscome has received final authority from the board of trustees to institute layoffs, and they'll be announced this week."

Beth took a step back and her mind went numb at the edges, threatening to shut down at the careening course of her thoughts in the past several days—missing student, Sally, murder, Sally, Mother, Sally, layoffs…

"Layoffs? Of whom? We're at a barely functioning level as it is. And who told you this?"

"I'll not reveal my source, Beth. She'd lose her job. Just understand that she's in a position to know."

"Know what, exactly?"

"He's laying off all assistant administrative department heads and all non-tenure-track teachers. Unless we do something quick to get Katie into Barrow's position, she'll be gone."

Beth sat hard on the porch railing. "How can this be true? He's going to ruin this school."

"No shit." Delilah crossed her arms over her flat chest. She was big in all ways but one.

Beth stood and started for the door. "I'm not going to discuss this until I get more information."

Delilah followed her into the house. "How can you not be screaming right now? You know who is going to have to handle the layoffs, don't you? It's going to be you. There's no way that miserable excuse for an academic leader will pull the plug on these people himself."

"Just shut up, Dee. See if you can keep something to yourself for once. I'm not going to do or say anything until I confirm this, and as your dean I'm ordering you to not say anything to anyone about it."

"You're ordering me?"

"That's right."

Delilah came right up to Beth's face. They were standing off to the side of the foyer, now empty of passersby. She put one pudgy finger on the front of Beth's shoulder and pressed it. "There is not a single scenario I can imagine in which you get to order me around. Not even in my wildest fantasies and certainly not in the present circumstances."

The door opened and Sally walked in. She paused a moment and then moved directly over to them as Delilah removed her finger and relaxed her stance.

"Chief, so glad you could join us. I know I don't need to introduce you to Dean Ellis."

"No, I know the dean." Sally looked Beth in the eye. "Everything okay here?"

Delilah clapped her hands and let out a whoop. "Oh, that's

precious. I just knew you had your eye on her, Chief, and the protective butch act is adorable."

Beth raised her hand. "Hello? I'm right here, fully grown and blessed with the gift of hearing." She turned to Sally and threaded her arm through hers. "Come on. I'll take you into the den of iniquity. Dee was just delivering some bad news with her usual verve."

Delilah called after her. "We have to meet about this, Beth. We can't sit back and do nothing." Then she moved away to greet more people at the door as Beth led Sally into the double parlor. The room was crowded, the men in corduroy and tweed, as if they came from central casting. The women wore more varied garb, from the all-black, post-Goth chic of Andi Vancaro the librarian, to the tailored pantsuit and Hermès scarf of Monica Trant of Modern Languages, to the pleated khaki trousers and Lands' End blazer of Dorothy Stanmeyer, wife of Don Stanmeyer of Psychology. The crowd was bunched around the sideboard and the dining table, both piled high with a mélange of food. Those who finished loading food on their paper plates turned around and moved away with their elbows tucked in, the gap left behind instantly filled.

Beth and Sally stood in a corner of the room, opposite the food tables. Beth remained silent, trying to wrap her mind around the idea of layoffs. Sally touched her arm.

"I hate to sound like I'm always asking if you're okay, but are you okay?"

Beth shrugged. "I'll be fine."

"How bad was the news that Delilah gave you?"

"Pretty bad, though it's hard to rank it in the cavalcade of bad news I've had recently." Beth took a deep breath and turned to smile at Sally. "But I don't want to sound like I'm always in the middle of a crisis, even though that's exactly where I have been ever since I met you."

"I hope that's just coincidence," Sally said.

"Yes, I assure you, it's just coincidence. You've been a little pocket of sanity for me."

Beth thought Sally looked pleased at that. And it was true that Beth felt calmer, a little more on top of things, when Sally was around, despite the alarming physical reaction she had to her. It felt surprisingly sexy to her, and not in any way she associated sexiness with before. It was almost as if Sally's solidness was what made Beth's heart beat a little faster when she saw her, not her tall, lean body or her beautiful smile or the fact that she wore a uniform and a gun. Sally seemed to hear her, understand her, care for her, without any of the games or flirtations that usually would occur before Beth wanted to fall in bed with someone. That was definitely sexy.

Sally was speaking as Beth's mind whipped through these thoughts. "I really didn't know how to dress for the occasion."

She was wearing dark gray moleskin pants and a blue button-down oxford shirt. The sleeves were rolled halfway up her forearm, showing a band of pale skin on her left wrist where her large watch usually lay. In its place was a woven dark brown leather bracelet. Beth found this almost unbearably sexy—the muscular forearm, the crisp shirt, the bracelet she brought out for the party. *Did she put that on for me?*

"I think you look fantastic," Beth said. "You chose well."

Sally blushed, which Beth could see caused her agony.

"Not so well as you, I think. You look beautiful."

Beth was wearing skinny black pants and a gauzy, skirt-length top that she felt hid a multitude of sins. She held back her usual self-deprecating comment and just felt the awkwardness of the moment. They were both noticing each other's bodies, feeling out the possibilities, weighing the desire against the shyness in the face of something this new and intense. Should she connect the dots out loud? Ask Sally if she'd like to see how she looked without these clothes? Beth was not shy about getting someone in bed, but she suspected Sally was. She also knew that this was a much different situation than with the women she'd taken to bed before. The stakes felt much higher—a wrong move could lead to a loss she would feel keenly.

Sally looked past Beth and toward the front door.

"Oh, boy," she said.

Beth turned around to see Katie standing at the front door, enduring a hug from Delilah. Katie's arms hung limply at her sides, her face contorted in a grimace that Delilah could not see but Beth and Sally clearly could.

"Katie didn't bring Mel with her, thank goodness," Beth murmured.

"Looks like Katie hasn't told Delilah yet that she's breaking up with her to be with the town's sex machine." Sally sounded like she was talking about the weather. No judgment, just the facts as she'd heard them.

Beth whirled back to face Sally. "What?"

"If I were a gossip," Sally said, "this would be the best town ever to live in. But I'm not."

"No, that's not fair. You can't drop a nugget of gossip, especially one that includes the words 'sex machine,' and then announce that you're not a gossip."

Sally seemed to consider this for a moment. She kept an eye on Delilah and Katie, who were in deep conference in the foyer.

"You're right, Beth. It was wrong of me to say anything at all."

Beth was not mollified. "You're not a priest. You are allowed to talk about what you see and hear. And I want to know what you meant by sex machine."

"You know I'm talking about Mel," Sally said mildly. "Katie was with her last night, which means that Mel's truck was parked in Katie's driveway, just as it's been parked in your driveway and the driveways of half the women in this town, married or otherwise."

"I can't quite tell if you're judging Mel or the women she visits, myself included. Or is it that you simply envy Mel?"

"I don't envy Mel. And I'm not judging anyone either."

"Oh, please," Beth snorted. "You may be in luck, however. It seems Mel and Katie might keep each other occupied for a little while, at least. Maybe you can take over her route."

Sally's posture became stiff, her lips pursed as if she were holding back something. "I'm sorry, Beth. I shouldn't have said anything."

"That's okay. I shouldn't have been sarcastic. It's just that you keep bringing Mel up and I don't know if I'm supposed to be apologizing for knowing her, explaining her actions, or what." Beth was concerned Sally was going to bolt. "Let's start over, shall we?"

Sally looked around the room. "Actually, my purpose in coming here was to mingle a bit and pick up what I could from the faculty about John Barrow. Maybe I'll catch up with you a little later."

Sally stepped away, leaving Beth feeling the conversation had completely gotten away from her. One reason she came to the party was to get a little more from Sally, some idea whether they were both on the same beam, whether there was a mutual attraction or not. She'd been certain there was, and now she wasn't, and that was what she hated about the whole relationship thing. If Sally were someone Beth just wanted to sleep with, she wouldn't be feeling bereft right now. Just horny, perhaps. Was there really a higher reward for this greater risk? There must be some hope within everyone that there was, for Beth found herself wanting to let Sally know that the casual sex she had with Mel was not what she wanted with her. There was something more going on, God help her. She realized that she had long lived in a state of sheltering her heart, of not exposing it to another and therefore not being disappointed or hurt. But through some sort of stealth attack, Sally had entered her heart, and there was no sheltering left to be done. She would be disappointed or hurt if nothing came to be with Sally; she might as well go for it, find out if something was there.

Just before opening the door, Beth turned back to see if Sally might be following her. She knew she shouldn't look, because then Sally would know Beth wanted her to follow her out. Sally was picking up a plate at the far end of the table and standing in line for some food, chatting with the couple in front of her. Beth left without saying good-bye to anyone. She wasn't going to jump right into Sally's arms. She was going to need some kind of sign from her.

CHAPTER THIRTEEN

When Beth got back to her house she went straight for the kitchen and made a stiff gin and tonic. Her brain felt like it was going to explode.

The drink was half gone and Beth was still standing in the kitchen when her mother walked in.

"Can I join you in one?"

"Sure. But I'm going to have more than one, I can tell you that."

Mae went about fixing a drink, pulling a bottle of Scotch from a cupboard and adding some ice. "What else can you tell me?"

"You don't want to know about the college. You've already said how ridiculous all the drama sounds."

"Did I say that? I don't recall that I did. I think I said that it seemed ridiculous to murder someone over tenure, and if you don't agree with that, I have more to worry about than I thought."

Beth fixed another drink and moved into the living room. Mae followed and sat next to her on the sofa.

"I've always thought the craziest, most upsetting thing in my life was being raised in a whorehouse. Now I think there is some serious competition."

"I really, really wish you wouldn't call Liaisons Fantastique a whorehouse. It makes it sound so sordid."

Beth was incredulous. "I don't know how you've managed to live in such a dream world, Mother. Legal or not, a house of prostitution is a whorehouse is a bordello is whatever you want to call it and always the same thing. It's not going to be mistaken for anything else."

"No, it's not the same thing. A whorehouse is what I used to work in. A call-girl ring is what I used to operate—both back in New York, during that time you never want to talk about. Being illegal meant no protection for myself or the women who worked for me. You can try to be careful, you can pay off cops, but in that world there are too many variables. Being illegal meant that at any time I could be busted, and because I was operating a business, that meant jail time. Once I had you to take care of, that wasn't an option for me."

Beth took another drink. "You've told me all of this before."

"Many times. And I know that one day you'll actually hear me. We all have times when hard decisions have to be made, when we realize that life as we've been living it no longer serves us. For me, that meant leaving a city I loved, a life that was the only one I knew, to move to godforsaken Nevada. I've never regretted it."

They both drank for a bit, the silence strangely comfortable for Beth. It was normally the part of the conversation when she would become agitated and argumentative.

"For some reason, I don't hate you as much as I usually do," she said.

"We're making progress, then." Mae patted Beth on the hand and went into the kitchen to put some dinner together.

After they ate in front of the TV, both fell asleep on the sofa, inches apart from one another. Beth woke with a start, having dreamed that she left her position as dean of Grafton College to work the front desk of Liaisons Fantastique. In the dream she was happy, which was a nightmare. Her mother still slept beside her, gently snoring. Beth put the sofa blanket over her and left the house for a walk. The dream was still uncomfortably with her, just starting to be chased away by thoughts of the campus crises and Sally. She felt exhausted and agitated and a little short of breath.

She headed up and across campus, turning left at Old Main to head down into town, then circle around toward home. On Main

Street a police car headed slowly toward her. Beth wondered why it was that she'd barely seen Sally in the two years since she became chief of police, and now she seemed to run into her all the time. She wasn't sure she wanted to see her now.

"Can I give you a lift?" Sally asked, leaning toward the passenger side to look up at Beth.

"No, thank you. I'm enjoying the walk."

Sally put the car in park. "Can I join you for your walk, then? There's something I want to say."

Beth wanted to make Sally work a little. It was a passive-aggressive tendency of hers that she was starting to hate.

"I'd prefer to walk alone, thanks."

"That sounds a little sad," Sally said. "The truth is, I'm not comfortable with you walking alone. There's a murderer out there, you know."

"So you don't have something to say to me?" Beth asked.

"I do. In fact, I have a number of reasons for wanting to talk to you."

Beth leaned down and looked into the car. "I guess you better walk with me, then."

Sally locked the car and joined Beth on the sidewalk. She was back in uniform, her gun on her hip. Beth had to admit it was a turn-on, though that gun would have to be pointed at her head before she'd admit it. *Why are a uniform and gun sexy?* It was far too much for her relentlessly curious brain to explore at the moment, but clearly it was sexy. Beth was having a hard time remembering she was supposed to be a little mad at Sally for ditching her at the party.

"Are you on duty?" Beth asked.

"Pretty much all the time while we're investigating this murder. I changed at the station after Delilah's party."

They walked for a bit. "How's your mother?" Sally started off.

"She's fine, thank you. However, I don't want to talk about my mother. I want to hear your multitude of reasons for wanting to talk to me."

"I'm not sure 'multitude' is accurate. Let's say I have a few."

They were walking now along Main Street, the stores closed up on a Sunday evening, the traffic very light. Beth zipped her jacket against the growing coolness while Sally seemed comfortable in her shirtsleeves.

"The first thing is that I want to apologize if I offended you earlier."

"Offended me?"

"With what I said about yours being one of the driveways I've seen Mel's truck in. I have no way of knowing what she's doing there. And it's none of my business, anyway."

"Why did you say it?" Beth picked up her pace and crossed the street, heading toward the municipal park. Sally trotted to catch up and then matched her stride.

"I'm not the best at analyzing why I do or say things, but I guess it doesn't take a genius to see that I was jealous. And jealous people tend to act like asses. The truth is that I want it to be my truck parked in your driveway."

Beth stopped and turned to Sally, amazed that she'd said something so frank. The elephant in the room was the growing attraction between them, and Sally had just mentioned the elephant for the first time. But Beth needed more.

"How do you mean jealous? Jealous of Mel having a lot of girlfriends?"

"Hell, no. That's not for me."

"Then what?"

"Somehow I thought you'd make this easier for me." Sally took in some air and blew it out slowly. "I was jealous at the thought of Mel sleeping with you. I'm worried that you have feelings for her. I'm scared to death right now that you are going to blow me off or laugh in my face."

Beth turned and started walking again, heading into the park. To the right was the Little League baseball field, to the left a large playground. Beth turned right.

"Tell me what went on at the party after I left," Beth said. Sally looked crestfallen at the change in subject. It was enough for Beth. She could see that Sally really was making herself vulnerable.

Sally reported as requested. "The word was all over Delilah's party that there are going to be layoffs at the college, so I imagine you've got that on your mind. Also, Katie hasn't broken up with Delilah, it seems. Delilah was dragging Katie around by the hand from group to group at the party, telling everyone they were going public with the relationship now that the tenure vote was not an issue. Katie looked like death warmed over."

"I didn't even know they were seeing each other. It's not like Delilah to keep that sort of thing quiet. Katie's probably dreading having to tell Dee the truth."

Sally fell quiet and Beth led her over to one of the dugouts on the field. It was nearly dark, and when they sat in the three-sided structure the dark deepened. Beth moved a little closer to Sally, who was sitting hunched forward, her forearms on her thighs, her hands clasped between her knees, her face pointed straight toward the field. She looked ready to pick up a bat and drive in the winning run. She was clearly struggling to stay still.

Beth placed her hands gently on Sally's shoulders, pushing her against the back wall of the dugout, pivoting to face her and sit on top of her thighs. Beth thought they might be trembling a little bit.

"That's an awful lot of news to tell me all at once," Beth said. "Let's just concentrate on the first thing you said."

Sally kept her eyes on Beth's. "You mean about wanting to park my truck in your drive?"

Beth smiled. "Yes. Exactly that."

Sally's response was muffled when Beth's lips met hers, her hands holding both sides of Sally's face. Sally's hands came up to Beth's hips and pulled her closer as the kiss deepened and lengthened. They kissed until Beth realized she had moved so she could rub herself against Sally's thigh—her very rigid thigh—and that things were about to get completely out of control. Sally, in response, moved her thigh up and pulled Beth more firmly down on it.

"Can we go somewhere?" Beth asked, her voice husky.

Sally nodded and stood with Beth still in her arms. She placed her down on the dugout floor and then led her by the hand to the squad car.

"Are you okay?" Sally asked.

"I'm a little, um, agitated, I'd say, but in a good way. For once."

"Yeah?" Sally sounded relieved.

"Yeah, a very good way."

"Thank God."

"What do you mean?"

"I was nervous," Sally said.

"You were nervous? I was really nervous, until you told me how you felt, that is."

"You didn't kiss me like you were nervous."

"I was a little nervous then, but mostly I wanted to touch you."

Sally's phone rang as she opened the passenger door for Beth. She picked up the call as she got in behind the wheel.

"Ted, where are you?" Sally looked at Beth as she talked, holding her thumb and index finger an inch apart. Beth kept her eyes on Sally. She wanted her badly. She scootched over and put her left hand on Sally's thigh and then moved it a little higher. It went all rigid again. *Good*, Beth thought. *She's going crazy as well.*

"Okay, Ted. Stick with it. Don't give up now."

Sally closed her phone and then pulled onto the street, accelerating east out of town.

"Where are we going?"

"To my place. You can meet my dogs."

"Yippee."

Sally grinned. "I hope you mean that, 'cause they're part of the package."

"Oh, I like dogs, in general. I just don't like dogs at this particular moment."

"Why is that?" Sally asked.

"Because I only have enough focus for you right now. How far to your place?"

"It's just two miles."

"Can you use your lights and sirens?" Beth asked.

Sally shifted uncomfortably as Beth kept her hand on her thigh, moving it up and down and over into very dangerous territory. She grabbed Beth's hand and held it tightly for the rest of the short ride while Beth nibbled on her neck.

"If you don't stop this while I'm driving, I'm going to handcuff you," Sally said.

"Please don't tease me, Chief. I'm about to explode as it is."

Sally dealt with the dogs while Beth took a quick look around the kitchen and living room of Sally's house. It didn't surprise her that everything was neat and well organized, but it did surprise her to see the furnishings and art work that spoke of a good eye and an appreciation for modern design and style. More Manhattan than Mount Avery. Beth sat on the sofa and soon Sally joined her.

"Let's reenact that moment in the dugout," Sally suggested.

"That moment when I first kissed you or the moment I almost, um, had an orgasm?"

"The first. I promise to have you in my bed for the second."

And she did.

❖

At three in the morning, not long after realizing that they couldn't possibly make love one more time and were giving in to sleep, Beth's cell phone alarm went off, waking them both up. Sally scrambled for her phone.

"It's mine," Beth said. "I'm supposed to call London."

"Forget it."

"Good. I don't think I can do it." Beth was practically slurring her words.

"Yeah, forget it. We'll call first thing in the morning." Beth was just drifting off when Sally said, "How about your mother?"

"My mother?"

"Won't she worry if you don't come home all night?"

"She never did when I was a teenager. I doubt she will now."

Silence.

"You should call her," Sally said. "My mother would be frantic."

"How old are you?"

"No, I mean if she were staying with me and I was gone all night, she'd expect the worst. That's normal for mothers."

Beth sighed. "Ay, there's the rub."

"What?"

"Shakespeare. I just mean that my mother is not normal. Don't worry about it."

"Would that be William Shakespeare or his sister?" Sally asked. She was now leaning up on an elbow, her hand finding Beth's breast.

"His sister?" Beth's eyes opened and she looked up at Sally. "What are you talking about?"

Sally smiled. "John Barrow apparently thought it was a feminist conspiracy to suggest that Shakespeare's works were written by his sister."

"How can you be this awake?" Beth closed her eyes again, holding Sally's hand to her breast.

"Why don't you just leave your mother a message so she doesn't panic in the morning?" Sally whispered.

"You're not getting how unnecessary this is. Soon you'll learn that the idea of my mother panicking is comical. You should hire her on your police force—she'd be great on a SWAT team." Beth turned to find her jeans on the floor and pulled out her cell phone. "I'll text her."

"Your mother does texting?"

"She has the unlimited plan." Beth punched in a message and threw the phone on the floor. "Can we sleep now?"

Sally gathered her up in her arms and poised her lips over Beth's. "Do you want to sleep now?"

"I do, but I'm open to persuasion," Beth said, pulling Sally down to her.

CHAPTER FOURTEEN

When Beth walked in the door to her house Monday morning, she found her mother sprawled on the sofa, remote in hand. The TV flickered as she scrolled through channels.

"I'm bored, Beth. Really, really bored."

"I'm not talking yet. Is there coffee on?"

Mae followed Beth into the kitchen. "I just made a fresh pot. Who were you with last night? The auto mechanic?"

"No, the police chief." Beth poured a cup and started drinking the coffee as if it were medicine. "And I'm not talking."

"I like the police chief. She's solid. You could do a lot worse."

Beth thought her mother had perhaps understated the case, but she agreed with her and she found that unsettling. She remained silent and Mae left the room to resume her channel surfing. Beth picked up the kitchen phone and called to check her office voicemail.

"Dean, it's Cora at President Landscome's office. He'd like to see you here at nine this morning, if that's convenient for you. Frankly, even if it's not convenient for you. Would you give me a call to confirm, please?"

The stove clock showed 8:45. Beth was in need of a shower—surprised that her mother didn't say anything about her smelling like sex—and in no mood to have her happiness destroyed by Nigel Landscome. She picked up the phone and told Cora she'd be there at 9:30, without offering any explanation, and then hurried to get ready and to her own office in time to make the phone call to London.

Cora showed Beth into Landscome's office at 9:40, and Beth could see from his furrowed brow that he was not happy with her.

"Dean. So pleased you could join me. Not a terrible inconvenience, I hope?"

"I had some matters I had to see to first thing this morning, so I got here as soon as I could. What can I do for you?"

They sat in their accustomed places, she on one of the leather chairs facing his desk, chairs that were slightly, but noticeably lower than she thought they should be, and he behind the massive desk, his leather executive chair pumped up just a little higher than you'd expect. She imagined his legs dangling, the tips of his cap-toed shoes just touching the floor.

"Obviously, Dean, we have a lot of ground to cover. Will you report to me everything you know about the murder of John Barrow and what's being done to deal with the situation here on campus?"

It was strange, Beth thought, that he'd never called her yesterday for such a report. She knew from Sally that Landscome had arrived late on Saturday. Jet lag aside, there was time on Sunday to pick up the phone. She gave him a full report of the security measures taken on campus, the announcements made to students and parents. She told him what she knew of the investigation, which was basically that the police were interviewing people associated with the tenure controversy.

"The chief asked me to release the names and contact information of everyone on the tenure committee and I made the decision to do so."

"That's appropriate. This is a murder investigation. We have to help however we can."

"Okay. I'll get her that information this morning," Beth said.

"There doesn't seem to be any other line of inquiry?"

"Not that I'm aware of. Why, can you think of anything about Barrow that the police should be aware of?"

"Of course not. The idea of anyone having a reason to kill him is absurd. He was a good man."

"That reminds me. I was following up on getting copies of

Barrow's letters of recommendation. I called the LSE this morning to ask them to forward a copy to me, and they claim not to have any letters at all in his file."

Landscome's eyebrows drew together. "Is that what delayed you for our meeting? Why did you do that? I told you I would provide you with copies."

"Yes, several times. I thought I'd save you the trouble. I know how busy you are. But our file really needs to be complete, especially with the police asking for it."

"I think the source of the confusion here is that many universities now have a policy where they are not taking any responsibility for recommendations coming from their files. Too much liability, apparently, when a recommended employee goes wonky at their new place of employment. That must be what happened here."

"Where did you get the letters from?" Beth asked.

"From Dr. Barrow, of course. I don't know why Cora's been unable to find them. I'll have her do a thorough search today."

Beth decided to leave it at that. Landscome was clearly scrambling a bit, and none too artfully. Beth had not heard of any such policy at universities in regard to referrals at the professor level, and she felt she would be in a much better position to know that than Landscome. Talk about wonky.

"Dean, the other reason I brought you in this morning was to discuss a sad but entirely necessary decision I've had to make about our staffing level."

"What is that?" Beth suspected it was Cora who had leaked the information that came to Delilah and she didn't want to jeopardize her job by letting on she already knew about the layoffs. Knew, but had held off thinking about by having sex with Sally for hours.

"With full authorization from the board of trustees, and with the goal in mind of balancing our budget and ensuring the long-term financial health of the college, I'm ordering a reduction in staff."

Beth tried to look startled. "We just had layoffs last year before you arrived. The administrative staff is already running on empty. I think it's a terrible mistake."

"Frankly, Dean, I expected you to say as much. And to be equally frank, your opinion doesn't concern me. I want you to begin notifying the employees on this list."

"Wait a second. Why should I be involved if you're laying off admin staff? Shouldn't that be the V.P. of Operations?"

"It will be, for the administrative people. You are informing all of the adjuncts. They must go as well."

Beth gave Landscome a hard look before rising and pacing about. She was very close to yelling, screaming, stomping the floor, leaving the room and slamming the door, or calling him a fucking idiot. Out loud. She was tired. She wanted to be happy, like she'd been the night before with Sally. It felt very hard to keep up the fight.

"If you reduce our faculty further, you are going to endanger the quality of the teaching at this school. That alone will threaten the financial future of this institution. Its reputation is everything."

"I agree it's not something we would want to do. But we have no choice. The faculty will have to sacrifice just as everyone else has. Here are the names of the adjuncts and the non-tenured assistant professors."

Beth took the list and scanned it. The English department seat made vacant by John Barrow's death had been eliminated completely, which meant Katie Murphy was out of a job.

"It's bad enough that you are giving this order without any apparent sense of the damage it's doing. But why now? Why in the immediate aftermath of a campus crisis?"

Landscome pushed his chair back and rose, heading toward the door of the office to signal the end of the meeting. "The two things could not be less related. We have to move on, business as usual. This is never an easy thing in the life of a leader, but as president I am left to make the hard choices. You are left to carry them out."

Beth walked through the door and turned to say a last word, but the door was being shut in her face. She felt tears of frustration threatening to spill over. Cora eyed her sympathetically.

"How do you stand it, Cora?"

"I drink a lot. And I retire next year. It helps."

"I'm not going to do either, but neither am I going to carry out these orders." Beth looked at the closed door. "And if he just heard me say that, so much the better."

Beth crumpled up the piece of paper and threw it in the garbage before leaving. As if on autopilot she walked across campus and headed for town, down the hill, across Main Street, and then east a block or so to the police station. She wanted to see Sally, rather desperately. For once, she enjoyed the rich and sweet feeling of feeling sure of her lover, of not trying to look to the uncertainty beyond. If she went to Sally, Sally would be there for her, and that was all she wanted at the moment.

A stout female sergeant stopped her at the front desk. Beth paced as the sergeant called Sally, and relaxed when Sally came out and took her back to her office, closing the door behind her.

"What's up?" Sally asked. "You look like a caged animal."

"That bastard Landscome is making me lay off all of the adjunct faculty. It's going to kill this college."

"Sit down here for a minute and just try to relax." Sally sat next to Beth and took her hand. "Let me know what I can do."

"I don't even know why I'm here," Beth said. "I walked out of Landscome's office and I couldn't even see straight. I just came here without even thinking about it."

"I'm glad you did."

"Really? Do you think you'll want me if I'm not the dean of the college? Or maybe you won't really want me at all. You don't know that much about me." So much for her resolve to stay in the moment. It didn't seem to matter. Sally kept holding her hand and it felt good.

"I want you despite the fact that you're dean. Is he threatening to fire you?"

"No, but I'm thinking of submitting my resignation. I just can't do what he asks me to do."

Sally looked a little alarmed. "If you quit, would you have to move to some other college?"

"No, that's the beauty of tenure. I could just go back to teaching, which actually sounds wonderful."

"Then that's what you should do."

Beth leaned over to kiss Sally. "I also wanted to see you to check."

"Check?"

"Check whether you still liked me. Sometimes what seemed like a good idea late at night seems foolish in the light of day."

"Ah. That may have happened a few times when I was in my twenties and drinking like a Chicago cop in her twenties generally does." Sally now leaned toward Beth to kiss her. "I can assure you that is not the case today."

Beth moved onto Sally's lap, facing her and straddling her thighs again. She leaned toward the door and locked it, smiling at the nervous look on Sally's face.

"I don't think you should sit like that," Sally said. "Nothing good can come of it here."

Beth laughed. "Do you want to rephrase that? From my perspective, only good things can come of it, as you put it."

Sally sighed and stood, holding Beth up by the rear before setting her down on her own legs. "Have mercy on me, please. I have no defense against you. I want to swipe everything off my desk, lay you on top of it, and make you come."

They were standing very close, arms wrapped around each other, and Beth leaned in even closer and whispered, urgently, "Do it."

"You know I can't. Fuck, I want to."

Beth wrapped her legs around Sally's waist. "Do it."

The sound of boots clomping down the hallway outside the office caused Sally to move out of Beth's embrace.

"We'll have to pick this up later. And aren't you worried about the layoffs and Landscome and the murder and every other damn thing?"

"Apparently not." Beth stepped back and turned to pick up her bag. "But luckily you're still able to act with some conscience."

Sally smiled ruefully and unlocked the door, then turned back.

"I almost forgot. I called about those recommendation letters." Beth described Landscome's fumbling explanation as to why they were missing.

"I think he's a pretty poor liar. That's my sense, anyway. There's definitely something going on with him," Sally said.

Beth stepped back into Sally's arms. "Do you think anything is going on with us?"

"Oh, yes. As much as you'll allow is how much is going on with us."

"It's big, then, isn't it?" Beth asked.

Sally kissed her. "I think it's huge. But we don't have time to even talk about it now. I have to find some wedge into who killed Barrow, and I'm itching to find out more about Landscome."

"Yes. You make perfect sense. I'm just not feeling very sensible. I want to go back to your place and spend the rest of the day in bed."

"Sounds great, but we can't. Not now."

"You're very good in bed, by the way. I'm putty in your hands." Beth had her arms wrapped around Sally's neck.

"I'm afraid flattery won't work."

"It was worth a try."

Sally leaned over to open the office door, extricating herself from Beth's arms. "You're making me feel like an ass—turning you down when we've only just gotten together. I'm not a killjoy normally."

"I know. I'm not being fair." Beth picked up her bag.

"So what do you think about resigning? Is it something you would have to do right away?"

Beth leaned over to pick up Sally's coffee cup and take a sip. "Landscome expects me to start meeting with the adjunct faculty today to let them know they are being terminated, and that includes Katie, by the way. I don't know how I can delay the layoffs or my decision, but I'd love a day to think things over."

"Just make yourself scarce, then. Hide out. He'd probably wait a day to fire you. You'll know what to do."

Beth stared into the cup. "I was so excited when I was made dean. It was like I'd been crowned queen, or elected president of the United States. It was the top of the only world I've known as an adult. The idea of going backward from that is a little hard to swallow."

Sally took hold of Beth's hand again. "It felt like that when I moved back here. I'd been a homicide cop in Chicago and then I was back in the small town I was raised in. It did feel like going backward at first, but it doesn't anymore. I love running the police department, and the town suddenly seems a lot more attractive."

Beth smiled. "There is so much I don't know about you."

"I know. That's what scares me."

"It shouldn't. And I'm sorry we're always talking about my crises."

As they stood the desk sergeant came through the intercom. "Chief, Henry's on the phone. Says it's important."

"Thanks, Dolly. I'll pick up."

"Her name's Dolly?"

"Just give me a second here and I'll walk you out to the door." Sally put the phone on speaker. "Henry, what've you got for me?"

"I've got you some word on that hotel registration in London. I had to go to Scotland Yard, can you imagine that, and ask one of them bobbies to go to the hotel and ask for the information. They've got all kinds of rules and regulations about privacy and such. Anyway, the fact is that Landscome did have a reservation at Brown's, but he never showed up. Seems the alibi he gave you was bullshit, excuse my French."

"Good work, Henry. Did they fax over a statement of any kind?"

"It's on its way to the station, Chief."

Sally hung up. "I wouldn't worry too much about Landscome firing you today. I might be keeping him pretty busy."

❖

Lou's Diner was on the other end of Main Street and Beth headed there next to get a bowl of grits. It was almost as soothing as ice cream, but more acceptable before noon on a Monday. Mel was at the register when Beth walked in, paying her bill and teasing Mona, Lou's daughter.

"Beth! Just the person I wanted to see. I was going to call on you later."

"Call on me? Sometimes you sound like something out of *Anne of Green Gables.*"

"Don't start talking dirty to me, 'cause I'm worn out in that department."

"That'll be the day."

Beth sat in a booth and slumped against the wall, stretching her legs across the seat. Mel sat across from her. Mona put two cups of coffee in front of them and headed off to get Beth's grits.

"You're not still mad at me, are you?" Beth asked.

"Hell, no. I can't ever stay mad at you." Mel flashed her brilliant smile. "You're one of my favorite people, Beth."

"That's sweet of you. What do you want to talk to me about? I hope it's not anything bad."

Beth knew Mel was going to bring up Katie and she was determined to keep news of the layoff to herself for now. Maybe there was still some way around it so Katie could keep her job and stay in town.

"I know you're friendly with Katie Murphy, right?" Mel was tapping a pen on the tabletop and Beth reached over and took the pen away from her.

"Is this about how you're sleeping with Katie Murphy?"

"Sort of. I mean, it's not like you and I ever had anything exclusive, but I still wanted to let you know that something's changed."

"What do you mean?" Beth sat up and swung her legs back on the floor.

"I mean that I'm not going to be sleeping around anymore. It's just Katie for me, and I hope I for her, once she gets rid of that cow."

Beth was stunned. She knew Katie and Mel were attracted to each other, but she'd never heard of Mel having the slightest interest in changing her ways.

"Wow, this is serious."

Mel drank her coffee and nodded in agreement. "It's very serious. I think I might love her."

"Mel, you've only known her for a day or so. Does she know you feel this way?"

"She knows it, but she doesn't want to make any plans yet. She needs to break up with Delilah, but I really don't know what the holdup is there. And what's the story with that woman, anyway? You have history with her, don't you?"

"Yes, and I can understand how Katie got involved with her. Dee can be a lot of fun and she throws her energy at you. It's really flattering. But it can take a couple of months to break up with her. She takes some convincing."

"She should leave it to me. I think I could convince her real good."

"Please, Mel. There is so much going on around here, the last thing I need is a showdown between you and Delilah Humphries. Just let Katie handle it."

"I don't feel very patient. I'm really crazy about her, Beth."

Sadness touched Beth, a little behind the eyes, a little in the throat. Everything was changing, even the simple pleasure of making love with Mel with no strings attached. She knew that if Mel hadn't changed the rules she would have herself because of Sally. But it was still a loss. Beth felt like she was sliced open by losses. Mona put the grits in front of her and she ate silently as Mel sat with her, chattering on about how wonderful Katie was. As Beth paid her own bill, Mel gave her a kiss on the cheek and bounded out the door, happier than Beth had ever seen her. She felt small in her jealousy, forgetting for the moment the happiness she felt herself about Sally. She would miss Mel.

CHAPTER FIFTEEN

"Ted, where the hell is that laptop? It's almost eleven in the morning."

Sally was in her office, anxious to develop some kind of approach regarding Landscome's false alibi. She wanted to take Ted with her when she went to see Landscome again. And she wanted the damn laptop.

"Chief, I'm just a few minutes away. That fellow finally opened his shop at ten this morning after I sat there all night in my truck waiting for him. I made him start the laptop to make sure it worked. He didn't even know that Barrow was dead."

"Just bring it into my office when you get here. And good job, Ted. I appreciate you hanging in there."

"Thanks, Chief."

Within fifteen minutes Sally had the laptop plugged into the wall and booted up. She scrolled through the files in the directory, seeing many that were duplicates of those on his office and desktop computers.

"Looks like he might have them all synched," Ted observed.

Sally kept scrolling, clicking on directories to reveal file names and subdirectories, drilling down each subdirectory to see all of the file names and extension types. She finally hit a subdirectory in a parent directory called "Freelance," which was buried under another two layers of subdirectories. A long list of filenames appeared, all with .jpg extensions. Photographs. Sally clicked on the first file and the image opened on the screen.

"Oh, dear Lord," Ted said, turning his face quickly to the side.

Sally studied the photo of a girl, maybe thirteen or fourteen years old, fellating a corpulent man. The man's head was not visible, but he appeared to be middle-aged or older. The room was small and dark, with what little light there was coming from a lamp next to the cot-sized bed. She could see a covered window at the top of the wall behind the girl, and knew the room was in a basement. Other than that, she could see nothing that would identify the location or the subjects, both of whom were naked. She clicked on the next photo.

"There we go," breathed Sally. "Ted, take a look at who we have with the underage girl."

Ted turned and screwed up his face. The scene was essentially the same but now a rear-angle shot of the man's head provided a partial view of his face. Sally recognized President Landscome. He was holding the girl's head to him. They could also see that her hands were bound behind her and that her thick mascara had begun to smear with the tears running down her face. "Who is that filthy son of a bitch?" Ted exploded. "That's just a little girl."

"Don't you think that's Landscome? I think it's him. It would explain a lot."

"Let's go get him, Chief. God, I'd love to beat the crap out of him."

Sally continued to click through the photos, searching for a shot with a clearer view of Landscome. In her mind there was no mistaking him, but she wondered how it would play as evidence. All of the photos were from a similar angle, which focused primarily on the girl. The man's face, Landscome's face, was sometimes tilted up, sometimes down, but never at an angle that gave it a fuller view of the face.

"I'd love to beat the crap out of him too, Ted, but we can't do that. We're going to get this fucker and we'll do it right so it sticks in court. Put some of that photo paper we've got in the copy room into my printer. I'm going to print a couple of these to share with the esteemed president."

Bob Geddings poked his head in the office. He always took

his day off on Sunday, whether the department needed him or not, because that was the Lord's Day and off-limits for work. Before he had a chance to ask what was going on with the murder investigation, he saw the photo on the laptop screen.

"Jesus H. Christ, what the hell is that?" Bob said.

Sally knew her officers would be stunned by what was to be seen during one day working a beat in Chicago, but she found it refreshing. The world weariness of an urban cop became dispiriting.

Sally waved him into the office. "This is what we call a big fucking clue as to why John Barrow was killed. It looks like President Landscome here is a pedophile and John Barrow got hold of this evidence of it. He was blackmailing Landscome, and my guess is that Landscome murdered Barrow. And you're going to help me figure out how we can nail him for it."

"What do you mean, how? We go over there and arrest him, that's how." Bob was looking everywhere but at the photo on the screen. "Do you think you could close that thing?"

Ted came back in with the photo paper and Sally printed four shots, all showing the clearest angle of Landscome's face. Then she closed the laptop.

"Here's the problem. I'm not saying we're not going to arrest him, but just hear me out about our evidence issues. First, we really have no evidence that Barrow was blackmailing Landscome to bring him to the United States and set him up in a tenured college position. It makes sense, but the photos aren't direct evidence of it. Landscome was pushing hard for Barrow and no one else seemed to like him, but so what? If Landscome doesn't admit to being blackmailed, the motive is pretty shaky. Secondly, we have these photos, but we have no foundation for them. Unless we find the same or similar photos in Landscome's house, we can't really prove this is him on the charge of having sex with minors or child pornography. What if Barrow found a Landscome look-alike and had him pose for these pictures? These are pretty poor photos for identity purposes."

"That's ridiculous, Chief. No one would think that it's not Landscome, given all the other circumstances," Ted said.

"They would if the defense attorney presented it the right way.

All he has to do is introduce a reasonable doubt that the man in the picture is the man charged with the crime. Unless we can find these girls or the person taking the photographs, there's no one to testify that it's really him. The person who had possession of the photos is dead."

"Fuck," Geddings said.

"You swear a lot for a religious man," Sally said.

"This is bad, Chief. It calls for some swearing."

"So now let's look at the murder. We've just had motive and opportunity dropped in our laps. Henry has gotten proof that Landscome's alibi is blown, and these pictures indicate the murder victim was blackmailing him. The blown alibi is a solid piece, but the motive is going to be supposition at best. If we can't prove that's Landscome in the photos, and Landscome doesn't confess that he was being blackmailed—and why would he since that would mean admitting he's a pedophile—then the motive is leaky. We have no physical evidence linking him to the murder scene, no eyewitness, no murder weapon. We have, in a word, fuck-all."

"What are we going to do then?" Ted asked.

"We can try to get a confession out of him," Bob said. "I'd love a turn at that."

"Yeah, we're going to interrogate him. Or rather, I am. And we're going to search his house and his office. If nothing else, that'll probably make the top of his head come off. But unless we find something, we might have to cut him loose. If he doesn't confess and lawyers up instead, we will definitely have to cut him loose. I just want to prepare you guys for that."

Sally had Bob organize a few plainclothes vehicles and officers to watch Landscome's office and home while she called the state's attorney at the county seat to get the warrants processed.

By three in the afternoon, Sally had managed to obtain a warrant for the search of Landscome's home and for his arrest. The county prosecutor was convinced that the photos on Barrow's computer were a strong motive and that the false alibi further supported a warrant. The officers watching Landscome's campus office would radio her as soon as he left. She assembled a search team and waited for him to return home.

Sally's radio crackled and Ted Benson reported that Landscome appeared to be leaving for the day, heading to his car with briefcase in hand. Ted followed as Landscome went directly home, a distance of approximately two city blocks. Jake, who was posted on Landscome's street, radioed that Landscome was pulling into the carriage house garage. Sally and the search team headed to their squad cars and made the short drive to the residence. The array of police vehicles would provide a fair amount of humiliation and fear, Sally thought, but nowhere near as much as that young girl in the photos suffered. Sally cared a hell of a lot more about her than she did about the murder of someone who used the photos to further his career. The only unfortunate thing about John Barrow's murder was that it deprived Sally of getting him on whatever role he'd played in those photos existing in the first place.

The squads pulled up en masse and Sally led the way to the door. Bob and Ted stood behind her with their hands at their holsters. Other officers fanned out to the back and sides of the property. A student mowing the back lawn was sent on his way. Sally was about to ring the door a second time when Landscome yanked opened the door. His face was at war with itself, the desire to show outrage losing the battle to fear. The blood drained from his odd, Kewpie doll lips.

"David N. Landscome, I am serving you with a warrant to search your home. And I'll ask you to come with me to answer questions at the station house."

"Are you out of your mind? What is this about?"

"If you don't come to the station house voluntarily, I have a warrant here for your arrest. Your choice."

"I won't allow this. I'm calling the mayor." Landscome reached into his pocket and Sally instantly grabbed him and turned him around with his face pushed into the doorjamb. She heard guns come out of holsters as she did so, and after cuffing him she moved him into the foyer of the house.

"Bob, will you pat him down and read him his rights?"

Bob recited the rights while pulling a wallet, a cell phone, and an asthma inhaler out of Landscome's pockets. "That's it, Chief."

"I'm delighted you weren't attempting to shoot me, Mr. Landscome. Nevertheless, I'm arresting you for the murder of John Barrow." Sally turned to the crew behind her. "Jake, grab one of the other guys and take him down to the station. You can put him in the interview room."

"I will have your job for this, Chief Sullivan. You have no idea what you're bringing down on yourself."

"Jake?" Sally motioned to the officers to take Landscome away and then got the search team started under Bob's supervision. "Call me as soon as you find anything or finish up, whichever comes first."

When Sally walked into the interview room at the station a short while later, Landscome's face was a terrible shade of white. He was still cuffed, and where Sally expected an explosion of abuse she found him subdued. She unlocked his cuffs and asked him if he'd like some coffee.

"Tea, if you could."

Sally sent the officer stationed outside the room on the errand and then turned on the recording equipment on the table, stating the date and time of the interview, the names of the parties.

"Mr. Landscome, do you acknowledge having been read your rights at the time of your arrest?"

"Yes."

"And do you understand those rights?"

"I'm a college president. Of course I understand them."

"And do you waive those rights at this time?"

Landscome was silent for a moment. The tea was brought in and he fussed with it a bit before answering. "I did not have anything to do with John Barrow's murder. If I bring a lawyer in, he will not allow me to answer any questions and you'll not see that you have nothing to hold me on. So for the time being, I waive my right to counsel."

"Mr. Landscome, you say you didn't have anything to do with

John Barrow's murder. Can you explain to me, then, why you lied about your whereabouts on the night of the murder?"

Sally thought he was a little relieved. "Yes, well, that was daft of me, frankly. I should have realized that you would actually call Brown's Hotel to verify my stay there. They answered your questions, did they?"

Sally took a piece of paper and slid it across the table. "An affidavit from the manager of the hotel saying you never checked in."

"Ah. Well, here's the thing of it. You may or may not know that I have lived in this area of the country for a long time and ran a successful Fortune 1000 company in Center City for many years."

"And?"

"My late wife and I bought a lovely cottage on Lake McDeere and spent many weekends there. That's where I was."

"Why would you tell your staff you were in London when you were at Lake McDeere?" Sally asked. "And then lie about it to the police?"

Landscome took off his glasses and polished them with a handkerchief, taking his time putting them back on. "You've no idea how stressful it is running this college. I think running AgriCorp was easier; in fact, I'm sure of it. I just found that I needed to get away for a bit without anyone bothering me. It seemed a perfectly good idea at the time."

"Who would be able to confirm that you were at your cottage last Friday?"

"No one, I'm afraid. Unless someone saw me drive up, but I don't know who that would be. The place is well stocked, you see, and I'd brought a few things from home for the fridge. I didn't stop anywhere on the way."

"I still don't understand why you felt the need to sneak around. As you keep reminding us, you're the president of the college. Can't you do what you want?"

A brief scowl came on Landscome's face. "Really, the pressure is enormous to always be pushing something forward, assuaging people's wounded egos, hitting up the most tedious of alumni and other donors for ever more money, putting out fires, and the like, all while looking 'presidential.' I just returned from a long vacation a few weeks ago and I didn't feel the administrators would understand my need for more time away."

Sally opened her file and leafed through a few pages. Landscome resumed. "Tell me, Chief Sullivan. What do you have that puts me at the scene of this murder? It can't be anything, because I wasn't there. So perhaps we are at an impasse?"

"No, I don't think we're at an impasse," Sally said, pulling the four 8 x 10 inch photographs from the bottom of her file. The last bit of color drained from his face as she spread them out on the table. "I think your troubles are just beginning."

"I want to call my attorney," Landscome said. And then he shut up.

"Do you know where we found these, Mr. Landscome? We found them in Barrow's computer," Sally continued. "But it looks to me like you know that already."

Sally shuffled the photos around in front of him, knowing he could hear them. He kept his eyes clamped shut.

"I'm sure any jury—particularly once they see this young girl—is going to find it easy to return a guilty verdict on the child sexual abuse charges. I'd say that's a slam dunk, there. Tying her hands behind her back will certainly make an impression."

Landscome's breath was coming in short rasps.

"Are you feeling a little panicky, Mr. Landscome? I would be too if I was thinking about doing time for this crime. They are so nasty to people like you in the penitentiary."

Landscome leveled his gaze at Sally. "I said I want my attorney."

"Sure, sure. We'll get you to a phone in just a minute. I think you'd be making a mistake, though, not helping us clear up a few things. It would help you out, for instance, if we knew that it was Barrow taking these photographs. Chances are you wouldn't be the only one he's been blackmailing."

"Get me a phone, Chief Sullivan. I know my rights here."

Sally went at him a couple more times, but he was clammed

up. She left him in the interview room while an officer brought him a phone and left the station to check on the search at Landscome's house. She found Bob in the kitchen and asked him what they'd found.

"Not a damn thing, Chief, unless you count a collection of vintage *Playboy* magazines in his closet," Bob reported.

"Have you been through everything?"

"We're just finishing up in the garage and car, but there's nothing here. He lives like a slob, though."

Sally found Ted and briefed him on Landscome's new alibi before sending him to Lake McDeere to check it out. Then she got in her squad to return to the station and called Beth on her way.

"It's Sally."

"I know. You're already programmed into my phone. There's no going back now, Chief."

Sally laughed. "You sound a little more relaxed."

"I shouldn't be, but I am. Go figure. Word has already hit us that the police have invited the president to the station for a chat. Is it true?"

"You didn't hear it confirmed by me. You were with me when I heard about the alibi being blown. Now he's saying that he wasn't actually in London, he was at his cottage at Lake McDeere. Apparently you all were working on his last nerve and he needed to get away."

"So he was in the area the night of the murder? But why would he want to kill Barrow? He was the only one who liked the man."

"I actually can't tell you everything just yet, plus I've got to get going. I just wanted to call to say hi."

"Any chance we can connect later?"

"Not much, I'm afraid. It looks like we'll be at the station for a while. Can I call you later?" Sally wanted to put the investigation on hold and concentrate only on Beth. Compared to the feelings blossoming for her, the urgency of finding whether the loathsome Landscome killed the boorish Barrow seemed much diminished. But duty was not only what was required of her, it was also her habit.

Beth told her to be careful and they hung up. And as soon as they did, Sally felt an intense desire for her, that physical thrum that shoots through the body when you're newly with a person, originating with a thought, terminating between the legs. Sally thought it was remarkable, one of the marvels of human existence, and at the moment, really inconvenient.

There were several officers congregating around the rear entrance to the station, a couple smoking and a couple others keeping them company, Jake among them. As Sally pulled into her parking space they started to break up and head inside, Jake waiting with the door held open.

"Chief, Landscome's lawyer just showed up. He looks younger than me."

"How old are you, Jake?"

"I'm twenty-two."

"Well, the lawyer's probably at least twenty-five, unless he is one of the genius types who go through college really early."

"I hope not, for our sake."

"I'm not scared, Jake. We'll get this guy if he's guilty."

Sally poked her head in the interview room to see what the young lawyer had to say for himself. Jake was right. His round face and bowl haircut made him look about eighteen years old. He sat in a chair next to Landscome, who looked mortified.

"There's been some kind of mistake at my attorney's law firm," Landscome said. "They've sent the wrong person, clearly, and we'll just have to wait until proper representation arrives."

The young man rose and reached a hand out to Sally. "I'm Ronald Liebson, from Hansen, Peters & Jones." Liebson's baritone voice was unexpected coming from his boyish face. "Mr. Landscome's chief counsel handles only corporate matters, so I was sent to take care of this misunderstanding, having just spent a year at the state attorney's criminal division, as I've just explained to Mr. Landscome. If you could give us another fifteen minutes, we will be pleased to meet with you and conclude this interview."

Sally left them to it, returning in a quarter hour with a fresh cup of coffee in her hand. Ronald Liebson began talking before Sally sat.

"I have had a chance to learn what my client knows of this situation, and as you can imagine, he's anxious to get this cleared up. Therefore, we will continue the interview, obviously with me present."

"Then we'll pick up where we left off," Sally said. "Mr. Landscome, when and where were these photographs taken?"

"I have no idea."

"And how is that possible?"

"It's possible because that's not me in the photos and therefore I have no idea where and when they were taken. They have nothing to do with me."

Landscome had clearly regained some of his confidence. Sally peered at each of the photos.

"When I look at these, there's no question in my mind that it's you. Same hair, same build, same face."

"Chief Sullivan, perhaps we can clear this up with a simple bit of show-and-tell." Liebson took the photos and lined them up. "I observed on three of these photos that the angle is such that a large mole or birthmark can be seen on the upper right thigh of the male subject. I asked my client whether he had such a marking and he said that he does not. He has consented to demonstrate this to you."

Sally wondered about the sudden rapprochement between Landscome and Liebson, and now realized it came about because Liebson sounded like someone who knew what he was doing.

Sally sighed and pushed herself up from the table. "Fine. Let me arrange for a photo to be taken." Within a couple minutes Jake came in with a digital camera. Landscome stood and lowered his trousers. Below his blue-striped boxer shorts was an angry red scar that extended an inch or so above and below the area where the photo subject's mole appeared to be.

"Did you have a butcher remove your mole, Mr. Landscome? That seems like a big scar."

"I had no such thing removed, and no examination will indicate that there was any mole in that spot. It is simply bizarre coincidence that I fell upon some broken glass a month or so ago and required sutures."

"Exactly in the spot where a mole appeared on the leg of a man forcing a pubescent girl to suck him off. Lovely. Jake, take a photo so this fucking animal can pull his pants up."

"Excuse me, Chief, but there's no call to abuse my client."

"There isn't?" Sally swept up the four photos and threw them at Landscome in disgust. "I'd say that's plenty of reason."

She leaned back in her chair and took a breath. "I'm going to ask you these questions one more time, and as your attorney can tell you, things will go a lot easier for you if you answer them truthfully. One, and this goes back to our first interview in your home, why did you insist on bringing John Barrow to the college?"

Landscome acted both bored and annoyed. "As I've said, it was simply my ongoing desire to set a higher tone here at Grafton College. The man was highly qualified."

"And yet there's nothing in his file that speaks to his qualifications. Why is that? Did you just make up the fact that he was highly recommended by senior faculty at the London School of Economics, just the way you made up your recent trip to London and your run-in with the broken glass?"

Liebson jumped in. "Chief, I don't know what these letters have to do with anything at issue here. I understand that the murder victim was a member of the faculty. If letters were missing from his file, surely that's an administrative matter."

"No, it's a piece of the puzzle that shows Landscome brought Barrow here for some reason other than his competency—like blackmail, for instance. But we'll get back to the letters. Number two, do you deny that you told me, in my official capacity, that you were in London at the time of Barrow's murder, when in fact you were here in the area?"

"I do not deny it. If that constitutes obstruction of justice or some similar charge, then I'll just have to deal with it. It never occurred to me that I would be charged with Mr. Barrow's murder. My lie was to cover up my whereabouts from my staff, as I've explained."

"And three, do you deny that this is you in these photographs in front of you?"

"I deny it without any hesitation."

Ronny Liebson now leaned forward and folded his hands. "Chief, I think a call to your state's attorney will result in him instructing you to release my client. There will be nothing found in your search of my client's home and you have absolutely no evidence that the man in these photos is my client, other than a passing resemblance. We both know that without further foundation, a defense lawyer will destroy their credibility. We don't know who took them and we don't know where they were taken. You will have no evidence of motive. In addition, you have absolutely no physical evidence that my client was at the scene of the crime—ever. With all due respect for your zeal, I suggest that you cut my client loose before he gives any serious thought to an unlawful arrest action."

Sally once again pushed back her chair and headed out the door, motioning Jake with her. In her office she called the state's attorney she'd spoken to earlier, a bulldog of a prosecutor named Rhonda Lenski. As soon as Rhonda heard there was no confession and no physical evidence found at his house, she told Sally to release him.

"But what about that ludicrous scar on his leg? It's so obvious he cut out the one thing on his body that someone could match to the photos."

"Ludicrous, yes, but on its own it's not enough, not even with the lie about his alibi. It's too little and too circumstantial. Bring me something else, Sally, and I'll nail him. And if we can find out where those photos came from, maybe we can nail whoever provided those girls."

Sally sent Jake out to release Landscome. She didn't want to set eyes on the man.

CHAPTER SIXTEEN

L ou's Diner at nine in the morning was a crowded, noisy
place. The action started at five, when truckers and shift
workers came in to fuel up before they headed to the job, followed
by farmers after they'd finished up their morning chores. By nine
there were mostly town workers and college people in the diner.
Beth sat in a booth with a bowl of grits and the local paper. The
cowbells over the door to Lou's clanged and she looked up to see
Mel and Katie walk in. Mel spotted her and with a big grin on her
face steered Katie over to Beth's booth and sat.

"This is so cool that you're here. This is Katie. Isn't she
great?"

"Mel, I've known Katie for two years."

Katie shrugged and smiled at Mel. "I try not to dampen her
enthusiasm, Beth. It's so infectious."

Mona came by and took orders.

"So I guess you've talked to Delilah?" Beth asked.

"No, not yet. I'm seeing her tomorrow night—Wednesday is
sort of a standing date—and I plan to tell her then," Katie said.

"I say we go over there right now and tell her together, but
Katie seems to think that's a bad idea," Mel said.

"I'm with Katie on that. You have to treat her with respect,
Mel. You're just going to make this a big thing if you get all 'she's
my woman now' about it."

"Amen," Katie said.

"Anyway," Beth continued, "it's not like Delilah is unreasonable. She feels hurt like anyone does. I don't think she hurts more, it's just that she's very vocal about it. When I broke up with her we had to talk it over more than once."

"I thought you said it took a while for her to get over it," Mel said.

"What can I say? I'm hard to get over," Beth teased. "Seriously, though, we did talk several times over several months, and that was fine. She just had to understand that I wasn't going to change my mind."

Beth knew that Katie had bigger problems right now than how Delilah was going to react to her breaking up with her. Without a job at the college, it was almost a certainty that Katie would be moving away. Delilah wouldn't follow. Her full professorship at Grafton was worth more to her than any woman. But Mel probably would. Every town needs good auto mechanics, especially college towns. Beth wanted to tell them what she knew about the layoffs, but until she found out how the day would play out, she'd keep it to herself. Maybe she could save Katie's job—and her own.

Katie asked, "Can I come by your office today, Beth? I want to talk about my job, if that's possible. You'd mentioned the other day that you may be able to avoid the normal search process and just put me into Barrow's position."

"I can't say anything, Katie, and I can't do anything—not today."

"But the word out there is that the adjuncts are about to be laid off."

"There were administrative cuts yesterday. There is nothing definitive on cutting the adjuncts. Please just bear with me today and I hope to have answers for you by tomorrow. Okay?"

Katie picked up her coffee cup and shrugged. "I trust that you'll do what you can. I'm not going to worry about it."

On her way to campus a few minutes later, Beth called Landscome's office to see if she could get in to see him. She had her letter of resignation in her bag, but she wasn't sure she needed to use it. She would resign if he forced her to implement the adjunct layoffs, but she was hoping she could talk him into further budget study or at least some revisions to his list. She was also hoping that the fact that he'd been placed under arrest yesterday would weaken him a little. She knew from Sally that they'd had to release him last evening, though she was unwilling to tell her anything else. Whatever it ultimately meant for Landscome, it had to be a distraction for him in the short run.

"Cora, it's Beth Ellis. I'd like to see Landscome as soon as I can."

"I don't know where he is, Dean. He was supposed to be here for an eight o'clock conference call and he hasn't shown up. He isn't answering at home or on his cell."

"Maybe he's taking the call at home?"

"Maybe. He never has before," Cora said.

"I'm just leaving Lou's. I'll swing around and look in on him at home. I can talk to him there."

"Are you sure? He doesn't like surprises."

"I think I could have guessed that."

Cora snorted, which was as close as she came to a laugh. "When you see him will you tell him to call me? I've got a slew of messages for him."

Beth circled the campus rather than climb up and over it to get to Landscome's house. It was another gorgeous April day, no rain in sight, and the idea of a long run later in the afternoon would normally be something she looked forward to. She was tired, though. Everything associated with the college felt enervating. What once defined her life now seemed to be draining the energy right out of her.

Landscome's house came into view and she could see that the blinds and curtains were still drawn. His car was in the drive. *Maybe he got out of jail last night and got drunk.* She rang the doorbell and stepped back a bit, looking idly around. After the second ring and lengthy wait, Beth peered through the etched glass panels on either side of the front door. The panel on the right afforded a full view of the marble foyer and though the view was distorted by the beveling in the etched glass, Beth thought she saw something. On her knees, face plastered against the panel, Beth could clearly see that President Landscome was lying on the marble floor, blood and brain in a wide arc behind him, a pistol a foot or two from his outstretched left hand.

Beth threw up in the bushes next to the door and then called 911.

❖

For a second day in a row, police cars arrayed themselves in front of President Landscome's house, this time joined by an ambulance. The ME was on his way from his office across town and the CSI vans from the state police depot in Center City had been dispatched. Sally arrived within five minutes of Beth's call and immediately started securing the scene. She sent officers inside to clear the house while she examined the area around the body. Then she took a few minutes to speak with Beth. She found her sitting in the back of the ambulance and talking on the phone, legs swinging. As Sally approached, Beth hung up.

"That was my mother," Beth said. "I called her to let her know what happened."

"Can we talk about what you saw?" Sally asked.

"The weird thing is that I don't even know why I called her. It just seems like something she'd want to know about."

Sally took Beth by the elbow and walked her to the side of the house and toward the backyard.

"Anyway, she said she'd come pick me up. That's okay, isn't it?"

The backyard was large and lavishly landscaped. Off the rear of the house was a wood deck, and below that a flagstone patio. Sally steered Beth into a chair on the patio and pulled another up for herself, so they were sitting knee to knee.

"Are you feeling okay?" Sally asked.

"Why do you ask, because I called my mother?"

"I know that seems remarkable to you, but I was actually asking because you just found a dead body."

"Yes. I'm sorry. It really is horrible."

Sally got out her notebook and took Beth through everything she saw, heard, smelled, or otherwise noticed as she approached the house and rang the doorbell.

"I don't understand why people are being murdered at our college. It doesn't make any sense," said Beth.

"It may be that Landscome's death is suicide."

"But why? I know you found out he lied about where he was when Barrow was murdered, but surely that's not something to kill oneself over."

"Can you think of anything else about this morning that you may have left out?"

"And it's a strange place to commit suicide, don't you think?"

"You mean the entryway to his house? Yeah, it's a little strange, but I've seen much stranger. How about a doghouse? Or a grocery store? Who knows what's going on in their heads, unless they tell us in a suicide note."

"Was there a note?" Beth asked.

"We haven't seen one yet." Sally flipped open her notebook. "Was Landscome left-handed?"

Beth thought a moment before answering. "I don't know. I can't remember seeing him pick up a pen or sign anything."

"His secretary will know, I suppose," Sally said.

"Can I go now? I have another crisis to manage on campus, and this time I really am the top dog, at least for a while."

Sally walked Beth back out front just as Mae's Escalade pulled up. The two drove off together toward campus. The medical examiner arrived and she waited for him on the front lawn.

"Let's go in the back door, Dr. Rice. We'll have a cleaner approach from inside the house."

Dr. Rice put a hand on Sally's shoulder as they walked to the back of the house. "One murder in Mount Avery is alarming, but two is going to really frighten people. What do you think is going on?"

Sally wondered how many people felt that she should know by now. "Let's see what you think of the scene before we call it another murder."

The officer standing on the back deck next to the sliding door was maintaining the log book. Dr. Rice signed in and they proceeded through the kitchen and down the long hallway to the front. The red tape that marked the no-enter zone extended slightly into the hallway. Here they were stopped by another officer and given booties and gloves.

"Oh, Christ," Dr. Rice said as they entered the foyer. The room itself was large, the marble floors tiled in a black and white swirling pattern that came to a point exactly in the middle of the room. Above it was a huge and ostentatious chandelier. The fifteen-foot ceiling was trimmed with ornate molding and the walls with picture and chair railing. A few portraits of past presidents of Grafton College hung on the cream-colored walls. On the right side of the room the stairway curved its way up to the next floor, and lying on his back, with his head two feet from the bottom stair, was President Landscome. It appeared that a good deal of his brain had splattered on the carpeted stairway, the finely turned balustrade, the cream walls, and the portrait of President Hiram Hainsworth (1915–42).

Landscome was wearing pajamas and a silk paisley robe. One leather slipper was perched on his upturned foot, while the other seemed to have been pushed away as he fell. The body lay sprawled, right arm up by his head, left arm down by his side, and two feet away from his left hand lay a Walther PPK with a silencer attached.

"Have you found any note?" Dr. Rice asked.

"None so far. I've sent some officers up the rear stairs to start a search there. I don't think we'll find one, though."

"You don't think it's suicide?"

"I'm keeping an open mind," Sally said. "It looks like we found the weapon that killed Barrow, though. And that silencer explains why no one heard a shot in that quiet neighborhood, or this one, I imagine. But why put a silencer on a gun used in a suicide?"

Dr. Rice examined the body closely, taking its body temperature directly from the liver, noting the degree of rigor, the areas of lividity.

He looked closely at both hands, taking fingernail scrapings before bagging them for transport. Finally he stood and joined Sally at the edge of the red zone.

"I can do the autopsy this afternoon in Center City. We'll have our folks transport the body when the CSI team is done."

"What can you tell me right now?" Sally asked.

"Rigor is almost fully established, so the death occurred, most likely, at least ten to twelve hours ago. Lividity is consistent with that time frame and indicates he has not been moved since he died, though that will be confirmed on autopsy. And his body temperature indicates a similar range."

"So probably somewhere between ten and midnight last night?"

"That's just a preliminary, but yes. The fact that he's inside a controlled environment helps with the calculation. Also, I don't know anything about your investigation into the other murder or what the story is with this man, but a couple of other things do point toward suicide. First off, there's the obvious—putting the muzzle of a gun in the mouth and blowing out the back of the head—a suicide technique frequently used by men. Next, there is blowback on the man's left hand, which indicates he had hold of the gun when it fired. There are no signs of a defensive struggle. Lastly, the fact that the weapon is lying away from the body is telling. I don't have a lot of experience in this, but I do know that the gun is usually thrown from the suicide's hand by the kickback. It would be more unusual to see them gripping the gun."

"In other words, if someone was gripping the gun, it would suggest the real shooter might have placed it in the victim's hand, thinking that's where it would be in an actual suicide."

"That's what their logic would be."

"I don't think we'll find fingerprints other than Landscome's on the gun," Sally said.

"Yes, if it was murder, they'll know to do that at the very least."

Sally arranged with the doctor to meet up with him at the autopsy in Center City and then turned to the arriving CSI team.

She grabbed the investigator in charge, and once he was gowned up and the photographer had photographed the Walther and an outline of its placement had been drawn, they got on their hands and knees and took a close look. Sally could see that there was some blood and tissue on the gun and Landscome's left hand, the blowback that Dr. Rice mentioned. She also saw at the same time as the forensics tech that the serial number had been removed from the body of the gun. The bullet casing was found to the right of the body, by the staircase, indicating the gun was pointed at Landscome as if it were held in the normal position by someone else. Sally urged the tech to have the firearms examiner test the gun and examine the casing as soon as possible. Were the prints on the trigger from a thumb or from a forefinger? The bullet would be extracted at autopsy and delivered later in the afternoon for comparison with the bullet in the Barrow case. She expected that the examination would tie the gun to the two bullets, but that didn't prove Landscome committed suicide. If he was murdered, Sally had a whole new set of problems.

❖

The dean's office was crowded with administrators and faculty department chairs, all of whom looked stunned. Both Cora and Lillian had helped Beth gather them together to announce Landscome's death in a manner more personal and more secure than campus e-mail.

Beth addressed the group. "I was told by the chief of police that it will be a day or two before the medical examiner announces whether the death was homicide or suicide, and that ruling can always change based on new evidence. For the time being we are to say only that we heard Landscome died but we don't know what happened. I imagine some of you will get calls from the press after they become frustrated with me, so it's important that you toe the party line."

"I don't understand, Dean. Are we hiding something from the press? Can't we just say we heard he was shot?" This came from the giant dean of admissions, Ed Baker.

"Think about it," said Delilah, standing at the front of the crowd. "We've just had a murder on campus, and now another violent death. Even if it was suicide, there's likely to be an exodus of students from campus."

"I'm afraid that's true," Beth said. "Let me talk with the board and get their advice on this. Losing students is the very last thing we need now."

The group shuffled out the door, with Delilah staying behind. Cora peeked her head in.

"Chief Sullivan wants to talk to me, so I'll call her now, if that's okay."

"Of course, Cora," said Beth. "Take all the time you need."

Beth got up from her desk and sat on the sofa in the corner of the office. Delilah closed the door and came to stand over Beth, her arms crossed at her chest.

"You have to be strong now, Beth. The board will make you acting president."

"God help us all."

"Come on, now." Delilah grabbed Beth's hand and pulled her up. "You know you'll do a better job than Landscome. Things are only going to get worse if you drop the ball."

Beth shook her off and walked back to her desk. "No, you can't put that on me. I'll do my best, but there's no telling what's going to happen next. If another person on campus is murdered, it might be the end of the college."

"You're exaggerating. We'll be fine."

❖

"Mayor, it's Chief Sullivan."

"Chief. Please tell me that we don't have a serial killer in our town. Please."

Sally was driving back from Center City following Landscome's autopsy. Her stomach was still unsettled. No amount of experience would allow her to see a face being peeled away from a skull without feeling queasy. Dr. Rice had not seen anything during the postmortem that suggested it was not a suicide. Landscome's blood alcohol level was .19, which in most people would qualify as roaring drunk, and the preliminary toxicology screen did not reveal any illegal or other toxic substances. The fingerprint lab confirmed that the only prints on the gun were Landscome's.

Dr. Rice also examined the scarred area on Landscome's thigh where the photographs had shown a mole to exist. There was no remaining evidence that a mole had ever existed, but Sally thought it ridiculously unlikely that Landscome would accidently fall on broken glass and slash his skin exactly where an incriminating mole was located on someone else's thigh, someone who looked astonishingly like Landscome himself. She had no doubt that Landscome was the man in the photos and that the photos were the motive to kill Barrow. He also clearly had the opportunity; Ted had found someone in the Lake McDeere area who noticed the lights on at Landscome's cottage. That merely confirmed that he was within easy driving distance of Mount Avery at the time of Barrow's murder. With the appearance of the Walther by Landscome's body, it appeared that he had access to the murder weapon as well. If Landscome weren't dead, he'd be convicted.

And yet there was something that didn't feel right. The question at the moment was whether to pass along her doubts to the mayor and a worried town and campus.

"Everything points to Landscome having committed suicide after killing Barrow and being exposed as a pedophile. I have nothing that contradicts that."

"Good. I mean, the whole thing is terrible, really unfortunate for the college. But I'm relieved there's not a murderer still running around."

"How do you want to handle the press? They've been calling all day and we've not told them a thing at this point." Sally hoped the mayor would volunteer to handle it.

"Call the local people for now and tell them what you have. They're going to get wind of it sooner or later, and I want to get the story out right away so that everyone around here knows we have the matter resolved. There's no point telling them anything but the truth. And, Chief, I'd be ready for some national coverage too. It's a pretty sensational story."

They rang off and Sally made a call to a reporter she knew at the *Center City Times.*

"Sam, it's Chief Sally Sullivan in Mount Avery."

"How are you, Chief? You have something for me on the bloodbath taking place in your little town?"

Sam Toshima was the most like the big-city reporters that Sally was used to dealing with. He was unflappable, efficient, professional, and nastily sarcastic.

"I have an exclusive for you, but I want you to act as a sort of pool reporter on this. We won't have a press conference until tomorrow at the earliest, but I'd like word to go out today."

"Done. What do you have?"

"The official ruling on President Landscome's death is suicide, and based on evidence obtained in our investigation, it is also our determination that Landscome killed John Barrow."

"No shit? Why did he kill him? They were lovers, right?"

"No, Sam. They were not lovers. Evidence shows that Barrow had something on Landscome and was blackmailing him."

"What kind of evidence?"

Sally considered her response. If she told Sam no more than she already had, she and everyone at the college would be hounded by the press. If she told them everything she knew, they'd still be hounded by the press.

"This is the extent of what we are releasing at this time, and you now know more than anyone else does. It isn't going to do you any good to talk to anyone at the college. They won't know anything about it."

"Wait a second. If Landscome murdered Barrow to end the blackmail, why did he commit suicide? It's got to be because you now have the evidence he was being blackmailed over and it's incriminating."

"You said it, not me. And I've said all I'm going to say."

"Thanks, Chief, and let me know when that press conference is. I'll issue what you've told me to the other media here."

Sally hung up and drove to the station to grab her files before heading home. Her dogs needed some attention and she hoped to spend some time with Beth. By seven o'clock, she was starting to give up on the idea of seeing Beth. A call to her home was picked up by Mae, who said Beth was still at the office. Repeated calls to Beth's office and cell phones went right into voicemail. She was about to try both numbers one more time when her own cell phone rang. It was Beth.

"Hi. You should know you're programmed into my phone too," Sally said. She was trying to sound flirtatious, but didn't think it was coming off very well.

"Are you trying to destroy the college, Chief Sullivan? Because if so, you're doing a good job of it."

"What are you talking about?" Sally's throat closed a little at the sound of anger in Beth's voice.

"I've just been contacted by the *Center City Times*. They want to interview me about our murderous college president. What else would I be talking about?"

"I'm just not sure why you're yelling at me."

"Because they got all the juicy details from you. Details, mind you, that I was hearing for the first time, such as Barrow having blackmail-worthy material on Landscome."

Sally could hear Beth take a big, shuddering breath before she went on. "I just thought it would occur to you to talk things over with me before you talked to the press, especially after the other night."

Now Sally was really confused. "Do you mean that because we slept together, once, I should discuss with you my actions and decisions as chief of police?"

"What I mean is that this school has been skating on thin financial ice for several years now. The unsolved murder of a professor has not helped our recruiting efforts, and the news that we hired a president who murdered that professor is likely to severely damage our enrollment."

"Are you crying?"

"Yes, I'm crying."

"I'm sorry, Beth. It would never occur to me that the college would need to manipulate the news about these deaths."

Sally could hear Beth take in a deep breath. "Being forthright with the press is not among my top values, especially right now. I'm seriously worried this is going to finish off the school, and the school is the only thing I'm worried about." There was another pause. "It's practically been my whole life."

"I can't see how you'd have been able to keep this from the press, but I wish I hadn't been the one to tell them. Are you mad?"

"More worried than mad." There was silence on the line, and then, "Will you still want me if I become an unemployed English professor?"

"I thought you were only worried about the college?"

"That's what I'm used to—only being concerned about the college. But you are starting to mess up everything that I'm used to, Chief. Now, answer the question. Will you still want me without the titles and all that?"

Sally wished they weren't on the phone. Beth sounded as if she really believed that without a position as a dean or a professor, Sally wouldn't want her. As if Sally cared about any of that at all.

"Yes, I'll want you. I'll always want you, because I'm pretty sure you're what I've always wanted."

"I'm very scared. I should tell you that, in case I wig out."

"Let me reassure you. Can I come get you tonight so we can spend some time together?"

"That's sweet. But I do have to work late. And then I'm going to go home and be miserable. If you keep this up it might be my last chance."

Sally smiled as she hung up. Beth cranky and miserable was still more wonderful to her than any previous girlfriend on her best day.

CHAPTER SEVENTEEN

The clock on Sally's nightstand read 3:20, five minutes later than the last time she checked. There was no end to the night. Between the excitement about the new relationship with Beth and the nagging feeling there were loose ends in the murder investigation, she simply couldn't sleep.

At 3:30 she gave up torturing herself and got out of bed. The files of both the Landscome and Barrow deaths were spread out on her kitchen table. She made a cup of coffee and sat to pick up where she left off the night before. She was slowly moving through every word in the files, hoping that at the end of the review she would be satisfied that everything that could be done to investigate had been done.

It was getting close to time to shower and change for work when Sally came upon the report Jake and Ted had put together regarding sales of Walther PPKs. They had completed their survey of gun shops in the tri-state area, a task fairly quickly accomplished through e-mail requests and follow-up phone calls with non-responders. Jake had been thorough in checking the shops off his list, and at the end of his survey had come up with several hits within the broader geographical range of his search, but only one in their area of the state. There was a purchase ten years ago by a woman in Center City named Lois Brandt. Jake had checked the state database for the woman's last known address and found it was the same one given by the gun shop owner. He'd found phone numbers for the two apartments located at that address, and neither was currently occupied by Lois Brandt. It seemed highly unlikely that this could have anything to do with the killings in Mount Avery, but Sally was inclined to run everything down. Their database resources did not give any further information on Lois Brandt, but maybe her old neighbors would remember something.

After taking care of a morning's worth of paperwork, most having to do with Landscome's death, Sally drove to Center City. Her lack of sleep caught up with her and her head nodded once before she shook herself awake, alarmed when she realized she'd actually fallen asleep, for just a moment. She pulled over and closed her eyes, waking a full hour later, thoroughly disgusted with herself, like a drunk waking up with her head resting on the bar, life and merriment still going on around her with nothing but darkness inside. She recognized the feeling as the creeping tentacles of depression starting to get a grip on her. She roared back onto the highway, trying to outrun it.

The last known address for Lois Brandt was not far from the university in Center City. Many of the houses on the street were divided into apartments, rented out to graduate students for the most part. Sally knew the chance of anyone remembering someone from ten years ago was remote, but she started at one end of the block and worked her way down. Because they were graduate students, many of the tenants were home at one in the afternoon. Most stared at her blankly when she asked her questions about Lois Brandt and whether anyone on the block or in the area might remember her. Toward the end of the street, one young woman was just heading out the door of a house as Sally turned into its walk. The woman stopped when she saw Sally's uniform and waited for her to approach.

"Good morning," said Sally.

"Good morning, Officer, what can I do for you?" Sally felt suspicious of her warm greeting. She was used to students of all ages adopting a bad attitude toward police. This woman, with her jeans patched with peace signs, Vote the Environment T-shirt, and orange hair would almost certainly be one such student. Instead, she sat on the front steps of the house and patted the space next to her. "Are you doing a door-to-door?"

"Actually, I am. Has word gotten around so quickly?"

The woman laughed. "No. But my dad and my brothers and sister are all cops, so I know all about door-to-doors. Generally, they hate them."

Sally took a seat next to her. "I'm Sally Sullivan, chief of the Mount Avery Police Department. And it's good to meet someone who understands the job."

"I'm Diane Swearingen. How can I help you, Chief?"

Sally told her exactly what she was trying to run down. Diane had only one bit of information to offer. "There's a woman named Rosa DeLuca who owns a lot of the houses on this block. She lives the next street over. I can walk you there if you'd like. I go there every month to drop off my rent and I know from chatting with Rosa that she's been here a long time and seems to know most everything about her tenants. Maybe she'll remember something."

"Do you mind if we drive over? I don't want to get too far from my squad."

Diane rode with Sally to Rosa DeLuca's house and then walked off to class, leaving her contact information behind. The DeLuca residence was a three-story frame house with each level painted a different color. There was an unpaved side driveway that ended at the end of the lot line. The carport that stood there was festooned with a wild assortment of Mexican plates, string lights, lanterns, piñatas, statues of Our Lady of Guadalupe, flags and banners, and several festival posters. There were no cars in the carport, just a number of picnic tables in the middle and folding chairs around the perimeter. Sally could see a middle-aged woman in the carport, holding a black trash bag and dropping cans into it. Sally approached her, holding out her identification.

The woman stopped what she was doing and put a hand on her hip. "What? It wasn't enough that you people had to come three times last night to harass us? We were doing nothing but quietly celebrating."

"Are you Rosa DeLuca?"

"Like you don't know." Now the bag had been put down and both hands were on her hips. They were generous hips and easily provided a resting spot. The rest of her was equally well padded, but Rosa DeLuca was a beautiful woman. Her lush hair was rich and dark and framed a face with an elegant bone structure and large, very light brown eyes.

Sally identified herself and made clear she was not from the local police department. "I was referred to you by one of your tenants on B Avenue who said you would be my best source of information about a woman we are trying to locate who may have lived in one of your buildings there."

"Maybe. Why are you looking for her?"

"She's not in any trouble. But she may have some information I need to help find someone else."

"What's her name?"

"Lois Brandt. She lived here about ten years ago."

"Ten years is nothing. I feel like I blink twice and ten years goes by. And I have a very good memory. I'm most likely to remember tenants if they were trouble, though. I never forget those."

Sally gave Rosa the address they had on B Avenue for Lois Brandt and then joined her in the carport, where they sat opposite one another at a picnic table. Remnants of a rather large celebration were strewn about.

"Lois Brandt. I think I do remember her. She was a graduate student like most of them, and the reason I remember her is that she was studying mortuary science. Is that what they call it? She was going to be a funeral director. But I don't think she ever became one. I remember that she left suddenly, like she was running from something. Left her rent on the kitchen counter, which is more than most would do. It was the middle of the semester, so I know something must have happened. She was German. Maybe she had to go home."

"Is there anything else you remember about her, any particular friends, or types of friends?"

Rosa stared at that horizon point most people look to when they're trying to remember something, as if it were a teleprompter. "There was something, now that you mention it. I thought it was the mortuary science that made me remember her, but there was something else. I got a lot of calls from her neighbors, actually."

"What about?" Sally noticed Rosa had a smile forming at the corner of her mouth.

"She was very loud when her girlfriend came over. Do you know what I'm saying?"

"Yes, I think so. They made a lot of noise when they made love?"

"Who knew two girls could make such a racket?" Now Rosa leaned back, putting her hands to her lower back and stretching. "I think the neighbors complained so much because they didn't like the girlfriend."

"Why didn't they like her?"

"I don't know, really. I kind of liked her myself. People just assume that I am going to dislike the gay people because I'm religious, but I don't care. If someone could make me scream like that, I wouldn't care if it was a man or a woman."

Sally swung her legs over the bench and stood, ready to conclude the interview.

Rosa continued. "I can't remember her name, but I liked her because she was big like me, you know? Everything about her was big. Her voice, her body, her manner. She took up space and wasn't shy about it, I remember that very well. I respected that."

Sally sat down hard. "Do you remember what this woman did for a living?"

"Oh, yes. It's all smart people around here. Too many brain cells, too much studying. That's why they don't like my family having get togethers here. We're too happy!" She laughed.

"Mrs. DeLuca? It's important. Was she a grad student too?" Sally almost hoped that she would say yes.

"No, no. She was older than Lois, a teacher herself. I think she taught at one of the colleges outside of town here, in the country."

"Mrs. DeLuca, do you have a computer in your house, connected to the Internet?"

"Sure, for my son."

"I need to get on the Internet so you can help me. I need for you to look at a photo. Can we do that?"

Sally had to boot up the son's laptop and connect to the Internet. Rosa didn't know the first thing about it. Then she typed in the Web address for Grafton College and clicked over to the faculty biographies. As soon as Delilah Humphries's photo came on the screen Rosa shouted, "That's her! Bigger, even, than before, but definitely her."

❖

Despite having a hard knot of fear lodged in her chest, Beth faced her first day as acting president of Grafton College with resolve. These first hours were so crucial—reassuring the board of trustees, the students and the students' parents, managing the press. By three in the afternoon she was desperate for a break. She gathered up files and overstuffed her briefcase, planning to go home and work on through the evening there. She still had several conference calls to make with board members, as well as interviews to conduct with two recommended public relations firms. Both gave her preliminary assurances that the blow to Grafton's reputation from hiring a murderous president could be kept to manageable levels.

Beth was also reminded by Harriet Taylor, an encyclopedia of Grafton College history, that two other sensational scandals had touched the school in the past. Both seemed overwhelmingly bad at the time but were now long forgotten.

"The first," she said, standing at a window in Beth's office, looking out over the campus, "occurred in 1895 and was a rather pedestrian story of adultery and divorce involving the president of the college, his wife, and one of the first female professors of mathematics in the country, the offending parties being caught in flagrante delicto in the president's home."

"That was fairly stupid of him, don't you think? Right there in his own house?"

"Actually, it was the president's wife who was found between the sheets with the mathematician. The husband returned early from a fund-raising trip and found them in the bedroom. No one was positive how the word of the tryst first got out, but the suspicion was that a student working in the yard may have witnessed more than he bargained for when he peeped into a window while cleaning gutters. In any event, the scandal raged and the wife, the president, and the mathematician were sent away at once. All parties, including the school, survived."

Beth wished her scandal was like that one. It would hardly cause a ripple. "Was the second tale more or less scandalizing?"

"More, I believe, for as shocking as any act of lesbianism might be to the mind of a 1895 Methodist, it paled when compared to rumors of a Methodist dean taking his pleasure with undergraduate males, and covering up the repeated abuses through some arrangement with the president."

"Are you saying the dean was raping the students?" Beth was shocked.

"I don't think so. I believe there was some form of consent from the young men, in exchange for passing grades or free credits, or whatever. But they felt in 1910 as we do today, that it's absolutely wrong for someone in a position of power, in this case a professor or dean, to have sexual relations with a student. But you add to that the incendiary fact that it was two men and it changes in character altogether. I don't know why the reaction was so much stronger about male homosexuality than female. Perhaps it's as Gertrude Stein said—people don't really want to think about what two men do together."

"I don't know that that's ever really been true, no more so than people not wanting to really think about what Gertrude Stein and Alice B. Toklas did together or, I don't know, you and your husband, for instance."

"I beg your pardon." Harriet looked over her shoulder at Beth.

"I think the point is that the straight men in charge had a more violent reaction to men having sex with each other than they did when two women were caught. They simply didn't, and probably still don't take two women together seriously. But tell me how it was resolved."

"The dean, who was a Methodist minister, was discharged and defrocked. The students were expelled, and the president hung on until it became apparent that he had known it was going on for some time. That was the bigger scandal. I don't know how much it affected enrollments, but they certainly survived it, and we will survive this."

Beth shook her head. "Harriet, I'm not ready to bury the college, but I do think there's a big difference between now and a hundred years ago, or even twenty for that matter, largely due to the Internet. Now when something like this happens the news spreads like wildfire, and the distortions that occur are breathtaking. Already, one day after Landscome's death, there are blog comments out there about him being blackmailed for a dozen different reasons, each more horrifying than the next. It's crazy, but the people who will scrutinize how this came to pass will be wondering why we didn't know about Landscome when we hired him. They'll find it impossible to believe that such information was not obtainable, that we should have known it simply by Googling him. And I still don't know what Barrow had on Landscome."

"The school will survive. I guarantee it," said Harriet. As she left, Beth thought how very easy it was for Harriet to say it and then wash her hands of the mess.

When she arrived home, Beth found her mother in front of the TV again.

"Thank God for all the drama at your school," Mae said. "It's a lot more interesting than anything on the boob tube."

Beth whirled on her and flung her full briefcase at the front door, the bag exploding against it and papers and files pouring out in a huge jumble. Mae stood and leveled her gaze at Beth.

"What was that about?"

"That, mother, was frustration. Set off by the reminder that the most important thing on your mind, always, is yourself—your amusement, your comfort, your ability to pass judgment. In the meantime, I'm in a crisis. But by all means, store up the details of what's been going on here so you'll have some good stories to tell back at the brothel."

Mae stared at her and at the mess at the door. Then she turned and walked to the kitchen. "I'm going to make shepherd's pie."

Beth followed her. "That's it? You're not going to tell me that I'm taking things too seriously?"

"No, actually, I can see that having two deaths on campus would be pretty awful. I'm sorry I didn't seem to be taking it seriously." Mae started opening cabinets and pulling ingredients out.

Beth didn't know what to make of the apology, so different than Mae's usual admonishment to Beth to "have a sense of humor" or "suck it up."

"Put on your sweats, watch some TV, and I'll make dinner. Shepherd's pie will make you feel better," Mae said.

"If we're going to have that, I'll need the baking dish that I left at Delilah's. I'll run over to get it."

"You don't have to. We can have something else."

"No, that sounds like the perfect thing to have. I'm going to change and walk over. It won't take long."

Delilah's house was just three blocks away and Beth took her time walking over, trying to let go of some of the tension in her body, trying to figure out why her mother seemed different. Was she ill? That thought sent another frisson of fear racing through her, but she simply couldn't add something as big as that to her crowded list of possibly life-changing issues.

The house seemed vacant when she walked up—the front drapes drawn, the car gone from the driveway. The front door was locked. Usually Delilah's place had a welcoming feel to it—the front door propped open, classical music wafting out the open windows, often the smell of something baking. Delilah was home a good portion of the time, it seemed to Beth. She knew she even kept her office hours in her home, with students sitting in her kitchen, eating cookies and discussing anthropology papers. Beth rang the bell twice, but there was no response.

Beth knew where Delilah kept a key from when they were dating, but she'd never had cause to go in the back and dig it out from beneath a rock. She couldn't stand the thought of not having the meal she now had her heart set on, so she walked up the driveway toward the back to get the key. The blinds along the side of the house and in the kitchen were also drawn. It seemed very strange, and was starting to feel a little alarming as well, though the explanation could be a simple one. Perhaps she was upstairs sick in bed?

Beth found the key under the large rock next to the air-conditioning compressor. It looked like no one had disturbed it since Delilah last showed it to her years ago. She rubbed it clean and stepped up to the back door, ringing the bell and knocking loudly before finally letting herself in. She stopped in the kitchen and listened and then she called out again. Delilah's purse was on the kitchen table, her keys on a hook by the back door, so it would appear she must be upstairs, and she must be asleep—or really sick—if that were the case.

Beth really didn't want to go up there. One of the main reasons she'd ended things quickly with Delilah was the discovery of what a neurotic she was, the worst manifestation of which was her inability to throw anything out. As soon as you left the rooms designated for the "public" to see—the kitchen, the front stairs, the main floor bathroom, and the double parlor—the house was like a jungle of junk with the thickest undergrowth imaginable. A thin path had been carved through the mess enabling one to move about, though toppled towers of *National Geographic* magazines and collections of Nancy Drew and Hardy Boys mysteries cluttered the way. It was not only mind-boggling to see, but the expense of accumulating all of the junk sent Beth's mind galloping. She'd heard that this behavior was a real psychiatric condition. Surely there was medication to help? When they were dating, Beth was once left on her own in the house for an hour while Delilah was teaching. She'd opened a closet and found a five-foot stack of hooked pot holders, a craft that Beth had heard Delilah once ridicule as a hobby for the simpleminded, the comment coming out of the blue and apropos of nothing they'd been talking about. Apparently when you ran out of things to horde that you liked, the next step was to horde the things you didn't like.

Beth was still hesitating in the kitchen when the door to the basement opened behind her and Delilah walked in. She looked at Beth without expression on her face, as if she didn't recognize her.

Something is really wrong, Beth thought. Delilah was dressed in her fleece sweatsuit again. Her bare feet looked huge and overpadded somehow, like Fred Flintstone's feet only not comical. They were filthy too, dusty all over, with rivulets of mud leaving streaks across both feet. Beth was staring at them when Delilah seemed to come to.

"How the hell did you get into my house?" she snapped. Her voice was gravelly.

"I'm really sorry, Dee. I needed to pick up my casserole dish so I thought I'd just pop in. I used that old key under the rock."

"The rock? I forgot about that."

"Are you okay?" asked Beth. "You don't look particularly well."

Delilah didn't look too pleased at that, but she moved over to the kitchen and grabbed one of several dishes stacked there.

"There's always a fucking parade of people 'dropping' in here for days after my parties. 'Just stopping by to pick this up. Thanks for scrubbing it clean for me.' They have no interest in talking with me." Delilah whirled around and thrust the dish in Beth's hands. "Here."

Beth felt the force Delilah put behind the dish and stepped back. "I don't know what's going on, but clearly you're upset about something. Do you want me to stay?"

Delilah stood still again, and then pulled out a chair at the kitchen table and sat. She pointed at another chair and Beth sat too. Between them was a cutting board, a chef's knife, and two zucchini. Delilah pulled the chopping board over by its handle and started chopping the vegetable.

"My mother's making shepherd's pie, which is why I needed the dish."

"Your mother's here? I've never even heard you talk about your mother." Delilah paused in her chopping and gave Beth a hard look. "I mean I never heard you mention her, even when we were lovers."

Beth tried not to wince. She viewed her time with Delilah as having taken place when she was particularly vulnerable to someone willing to lavish her with attention and romance. The fact that she'd slept with Delilah was not something she was proud of.

"My mother and I have not been on particularly good terms for a long time. I really don't talk about her. We seem to be reaching some sort of détente lately. Who knows why."

Delilah resumed her chopping. The work was proceeding slowly, with each zucchini being cut into tiny pieces. "Are you sure, Beth, that it was not another incidence of you keeping something important from me?"

"Keeping something from you? Generally, you know more about everything than I do, don't you think?"

"Not when it comes to Katie. That's where I think you've known something I didn't—and you didn't tell me."

Beth felt the hair distinctly rise on the back of her neck. She wondered if Delilah knew about Mel and Katie. Her brain was now hyperalert from some animal-like warning system. She started to rise slowly from the table, not wanting to seem afraid, placing her hands flat on the surface and pushing herself up.

"I'm not aware of anything about Katie, but in any event we'll—"

The knife flashed through the air and came down with all the strength of Delilah's shoulder behind it, straight through Beth's right hand, pinning it firmly to the table. The handle quivered before holding still. A full second ticked by as Beth's brain caught on to the horror of what had just happened, and then she screamed, but only for the full second it took Delilah to get behind her and cover her mouth with her meaty hand. Delilah picked up a hand towel from the table and started to stuff it into Beth's mouth, just as Beth found the use of her left arm and started to pummel Delilah's head for all she was worth.

Beth had never fought before. She had no concept of what the force of her fist felt like, especially adrenaline stoked as it now was. Apparently, it didn't feel like much to Delilah, who appeared quite calm in battle. She easily grabbed Beth's wrist, held her left hand on the table, and using her prodigious strength, smashed the edge of the cutting board down on her fingers, bursting two of them open. Beth screamed again as Delilah pushed the towel farther in her mouth, securing it in place with the tie to an apron that she cut off with some kitchen shears. Then she sat back down in her chair across from Beth and started scraping the scattered zucchini pieces into a pile.

"You're right about one thing, Beth. I do know more than you do—about everything. Always have. Don't think you would have made dean without me guiding you along. And don't think you would have gotten through your first year without making a mess of things if I wasn't your consigliore. And in return you've been loyal to me, or so I thought. But then I find out that not only did you know that Katie was leaving me for that piece of shit auto mechanic, but you coached her on how to break up with me. I'm sorry, but if it's going to be left to me to see that this college doesn't run itself into the ground, I'm going to expect to be paid certain respect."

Beth hardly heard a word Delilah was saying. She was concentrating fiercely on not throwing up. She expected that Delilah would happily watch her choke on her own vomit and die. There was also the unholy pain of the broken left fingers. She had barely moved them an inch and the pain roared through her. The knife through her hand was not as painful, but it was more effective than leg irons at keeping her where she was. She forced herself to breathe slowly through her nose.

Delilah finished scooping the zucchini into a pile and then transferred it back on the cutting board. Before Beth could even realize what she was doing, Delilah reached over with both hands and pulled the knife straight up and out of Beth's hand and resumed cutting the vegetables into their tiny pieces. That was the last Beth saw before passing out.

When she came to, she was lying on a camp cot in the corner of a room that had red walls and fluorescent lights. She felt sick to her stomach. Her right hand had a meager amount of gauze wrapped around it, thoroughly blood soaked. The fingers on her left hand were swollen and bloody. She couldn't look at them, so she looked all around the room instead. On the opposite side of the room there was a big sink with stainless steel countertop and cabinets, and a stainless steel table stood in the middle of the room, a portable tool tray next to it. There were drains dotting the cement floor and the room smelled a little musty. Delilah was nowhere in sight.

She tried to rise without using her hands and as she swung her legs to the floor they hit something. Mel lay on the floor, unconscious, deathly pale, a pool of blood next to her middle. She was curled up as if protecting it. The blood matched the color of the walls.

Delilah did not appear to be around, but Beth did not trust any of her senses. She felt drugged with pain and fear. She touched Mel very gently with her foot, whispering her name. After a while Mel stirred and opened an eye, her face grimacing with pain. Then she seemed to understand that it was Beth and not Delilah above her. Unbelievably, she smiled.

"I told you she was crazy," Mel said.

"Shush. We don't know where she is. How bad are you hurt?" Beth was leaning over, trying to see the area of her abdomen that Mel was protecting.

"She stabbed me in the gut. Fucking hurts, I gotta say. She called me over to take a look at her car, and when I turned around in the garage to talk to her she stuck me. Just like that."

"Is it bleeding a lot?" Beth was really scared now. She wouldn't die of hand wounds. But gut wounds, those were really bad.

"I think I'll be okay if we can get out of here. The bleeding's slowing down."

"I guess we're in the basement of her house," Beth said.

"That's what I think. She knocked me out after she stabbed me, and I'm big enough that it would have been too hard for her to take me much further than that. Plus, the floor's cement."

Mel grew quiet while Beth thought. She gingerly felt along the pocket of her jeans, but her cell phone was gone. Her mother knew where she was. God, she hoped her mother wouldn't figure out where Delilah lived and come over looking for her. Chances were she would just stay at home, thinking that Beth blew her off again, and that thought was so painful that Beth's eyes stung. She didn't want her mother to think that of her. Not anymore. But she didn't want her showing up at Delilah's either.

A door in the center of the room opened and Delilah walked in.

She put a large paper bag on the steel table and then strolled over to Beth and Mel. She had changed into one of her signature Delilah outfits—black cape, leopard blouse, black pantaloons, black boots. Kind of a Zorro/Sancho Panza mix with the leopard print to mark it as her own. She nudged Mel with the toe of her boot and got a groan in response.

"Don't worry, stud. You won't be uncomfortable much longer. I've brought supplies. I'm going to put you right on that table and make it all better."

Mel's eyes grew narrow. Then she made a hacking noise and spat a big glob onto Delilah's shiny boot. Without hesitation, Delilah swung the boot back and kicked Mel in the head. Mel tried to hold back a scream, but a horrible noise worked its way out. The kick had shifted her body and must have torn at her midsection. Blood ran from the gash on the side of her head.

"That's the way it works, darling," Delilah said, addressing Beth. "When you're bad, you must pay. Spitting is bad. Fucking my girlfriend? Very, very bad."

Delilah walked away and started taking items out of the bag, setting them up on the tray next to the table. She was whistling.

"Delilah, Mel needs to get to a hospital right away. There's nothing you can do for her here."

Delilah threw her head back and laughed, the full-throated laugh that had sounded merry and infectious before and simply maniacal now.

"People think that anthropology is not a relevant area of study," she said, placing more items from the bag on the counter. "But I have extensive knowledge of all kinds of compounds and techniques. I am a healing master."

Beth got off the cot and walked toward Delilah. "Dee, please let us go. Or at least let Mel go. I don't know what is going on with you, but I do know you'll eventually get caught. Just think how much better things will go for you if we're safe."

She stopped two feet from Delilah and stood her ground. She did not harbor any notion of overpowering Delilah—her wounded hands and Delilah's great size advantage made that a nonstarter. If she could talk to her, though, find out what was driving this, find out what it was she wanted, maybe there was some hope.

Delilah picked up a long metal spoon and turned to Beth. "Do you know what has driven me crazy for years now? Everyone underestimating me."

"That's just not true, Delilah..."

Delilah whipped the spoon across her body and caught Beth right below her left eye, opening a cut. Delilah pulled back to strike again and Beth raised her hands to protect her face. The metal spoon connected with the broken fingers. Beth howled and fell to the floor, trying to protect her hands and her face with her back as Delilah struck her again and again. Then she stopped abruptly, stepped back, and delivered a mighty kick to Beth's ribs. Beth screamed again, until she realized that the screaming itself hurt.

All was quiet for a few minutes. Delilah finished unpacking her supplies and began measuring and mixing contents. Beth tried not to sob. She was now on her side, curled into a fetal position, her left hand and ribs more painful than anything she remembered feeling, her right hand bleeding at the entrance and exit wounds, the cut under her eye bleeding alarmingly. By moving her head slightly she could see Mel, who was flat on her back and appeared to be unconscious, her hands still covering the wound in her middle.

"Why are you doing this?" Beth asked, struggling to sit up. Delilah kept working, her back to Beth, apparently unconcerned that Mel or Beth could pose any threat.

"By 'this' do you mean what we're doing here today? Because you're right that it's separate from the Landscome/Barrow thing." Delilah hit the button on a blender and watched as a murky mixture whirled around.

Beth's head was a mess. What Landscome/Barrow thing? The only thing she was aware of now was the thing that was likely to kill her, the thing that less than an hour ago she thought was a friend and colleague.

"Everything's been going to hell since that nincompoop Landscome came to Grafton. I had about had it with his insistence on tenure for Barrow, but I thought the situation could be made tolerable by getting rid of Barrow. I wasn't about to have Katie lose that spot to someone as unqualified and asinine as Barrow. So I broke into his house a couple of times while he was away or in classes, looking for something I could use against him. You didn't know any of this, did you?"

"How would I?" Beth was feeling lethargic. She wanted to go to sleep next to Mel, but she knew she should be doing something to stay alive. *Just keep her talking, isn't that what they say to do?*

"Did you find something?" Beth asked.

"Bingo. I found photos of Landscome with a little girl, and they were disgusting. Nothing on Barrow, though, so I figured Barrow was blackmailing Landscome and now I would just blackmail both of them. Then I realized that was entirely too messy and complicated, so I just killed them."

"You killed Landscome?" Beth had climbed to her feet, swaying slightly. She thought her rib must be broken and it made breathing difficult and painful. Worse though was a new and awful realization.

"Yes, planned it all from the start, and I have to say, it worked beautifully. The conclusion is inescapable that Landscome killed Barrow and then himself. Case closed. I don't think that cop of yours will ever figure it out."

Beth knew she was going to be killed. Delilah had just confessed to two cases of first-degree murder. It would not be part of Delilah's plan to let Beth tell anyone about that.

❖

Sally raced toward Mount Avery, lights and siren on, talking on her cell phone to Bob Geddings. "Bob, I need you and all hands. I'm on my way back from Center City, where I learned that the Walther we picked up at Landscome's is connected to Delilah Humphries."

"She's at the college?"

"Yeah, and I'm pretty sure she must be the one that killed Landscome and Barrow. I need to figure out where she is right now, but I don't want to spook her."

"Okay. I'll track her down and get back to you."

"And, Bob? I need you to assemble as many officers as you can. Call people in. Distribute rifles from the armory, or have someone else handle that. We don't know what we'll need to do to bring her in. But keep everyone there at the station until you hear further from me."

Sally then called Beth. After no answer at the office or cell, she called the home number and talked to Mae.

"I don't know where she is, Chief. We were supposed to be making dinner and she's disappeared."

"What do you mean, disappeared?"

"She went over to Delilah Humphries's to pick up her casserole dish, and that was over an hour ago. I called there, but no one answered. She probably got involved with some college thing and forgot all about me."

God damn it, thought Sally. *She has Beth*. She started to panic, for just a moment, until the professional side of her took over. "Mae, I'd like to try to get hold of Beth myself. Would you do me a favor and text me all of the numbers you can find for Delilah Humphries? I'm driving and can't write them down."

"No problem. I've seen her number on a list by the kitchen phone. Is there something wrong? Should I be worried about Beth?"

"No, no. I just want to track her down to see if we can see each other tonight."

"I'll let her know if I see her. I think the two of you are cute together."

Sally was now five minutes away from campus. There was sweat forming on her brow and her breathing was rapid. *What if Delilah really has Beth?* She'd already killed at least two men, apparently with ease, so it didn't seem unlikely that she'd kill Beth. Sally got back on the phone with Bob and arranged to meet at Delilah's house. Bob reported that so far he'd not located Delilah. She was not answering her home or office number. He had not approached the house, but it looked like all the shades were drawn.

When Sally pulled up there were four other squad cars on the scene. Her officers wore their Kevlar vests and held their rifles at the ready, waiting for Sally to give them an order. They'd only done something like this in their training academies. She prayed that none would die from friendly fire, that none would die at all.

Time to act. "Bob, we're going in the house. There's no time for a warrant and all of that shit. This is a probable cause and I can give all the particulars later. She's got Beth. Where they are in there I have no idea. I want you and four others at the back entrance. We'll take front and on my mark we enter. Your team goes up, we go down. Just rely on your training and we'll be fine. Let's go."

❖

Delilah dragged Mel across the room, picked her up, and placed her face up on the autopsy table. The jostling around woke Mel. She tried to struggle as Delilah was lifting her, but she seemed so weak. Beth didn't think she was going to live long.

"Please, Delilah. We have to get help for Mel. You don't want her to die, I know you don't."

"Actually, I do. Ever since Mona at the diner told me about Mel and Katie, I've wanted to kill her. Someone needs to. I've never seen anyone so greedy in my entire life. She beds any woman she sees if the fancy strikes her, regardless of what it does to the woman or her loved ones. Do you know what that did to me to find out that Katie was sleeping with her? I'd just killed a man for Katie!"

"I don't understand any of this," Beth said. "When did you become the kind of person who murders people? That's not the person I know."

Delilah poured the glop from the blender into a bowl and put it in the microwave.

"I remember when we got together, Beth, that the most disappointing discovery I made about you was that you were unbelievably patronizing. You would tell me what I really wanted or didn't want to do as if I didn't know myself. You'd say things like

'You don't really mean that,' as if I didn't know what I really meant. It was a complete turn-off, believe me. But you were amusing in bed, so I let it go on longer than I should have."

The microwave dinged and Delilah took the bowl out, adding a few cups of a dusty powder to the hot mixture and stirring it with the spoon she'd used to hit Beth. Beth searched the room for any means of signaling where they were, anything she could use as a weapon, anything at all. She knew that if she made a break for the door it would be a matter of a second before Delilah had her back, and in restraints. Her wounded hands made any heroic move at all seem unlikely to succeed. There was a heavy feeling descending on her, made more so by the low ceiling in the room, the red walls, the awful, fluorescent lights.

"Where are we? We can't be far from your house. I know I wasn't passed out that long."

"You weren't, that's true. And we are in my house. This is a sub-basement, a fallout shelter that was built by some paranoid prior owner of the house, probably in the sixties. And in case you're wondering, no one is going to find us here. Theoretically, in order to keep nuclear fallout from getting in here, the room is surrounded by thick concrete. No one will hear you if you scream bloody murder. Even the ceiling above the drywall is concrete. Your girlfriend the cop is not going to find you."

Using a trowel, Delilah spread the mixture onto some linen towels she'd heated in the microwave and wrapped them into a tight package, securing it with fabric tape. "Okay, stand there next to Mel. You're going to help me nurse her back to health. This is my famous poultice, based on an ancient recipe that kept hunter/gatherers from dying every time they hacked themselves with an ax or got gored by a wild pig."

Mel had passed out again. Delilah stood over her and raised her T-shirt up, past her sports bra, so that it bunched around her neck. Beth gasped to see the knife wound in Mel's belly, a wide gash at least two inches long, about mid-abdomen and a little off center. How deep the wound was she didn't know, though it was still oozing blood. Mel's skin color made her think she didn't have any blood left in her, but she opened one eye and stared right at Delilah, as if daring her to do her worst. Delilah placed the hot poultice right on the wound and held it there. For the first time Beth heard Mel scream.

❖

Upon her signal, officers smashed open the front and rear doors with battering rams. The teams moved quickly to clear the first floor, but as soon as they got beyond the first-floor rooms their progress was slowed by the mounds of junk. Bob Geddings led a team upstairs, while Sally went down to the basement. Bob's voice came over the radio.

"Chief, it's unbelievable up here. You've never seen so much crap. She could hide twelve bodies and we'd never find them."

"Just clear the rooms, Bob and report back."

Sally was first down the stairs to the basement, holding her gun in front of her, the team behind her pointing at different angles as the room came into view. It looked impenetrable at first glance, other than a small area to the left of the stairs that was relatively clutter free and held the furnace, sump pump, and laundry. The rest of the large basement was nearly solidly filled with boxes, primarily, and an assortment of things that defied easy description. It was as if every category of goods for sale on eBay, with the possible exception of transplant organs and Ferris wheels, were represented in one room, a room entirely too small for the task.

A narrow path allowed travel to the end of the basement at the rear of the house, as well as side to side in the middle of the room. At the rear was a door leading to a few cement stairs that went up into the backyard. At the end of the midway path at the east wall were the gas meter and the electrical panel. The west wall had a clearing at the end of the path that seemed to be a staging area of some sort. There was a scattering of items that appeared ready to be boxed up—a collection of vintage advertising thermometers, a stack of magazines and books, piles of notebooks of all conceivable style. Sally opened the top few and saw that they were all blank.

A card table held packing material. Stacked against the wall were flat bankers boxes. On the floor by the card table was an assembled bankers box, empty, its flaps open, ready to be filled with more stuff.

Bob's voice came through the radio. "We're all clear up here, Chief. I think. It's hard to swear to it. What's it like where you are?"

"I see what you're talking about. It's nearly wall to wall boxes down here. I think we're clear, though. We'll meet you on the main floor."

Sally sent her team back upstairs, her heart sinking. Where was Beth?

❖

Delilah secured the poultice to Mel by duct taping it to her skin. With almost no ability to use either hand, Beth moved to the other side of the table and tried to bump Delilah away from Mel. Delilah laughed and caught Beth around the middle with both arms, holding her close to her front and whispering, loudly, into her ear. "Your spunk is adorable, as always. But I don't have much time for it now. If you prefer I tie you up to the cot, I will do so."

"No. I just beg you to take that off her. It's burning her."

In fact, there was some faint smell that might have been the poultice itself or might have been Mel's skin burning. From the look on Mel's face it was the skin. Her face contorted and the sweat on her brow fell freely down her face. Beth felt desperate to help her.

"Is there some kind of deal I can strike with you, Delilah? Something you want that I can exchange for Mel's freedom?"

"Nothing at all. And I'd get the idea of freedom out of your head. Now get back over by my patient and hold that poultice down on her belly. It will help your hand."

"No," Beth said. If they were going to die, she sure as hell wasn't going to make it easy for her.

Delilah sighed. "Then I'm going to tape your hands to the

poultice. Your choice." Delilah reached out and grabbed Beth's left hand, squeezing the bloody, pulverized fingers, bringing Beth to her knees with the pain. And while Delilah was turned toward Beth, Mel curled up and brought her right knee to her chin at the same time, grabbing something from her ankle. As Delilah let go of Beth and turned back toward the table, Mel lunged at her and drove a knife into Delilah's throat.

"Run, Beth. Get the hell out and get help!" Mel shouted. She struggled to a sitting position as Beth stood, transfixed as Delilah gurgled and slumped back against the counter, a dazed look on her face. "Run!"

Beth ran to the door of the room and tugged it open with her right hand, the pain searing through her. On the other side of the door was a narrow entryway and then some steep wooden stairs that seemed to lead to nowhere. It was nearly pitch black. Beth began climbing the stairs, unable now to hear anything behind her in the sub-basement, but aware of some sound above her. She yelled for help. She ran up the stairs. She prayed.

❖

Sally was turning to join the rest of her team when she heard something. It seemed to be coming from below and she looked around desperately trying to find the source. Another sound, closer now, a voice. The noise seemed to be coming from right below her, yet there was nothing that looked like a trap door to below. She kicked at the empty box sitting on the floor. It didn't move. She kicked again and then leaned over and tugged on it. The box had been glued and bolted to a door in the floor and when Sally pulled on the box the door opened. Beth's bloody face was moving toward her.

"Oh, my God, help. Mel's down there."

"And Delilah?"

"Mel just stabbed her in the throat. I don't…"

Sally pulled Beth up the rest of the way and told her to stay put. She radioed her team and went down the stairs, kicked the door open, and entered with her gun pointed at the center of the glaring red room. Mel was face first on the ground, not moving, with Delilah kneeling above her, blood pouring from her throat, a bloody knife poised to plunge into Mel's back. Sally shot her in the chest and she went down.

CHAPTER EIGHTEEN

O kay. We have the go-ahead on the pain meds."

"Oh, thank Christ."

Beth was not clear on everything going on around her, but the word that relief was on the way came through clearly. Her left hand felt like it was on fire, and the slightest movement of the mushy fingers brought on a wave of nausea. Her right hand had a sharp stinging pain that made her think of the chef's knife quivering as it pinned her hand to Delilah's table. More nausea. Her face was bandaged where Delilah had clobbered her. She knew that Mel was much worse off, but this was bad enough. Oblivion would be welcome for a while.

She could hear the sirens as the ambulances sped through the cornfields lining Route 20, heading toward the hospital in Center City. Mel's ambulance was in the lead, her own right behind it. Delilah remained behind in Mount Avery, her body lying where Sally shot her, the scene being processed by Bob and the medical examiner.

Next to her was Sally, just putting her phone back on her belt. She put her hand back on Beth's thigh, since holding either hand was impossible. "Are you feeling more comfortable now?" she asked.

"It's taking the edge off. I couldn't even think straight for a while. Was that my mother on the phone?"

"Yes, she'll meet us at the hospital."

"I can't believe I'm going to say this, but I'm glad she's here." Beth lay quiet for a moment. "How about Mel? Anything new?"

Sally looked at the paramedic riding in the back with them. "Say, Tonya. Any news on Mel?"

"She's stable, so that's good. I'm sure they'll take her right up to surgery." Tonya fiddled around with the IV line running into Beth's arm. "Is it true she stabbed that professor?"

"It's true. She told me that she always carries a knife strapped to her ankle, ever since she got jumped during a tow-truck call. Thank God she wasn't afraid to use it."

"Mel's handy, I'll give her that," Tonya said, as if Mel had just fixed a dishwasher. "How are you feeling now?" she asked Beth.

"Better. A little better. Groggy, though." Beth closed her eyes for a moment, then opened them and turned to Sally. The pain flared up.

"We'll be there in ten minutes," Sally said. "You should just rest."

"No, I have to tell you something. It's important."

Sally smiled and squeezed Beth's thigh. "You're not going to die. We have all the time in the world to tell each other everything."

"We do?"

"Absolutely."

"Let me tell you this while I'm high on morphine. You'll be doing me a favor."

"Okay." Sally looked at Tonya, who tried to take herself out of Beth's line of sight.

"It's all right," Beth said. "I don't care if Tonya hears this and tells the whole town."

Tonya started to protest, but Sally held up a hand to silence her.

"What is it, Beth?"

"My mother runs a legal house of prostitution in Nevada."

Sally's face looked crestfallen, the exact reaction that Beth expected. "I wanted to tell you so you could leave me now instead of later. Later is harder."

Sally frowned. "You think I'll leave you? Hell, we haven't even really gotten together yet."

"Well, you looked pretty disappointed."

"That's because I thought you were going to tell me that you love me. That's what I was hoping you were going to say."

"My mom worked at one of those places," Tonya said, pressing buttons on the monitor by Beth's head. "She said it wasn't too bad."

"I've heard the same thing," said Sally. "I always thought it would be much better if prostitution was legal. I worked vice for a few years in Chicago and I know what life is like for most of the women. It doesn't have to be that hard."

Beth didn't dare try to look closely at their faces. She suspected they were teasing her, humoring her because of her injuries. They acted as if Beth had just told them there was a great sale coming up at Macy's. It was of mild interest, something to talk about as you were passing the time together. As her eyes focused on the ceiling of the ambulance, her peripheral vision cloudy, she thought of how narrow her life had been, how devoid of those experiences that helped put things in perspective. She was like a child. That was going to have to change.

"Mae loves talking about the business," Beth said. "You can ask her all about it at the hospital."

"I think we'll have something else on our minds. The only important thing for me right now is for you to get taken care and feel better," Sally said. "Rest now. You're talking too much."

"I just have one more thing to say," Beth said. "And then I'll shut up."

"What's that?"

"I love you."

The monitor beeped in the silence and Tonya hit a button to quiet it. "Now that's something I'll spread around town."

About the Author

Anne Laughlin's short stories have appeared in a number of anthologies. In 2008 Anne was named a Lambda Literary Foundation Emerging Writer, and in 2009 she was awarded a residency at the Ragdale Foundation, where she will work on her next novel.

Books Available From Bold Strokes Books

Power Play by Julie Cannon. Businesswomen Tate Monroe and Victoria Sosa are at odds in the boardroom, but not in the bedroom. (978-1-60282-125-5)

The Remarkable Journey of Miss Tranby Quirke by Elizabeth Ridley. When love enters Tranby's life in the form of a beautiful nineteen-year-old student, Lysette McDonald, she embarks on the most remarkable journey of all. (978-1-60282-126-2)

Returning Tides by Radclyffe. Insurance investigator Ashley Walker faces more than a dangerous opponent when she returns to the town, and the woman, she left behind. (978-1-60282-123-1)

Veritas by Anne Laughlin. When the hallowed halls of academia become the stage for murder, newly appointed Dean Beth Ellis's search for the truth leads her to unexpected discoveries about her own heart. (978-1-60282-124-8)

The Pleasure Planner by Larkin Rose. Pleasure purveyor Bree Hendricks treats love like a commodity until Logan Delaney makes Bree the client in her own game. (978-1-60282-121-7)

everafter by Nell Stark and Trinity Tam. Valentine Darrow is bitten by a vampire on her way to propose to her lover Alexa Newland, and their lives and love are placed in mortal jeopardy. (978-1-60282-119-4)

Summer Winds by Andrews & Austin. When Maggie Turner hires a ranch hand to help work her thousand acres, she never expects to be attracted to the very young, very female Cash Tate. (978-1-60282-120-0)

Beggar of Love by Lee Lynch. Jefferson is the lover every woman wants to be—or to have. A revealing saga of lesbian sexuality. (978-1-60282-122-4)

The Seduction of Moxie by Colette Moody. When 1930s Broadway actress Violet London meets speakeasy singer Moxie Valette, she is instantly attracted and her Hollywood trip takes an unexpected turn. (978-1-60282-114-9)

Goldenseal by Gill McKnight. When Amy Fortune returns to her childhood home, she discovers something sinister in the air—but is former lover Leone Garoul stalking her or protecting her? (978-1-60282-115-6)

Romantic Interludes 2: Secrets edited by Radclyffe and Stacia Seaman. An anthology of sensual lesbian love stories: passion, surprises, and secret desires. (978-1-60282-116-3)

Femme Noir by Clara Nipper. Nora Delaney meets her match in Max Abbott, a sex-crazed dame who may or may not have the information Nora needs to solve a murder—but can she contain her lust for Max long enough to find out? (978-1-60282-117-0)

The Reluctant Daughter by Lesléa Newman. Heartwarming, heartbreaking, and ultimately triumphant—the story every daughter recognizes of the lifelong struggle for our mothers to really see us. (978-1-60282-118-7)

Erosistible by Gill McKnight. When Win Martin arrives at a luxurious Greek hotel for a much-anticipated week of sun and sex with her new girlfriend, she is stunned to find her ex-girlfriend, Benny, is the proprietor. Aeros Ebook. (978-1-60282-134-7)

Looking Glass Lives by Felice Picano. Cousins Roger and Alistair become lifelong friends and discover their sexuality amidst the backdrop of twentieth-century gay culture. (978-1-60282-089-0)

Breaking the Ice by Kim Baldwin. Nothing is easy about life above the Arctic Circle—except, perhaps, falling in love. At least that's what pilot Bryson Faulkner hopes when she meets Karla Edwards. (978-1-60282-087-6)

It Should Be a Crime by Carsen Taite. Two women fulfill their mutual desire with a night of passion, neither expecting more until law professor Morgan Bradley and student Parker Casey meet again…in the classroom. (978-1-60282-086-9)

Rough Trade edited by Todd Gregory. Top male erotica writers pen their own hot, sexy versions of the term "rough trade," producing some of the hottest, nastiest, and most dangerous fiction ever published. (978-1-60282-092-0)

The High Priest and the Idol by Jane Fletcher. Jemeryl and Tevi's relationship is put to the test when the Guardian sends Jemeryl on a mission that puts her not only in harm's way, but back into the sights of a previous lover. (978-1-60282-085-2)

Point of Ignition by Erin Dutton. Amid a blaze that threatens to consume them both, firefighter Kate Chambers and property owner Alexi Clark redefine love and trust. (978-1-60282-084-5)

Secrets in the Stone by Radclyffe. Reclusive sculptor Rooke Tyler suddenly finds herself the object of two very different women's affections, and choosing between them will change her life forever. (978-1-60282-083-8)

Dark Garden by Jennifer Fulton. Vienna Blake and Mason Cavender are sworn enemies—who can't resist each other. Something has to give. (978-1-60282-036-4)

Late in the Season by Felice Picano. Set on Fire Island, this is the story of an unlikely pair of friends—a gay composer in his late thirties and an eighteen-year-old schoolgirl. (978-1-60282-082-1)

Punishment with Kisses by Diane Anderson-Minshall. Will Megan find the answers she seeks about her sister Ashley's murder or will her growing relationship with one of Ash's exes blind her to the real truth? (978-1-60282-081-4)

September Canvas by Gun Brooke. When Deanna Moore meets TV personality Faythe she is reluctantly attracted to her, but will Faythe side with the people spreading rumors about Deanna? (978-1-60282-080-7)

No Leavin' Love by Larkin Rose. Beautiful, successful Mercedes Miller thinks she can resume her affair with ranch foreman Sydney Campbell, but the rules have changed. (978-1-60282-079-1)

Between the Lines by Bobbi Marolt. When romance writer Gail Prescott meets actress Tannen Albright, she develops feelings that she usually only experiences through her characters. (978-1-60282-078-4)

Blue Skies by Ali Vali. Commander Berkley Levine leads an elite group of pilots on missions ordered by her ex-lover Captain Aidan Sullivan and everything is on the line—including love. (978-1-60282-077-7)

The Lure by Felice Picano. When Noel Cummings is recruited by the police to go undercover to find a killer, his life will never be the same. (978-1-60282-076-0)

Death of a Dying Man by J.M. Redmann. Mickey Knight, Private Eye and partner of Dr. Cordelia James, doesn't need a drop-dead gorgeous assistant—not until nature steps in. (978-1-60282-075-3)

Justice for All by Radclyffe. Dell Mitchell goes undercover to expose a human traffic ring and ends up in the middle of an even deadlier conspiracy. (978-1-60282-074-6)

Sanctuary by I. Beacham. Cate Canton faces one major obstacle to her goal of crushing her business rival, Dita Newton—her uncontrollable attraction to Dita. (978-1-60282-055-5)

The Sublime and Spirited Voyage of Original Sin by Colette Moody. Pirate Gayle Malvern finds the presence of an abducted seamstress, Celia Pierce, a welcome distraction until the captive comes to mean more to her than is wise. (978-1-60282-054-8)

Suspect Passions by VK Powell. Can two women, a city attorney and a beat cop, put aside their differences long enough to see that they're perfect for each other? (978-1-60282-053-1)

Just Business by Julie Cannon. Two women who come together—each for her own selfish needs—discover that love can never be as simple as a business transaction. (978-1-60282-052-4)

Sistine Heresy by Justine Saracen. Adrianna Borgia, survivor of the Borgia court, presents Michelangelo with the greatest temptations of his life while struggling with soul-threatening desires for the painter Raphaela. (978-1-60282-051-7)